Former journalist S.D. Robertson quit his role as a local newspaper editor to pursue a lifelong ambition of becoming a novelist. His debut novel, *Time to Say Goodbye*, was published to rave reviews in 2016, and his second book, *If Ever I Fall*, hit the shelves in 2017. This was followed by *Stand By Me* in 2018.

An English graduate from the University of Manchester, he's also worked as a holiday rep, a door-to-door salesman, a train cleaner, a kitchen porter and a mobile phone network engineer.

Over the years, S.D. Robertson has spent time in France, Holland and Australia, but home these days is back in the UK. He lives in a village near Manchester with his wife and daughter. There's also his cat, Bernard, who likes to distract him from writing – usually by breaking things. *My Sister's Lies* is his fourth novel.

S.D. ROBERTSON

MY SISTER'S LIES

avon.

AVON
A division of HarperCollins*Publishers*
1 London Bridge Street,
London SE1 9GF

www.harpercollins.co.uk

A Paperback Original 2019

5

Copyright © S.D. Robertson 2019

S.D. Robertson asserts the moral right to
be identified as the author of this work

A catalogue record for this book is
available from the British Library

ISBN-13: 978-0-00-822348-9

Typeset in Sabon by Palimpsest Book Production Ltd, Falkirk, Stirlingshire

Printed and bound in Great Britain by
CPI Group (UK) Ltd, Croydon CR0 4YY

MIX
Paper from
responsible sources
FSC
www.fsc.org
FSC™ C007454

For Claudia

Also by S.D. Robertson

Time to Say Goodbye
If Ever I Fall
Stand By Me

PROLOGUE

She waves goodbye to him through the windscreen of her car and congratulates herself on a fine acting performance. She's fairly certain she managed not to give anything away while driving the short journey to the station. It wasn't as hard as it might have been with another person. Things were bound to be awkward between them anyway, particularly after last night and everything they discussed. But still. She could easily have said or done something to raise his suspicions – to signal her intentions – yet she didn't. Now she's confident he'll be almost as shocked as everyone else by her death.

Not long to go, but first things first. She drives the car a short distance until she spots a post box. Then she parks at the side of the road, unzips her handbag and pulls out the small padded envelope she placed in there earlier. She holds it in her hands for a moment, her eyes briefly scanning the name and address plus the postage label she printed off in the early hours, then lets out a slow sigh and feels a couple of tears trickle down either cheek. This little package looks like so many others she's posted out, selling bits and bobs on eBay, but it couldn't be more different. And by posting it, she will be sealing her fate. There will be no going back after that.

She gets out of the car and stands in front of the red pillar box. Hesitates for a moment. Looks at the name and address one more time, checking again that they're right, and shoves it through the open slot before she can change her mind.

It's done.

She returns to the car, looks at her pale face in the mirror and then drives on, one step closer to the end.

She arrives at Costa a few minutes later. It's the coffee shop branch they always used to go to together before doing the shopping on a Saturday morning; it's much quieter this early on a weekday. She orders the same as they always did – a latte and a hot chocolate – even though it's only her now. She's tempted to order a biscuit or cake too but decides she probably won't be able to manage it.

She sips the latte and pretends she's not alone. Trawls her memory for an image of another hot chocolate in a pair of hands on one of those glorious Saturdays, which she never properly appreciated until they were over. It's the same with so much in life, she thinks. You take wonderful things for granted, only realising how amazing they are when they're no longer there. It's incredible what imminent death does for your sense of perspective.

She doesn't actually drink much of her coffee, fearful the caffeine might upset her stomach. Ordering a decaf would have been more sensible, or drinking the hot choc-olate instead, but she wants to experience the taste exactly as it was in the days she remembers so fondly.

That and the smell certainly do the trick. When she closes her eyes, she's hurtled headfirst into the past. She stays there as long as she can, revelling in its warm glow, until the cup her hand circles grows cold, and wearily she returns to the present: her last morning on earth.

'Goodbye,' a chirpy staff member, barely more than a girl, says to her as she gets up to leave. 'Have a nice day.'

'Thanks. You too,' she replies with a smile, conscious of the fact that this could be the last thing she ever says to another person.

Before she starts the car, she has a moment of panic. For a second it feels like she can't breathe as a voice in her head tells her she's handling everything wrong. That she shouldn't go ahead with it.

It certainly wasn't her first choice of how to proceed, but it's the only option she has left now. Isn't it?

She stares at a tree in the distance and tries to focus her mind on it, counting the number of branches and watching its leaves flutter in the light breeze as she fights to slow down her breathing and take back control. Eventually it starts to work and, as she feels herself calming down, she speaks out loud in a bid to continue the process: 'You're doing the right thing. It's hard, but ultimately it will be best for everyone. Doubts are normal, but you mustn't give in to them. You're doing the right thing. You're doing the right thing . . .'

A few minutes later she starts the car and, still regulating her breathing, finds some classical music on the radio. It sounds like something from an epic film; she draws strength from its sweeping strings and triumphant trumpets.

Her final destination isn't too far away, but she's chosen it carefully. It's an unremarkable residential street with a mix of terraced and semi-detached houses on both sides. There are plenty of parking spaces at this time on a weekday morning, presumably due to many of the residents having left for work. She pulls into an empty spot outside one of the street's smarter properties, with neatly trimmed ivy nuzzling its red bricks and a colourful array of shrubs, pots and hanging baskets making the most of the small front yard.

Methodically, she removes her watch, rings, necklace and ear studs, placing them into the glovebox after first looking around to check no one's watching. She had intended to do this at home before leaving, but it slipped her mind.

Next she steps out of the car, pats her hand gently on the roof to say goodbye, locks it and walks towards the footpath that will bring her close to the railway and the broken fence that will give her access to it.

She passes a couple of dog walkers along the way, beaming a broad smile at them so as not to raise any suspicions. This is ridiculous, she muses, because why would they be suspicious of her looking grumpy or upset? They might if they later spotted her near the track, she counters, if they lived in a house that overlooked it or something. So no harm in being careful. She needs this to go the right way. Well, as right as killing herself ever could.

It would be a disaster if someone somehow managed to stop her.

This isn't a cry for help. She absolutely wants it to work – one hundred per cent, first time, instantly, no messing about. That's why she's chosen such a brutal method. With the right conditions, the mortality rate is very high. It's fast too. Even if she isn't killed instantly, she should at least be knocked unconscious straight away. There's still a small chance it could go wrong, of course, meaning survival with horrific injuries. But that's why she's done her homework, scoping out the optimal spot in advance; visiting several other possible locations before selecting this as the most suitable.

Fail to prepare, prepare to fail.

She originally intended to wait a few more days, to spend more time getting her affairs in order. However, the arrival of her unexpected house guest yesterday had forced her hand, since she'd told him enough to potentially put her plans at risk if he didn't do as she asked. The fact that he arrived and departed by train also felt like a sign.

As she arrives at the broken fence, she breathes a sigh of relief to see it hasn't been fixed. It was only a few days ago she was last here, and it looked like the fence had been that way for a while, but, in her experience, Sod's Law could strike at any moment. Well, not this time, she thinks, checking no one is watching before squeezing through the gap, catching her jeans in the process, but managing to pull free. Next she runs for the cover of a nearby bush.

She crouches there for a few minutes, catching her breath

and calming herself down once again. Then she continues to a better location, still sheltered from view by thick greenery but alongside the train track. 'This is it,' she whispers into the warm summer air.

Her heart's racing and there's little she can do to calm it now. No surprise really, considering where she is; what she's about to do. Her hands are shaking and her right eye is twitching like it does when she's stressed or tired.

It's no good resisting, her mind tells her worthless body. It's your fault we're in this situation. You'll do what you're told. That's the only choice.

It's a waiting game now. She just needs a train to come along. Either direction will do. Another reason she picked this spot, besides the broken fence and good ground cover, is that it's far enough away from the station for any passing train to be travelling at a decent speed. She can't see too far in either direction, thanks to the curved route of the track, but that's fine. It means no driver will spot her too soon and slow down. She'll hear it coming and then all she has to do is step out. At that stage, it won't matter about the driver seeing her. It'll be way too late for them to do anything about it. A fast-moving train takes a very long time to stop, as she discovered while researching the matter online.

All she has to do is step out. That sounds so easy, doesn't it? She knows in her heart that it won't be. That there's a chance she might chicken out. But she can't. And she's not going to let one train pass by first as a practice. That was her original plan, but she decided the sheer noise and power of it thundering by so close might shock her into changing her mind. No, she'll have to fight her natural survival instinct to do this, and she's convinced that will be easier without a dry run. Plus she could get spotted by that initial driver, who'd then be able to warn the next. So it has to be the first one.

She needs to do it without thinking. The time for rumination has passed. She's weighed up her options over and over again in recent days. She's made her final decision.

She's afraid – of course she is. She's scared death or unconsciousness won't come as quickly as she hopes and the pain will be excruciating. So she reminds herself that the odds of success are heavily in her favour.

The idea that she'll never see . . .

No, she can't allow herself to even think that name. Not now. Tears start to pour down her face as multiple images of the two of them together flood her mind. But she grits her teeth, squeezes her eyes shut and fights to block them.

'I can't. Not now,' she says under her breath. 'I have to do this. I have to do this. It's the only way.'

And then she hears a rumbling in the distance. This is it. She knows it is, without question. A train is fast approaching from her left. She can't see it yet, but it's definitely coming, so as late as she dares she moves from a crouch into a standing position. The sound quickly gets louder and, as she stares in that direction, hunched, waiting, her heart is like a jackhammer, her breaths tight and shallow, her whole body trembling.

After a fleeting hesitation, she steps on to the track, her

determination pushing her forward despite the continued resistance of her body.

Time crawls until the front of the train reveals itself, the noise deafening now, and she stares it down.

She can see the alarmed driver's bearded face looking at her as he does the only thing he can and sounds the horn. She feels for him in that split second, knowing this must be his worst nightmare – something that will scar him for life – and wishing she didn't have to be the one to put him through it.

But although it's his face racing towards her, at the last moment her tortured mind replaces it with another: the one person she loves more than anyone or anything else.

'I'm sorr—'

CHAPTER 1

Twelve days earlier

Hannah Cook was glowering at the computer screen, tempted to delete the pathetic collection of words staring back at her, when she heard the doorbell.

Her eyes darted to the clock in the corner of the display: 4.07 p.m. Who could be calling round at this time of the day? It was way too early for Mark to get home. Not that he'd use the bell anyway, unless he'd left his keys at the office or lost them somehow. And it would be unlike any of their friends to turn up unannounced. It was 2019, for goodness' sake; there was no need to risk catching people unawares in this time of constant connectivity. In fact, to do so was verging on rudeness.

Hannah decided it must either be a delivery – despite the fact she wasn't expecting anything – or someone selecting the wrong apartment number. In case of the latter, and since the bell had only sounded once so far, she waited for a moment.

It wasn't like she didn't want to get away from her

laptop. She'd already found countless reasons to do so throughout the day, procrastinating like a pro. The problem was that if she did so now, this late on a Friday afternoon, she'd probably not get back to it. And then she'd feel guilty all night and into the weekend, maybe even making herself work on Saturday or Sunday when she ought to be spending time with her husband.

She'd once read somewhere that being an author was like having homework for evermore. She'd laughingly dismissed this at the time, when having a book published had been her heart's desire: a dream she'd never expected to realise. But already, now, even though she technically wouldn't become a published novelist for several more months, she understood the truth of that statement. A dream job was still a job. And this particular one had expectations and deadlines that didn't disappear when she left the office at 5 p.m., because there was no office, nor regular business hours. There was just Hannah.

The bell rang again, longer and more insistent this time. Hannah saved her work, ignoring the reckless, frustrated part of herself who told her it wasn't worth saving, and walked out of the lounge into the hallway.

'Hello?' she said into the telephone-style intercom next to the apartment's entrance. As she did so, Hannah looked into the mirror opposite and frowned at the grey roots already showing in her shoulder-length, wavy brown hair.

There was a pause as the person on the other end of the line cleared their throat. Then, like a muffled gunshot, came the last words Hannah was expecting to hear: words with the power to flip her world on its head.

'Hannah? It's Diane.'

'So,' Hannah said a short while later, breaking the latest uncomfortable silence in a conversation so stilted she felt a desperate urge to run out of her own home to escape it. 'You've changed a lot since I last saw you, Mia. You were just a tot then.'

'She's still as beautiful as ever,' Diane said, 'but for some reason she likes to hide it away behind all that war paint.'

Mia scowled at her mother, next to her on the couch, who was chewing a fingernail like her life depended on its removal. The teenager gave a fleeting glance towards Hannah, perched on the armchair opposite, and shrugged her shoulders. Then she dipped her head forward so her green eyes, lined with dramatic, dark make-up, disappeared behind the long fringe of her straight, shoulder-length black hair. Although she was young to do so, Hannah was convinced she must have dyed it, as it had been dark brown when she was little.

Hannah had almost passed out at the sound of Diane speaking on the intercom earlier. She hadn't seen or spoken to her sister for nearly eleven years. She'd all but resigned herself to never seeing her and her niece again. And now here they both were, sitting in her lounge.

It had taken Hannah a few moments to get over the shock of hearing her sister's voice after so long. She'd actually dropped the intercom handset and let it swing against the wall on its coiled cord while she stood there

11

wide-eyed, frozen to the spot; covering her open mouth with her hands, desperately trying to grasp what was going on.

Then she'd heard Diane's voice again: a faint, tinny version this time, leaking from the speaker of the dangling telephone.

'Hannah?' she'd said. 'Are you there or not? It's Diane. I know you're probably surprised to hear from me after so long, but I really need to see you. It's important. I have Mia with me. Hannah?'

And so she'd reached over and buzzed them in. It was all she could manage at that point, needing the extra time it took the lift to reach the eighth floor to find her voice. And even then, seeing the pair of them appear at her door in the flesh – Mia unrecognisable from the child she'd adored – Hannah had struggled to find any words.

Instead, despite everything that had gone before, she'd instinctively hugged them both in one go and proclaimed how wonderful it was to see them. It had felt weird and awkward, so she'd ushered them inside, sat them down in the lounge and rushed to the kitchen to make a pot of tea. Because what the hell else was she supposed to do?

That was exactly the question she'd intended to ask her husband when, while in the kitchen alone, she'd phoned his mobile. Unfortunately, she'd got his voicemail, meaning he was probably in a meeting.

'Mark,' she'd said, trying to keep her voice steady as she left a message. 'Please get home as soon as you can. I've got a situation here.' She'd taken a deep breath before adding: 'You won't believe this, but Diane and Mia have turned up. They're here in the apartment right now. Call me.'

From her seat opposite the visitors in the spacious lounge, Hannah's eyes moved from Mia's low-hanging fringe to Diane's continued nail biting and then on to her mobile, sitting next to her on the right arm of the chair. Come on, Mark, she thought. Phone me back so at least I have a good excuse to leave the room again. She'd already been to the toilet once and returned twice to the kitchen to get sugar and biscuits.

It was so damn awkward. And since they were in her home, she somehow felt like it was her responsibility to keep the floundering conversation going, which was ridiculous when she thought about it. It was Diane, not her, who'd upped and left all those years ago. Now her sister, looking gaunt and frazzled, wearing navy leggings, pumps and a white blouse, was the one who'd turned up on her doorstep unannounced and utterly out of the blue. So why wasn't she discussing the reason for this? She always used to have plenty to say.

There had been an initial chat of sorts: a bizarre, staccato series of pleasantries about the weather, their car journey to Manchester from Bournemouth, her apartment, and other peripheral matters like the modernisation of the city. At one point she'd asked Diane how long she'd been wearing her hair, now dyed a striking burgundy colour, in a pixie cut.

'Oh, I don't know exactly,' she'd replied. 'Quite a while. A few years.'

Hannah hadn't been able to think of a suitable response

to this. Diane's words served as a harsh reminder of how long they'd been apart; how little they knew about the present-day versions of each other.

Was her sister aware, for instance, that she'd long since quit her job as an advertising copywriter and somehow – miraculously – written her way through the eye of a needle to win the elusive publishing deal that had been her childhood dream? She very much doubted it. It was out there on social media, of course, but Diane wasn't involved in any of that – not as far as Hannah knew. Nor, to her knowledge, was she in contact with anyone from their past who might have told her. Apart from their father, of course: the one person she knew to have kept in touch with Diane. However, after his initial attempts to mediate between the sisters had failed, he'd refused point-blank to take sides in what he referred to as their 'foolish feud'. As such, and as long as it lasted, he'd sworn not to speak a word to either of them about the other in order to maintain his neutral status.

He was a stubborn man, Frank Wells, so she couldn't imagine he would have breached his vow to reveal this one particular piece of news. While she could only assume he was the person who'd given Diane her address, this was no doubt with the intention that it might lead to their reconciliation.

As Hannah had lost herself for a moment in these thoughts, her guests had also kept quiet, leading to the first long, awkward silence of their visit. Suddenly aware of it and uncomfortable, she'd responded by taking the bull by the horns and attempting to get to the bottom of

Diane's shock return. 'You said something before about needing to see me,' she'd said, squeezing her palms together and raising her eyebrows. 'That it was important?'

'Yes, that's right, but can we talk about it later?' Diane had replied. 'How's Mark, by the way? He's still at work, I assume.'

'He's fine, thank you. He should be home before too long.'

'Good.'

Now Hannah, whose initial feelings of shock and panic had given way to unease and confusion, felt like asking Diane again why she was here and, if necessary, demanding an answer. It was definitely a reasonable question, but she couldn't bring herself to do it after the last response. So instead she found herself trying again with Mia, who was, after all, an innocent party in the family feud that had kept them separate all this time. Losing touch with her niece – the closest thing she'd ever had to a child of her own – had been one of the most painful parts of the whole sorry affair.

'So, Mia Wells, let me see,' she said, trying not to think about all those years and milestones she'd missed from her childhood. 'You must be fourteen now, right?'

Mia, who was pin thin and wearing skinny jeans with a black T-shirt, nodded without looking up at her.

'So what school year are you in now?'

'I've just finished Year Nine,' she replied in a monotone voice.

'Right,' Hannah replied, nodding her head as she tried to work out what that meant, recalling that the naming

15

system for year groups had changed since her and Diane's schooldays.

'It's what we used to call Third Year,' her sister chipped in, as if reading her mind. 'From September she'll be in the equivalent of Lower Fifth, working towards taking her GCSEs at the end of the following year.'

'So have you finished for the summer now, Mia?'

'Yes,' the teenager replied.

'They broke up earlier this week,' Diane explained, looking at the fingernails she'd just been biting, frowning and then shoving both hands under her thighs.

Old habits die hard, Hannah thought. Smiling at her niece in case she decided to make eye contact, she added: 'Wonderful. All that time off. I bet you've got loads of stuff planned. Are you going on holiday anywhere?'

'I'm not sure.'

'Right.'

'Can I use your toilet, actually?' Mia asked, adding a 'please' following a nudge and a glare from her mother.

'Um, yes. Of course. It's in the hall, next to the front door.'

Diane rolled her eyes. 'Sorry about Little Miss Grumpy,' she said once Mia was out of earshot. 'She's at *that* age.'

'Listen, what the hell's going on?' Hannah hissed, unable to contain herself any longer. 'You show up at my home after all these years of no contact and then you sit there, saying almost nothing. Why are you here? Is one of you in trouble? You need to give me something.'

'I will, but not in front of Mia.'

'She's not here now.'

'She'll be back any minute, and it will be better if Mark's around too.'

'Mark? What—' Hearing the toilet flush, Hannah changed tack. 'Come on, quick. Just tell me.'

'I can't now. Sorry. It'll have to be tonight – after Mia's gone to bed.'

'Gone to bed?' Hannah repeated, as it dawned on her what Diane's words implied. 'Where are you staying?'

'Um, well, I was hoping you might be good enough to put us up for the night.'

'What? You don't even have an overnight bag.'

'Our things are in the car.'

'You didn't think to phone ahead?'

'I didn't have your number to start with and then . . . Well, I got your landline from Dad, but I wasn't sure you'd take my call. Turning up here seemed a better option.' Diane threw her sister a sheepish look. 'I know it's a lot to ask in the circumstances, but . . . please don't make me beg.'

Mia walked back into the lounge at the same moment as Hannah's mobile started to ring.

'Sorry, you'll have to excuse me,' Hannah said, wondering whether her niece had overheard any of their discussion. 'That'll be a business call I've been waiting on. I need to take it.' She slid the phone from its facedown position on the arm of the chair, knowing it was almost certainly Mark calling, and raced to the relative safety of the kitchen before answering.

'Hi, love,' she said, speaking quietly despite having shut the door.

'Are you okay? I just got your message. Sorry, I was tied up in a meeting.'

Hannah brought her husband up to speed with what had happened so far.

'The whole thing is totally weird, right?' she said.

'Definitely.'

'So what do we do? Can they stay tonight or not?'

She heard the sound of Mark letting out a long sigh on the other end of the line. 'It's tricky, isn't it, darling? Despite everything, they're still family. And none of this is Mia's fault. It's hard for me to form a proper opinion without having seen them for myself. What's your gut feeling? Do you think Diane's here with good intentions or, I don't know, that she's up to something? How does she seem? Is she behaving strangely or—'

'She's like my sister, but older.' Lowering her voice to little more than a whisper, Hannah went on: 'She does look tired and anxious. Not chatty at all. There's definitely something weighing on her mind. My guess is she needs our help in some way. Money, perhaps? That might explain why she wants to stay with us rather than in a hotel. You can see for yourself when you get home. Let's wait until then and we'll make a joint decision about them sleeping over. How long are you likely to be?'

'I need to reply to a couple of emails and then I'll head straight back. I'll be home soon, I promise.'

'Good. Please hurry. I'm running out of things to say.'

Luckily, Mark's office was also located in the centre of Manchester, only a fifteen-minute walk from the apartment. True to his word, he returned home in around half an hour, although to a struggling Hannah it had felt like forever.

She'd almost resorted to turning on the television, although doing so in the presence of guests was one of her pet hates. Instead, she'd gone for an artificially extended trip to the bathroom before busying herself about the kitchen making another cup of tea for everyone.

'There you are,' she said, dashing to the front door as soon as she heard the key in the lock.

Mark was dressed in his usual work attire of a dark suit and open-necked shirt, his tan leather briefcase swinging from his left hand and his door key in the right. He looked as tall and handsome as always, his short but thick salt-and-pepper hair lightly ruffled, and a five o'clock shadow lining his square jaw. If anything, he'd got better looking with age. At forty-five, three years older than Hannah, he'd retained his slim and sporty physique, unlike some of his tubby contemporaries. But he'd done so in a natural rather than gym-crafted way, thanks to regular squash games and the odd run, combined with sensible eating and drinking.

Hannah had always been proud to call this dashing, intelligent and yet grounded man her husband. The fact he also had a good job as chief financial officer for a fast-expanding tech firm – well paid enough to enable her to pursue her literary ambitions – was the icing on the cake.

Now, with sibling rivalries suddenly back on the agenda, she recalled how she used to feel like she'd got one up on her sister by marrying such a catch. Looking at him standing before her in the hall today, she felt it again. Diane had Mia – but she had Mark.

In a loud voice meant for the ears of their guests, she asked: 'Did you have a good day, love?'

'Yes, thanks. It was fine.'

'I have a surprise for you,' she added, voice still raised. 'We've got some unexpected guests. You'll never guess who.'

Hannah really wished she didn't feel the need to do this: to hide from Diane that she'd phoned for backup. But she did nonetheless, tumbling back into bad habits, because Diane had always been so independent and fearless, like she could single-handedly take on the world without breaking a sweat. And now – perhaps even more so than in the past – she absolutely did not want to look weak and needy in front of her sister.

'Do we?' Mark replied, his mouth going along with the ruse while his eyes begged to know what was really happening. 'That sounds intriguing.'

CHAPTER 2

'I think I'll head to bed and read for a bit, Mum,' Mia said after they'd finished eating. She looked across the dining table, first at Hannah and then Mark, adding: 'Would it be all right for me to have a shower first?'

'Of course,' Hannah replied, even though the question hadn't ultimately felt directed at her. 'You know where the bathroom is. Help yourself to a towel from the pile in there and feel free to use whatever toiletries you need. The shower is pretty straightforward, but give me a shout if you need any help.'

She smiled at her niece, who pursed her lips and muttered, 'Thanks,' in response.

Mia still hadn't shown much sign of coming out of her shell – at least not to Hannah. Mark, on the other hand, had had some success at getting the teenager to chat when he'd started asking her about what kinds of TV shows and films she liked. They'd both seen a lot of the Marvel superhero movies, apparently. Plus they shared an affection for this weird, nerdy cartoon about space, time travel and that kind of thing. Hannah had seen Mark watch it a few times and dismissed it as nonsense. She couldn't remember what it was called, but it definitely wasn't her cup of tea. Neither was the Marvel stuff, to be honest.

Her ears had pricked up, however, at Mia's mention of reading. This was much more her field than Mark's, who rarely found time to read anything but the paper these days. So before her niece disappeared from the dining room, she asked her what she was reading.

'Oh, you wouldn't have heard of it,' Mia replied.

'Try me,' Hannah said, throwing Mark a glare designed to remind him not to say anything about the upcoming release of her own novel, which she'd warned him not to mention in front of Diane. It wasn't something she was ready to share with her yet.

Mia let out a tiny, almost inaudible sigh. 'Fine. It's called *Dust*.'

'Oh, you mean *The Book of Dust* by Philip Pullman?'

'No. It's called *Dust*.'

'I see,' Hannah replied, shaking her head. 'You're quite right, then. I don't think I have heard of that. Who's the author? Is it YA?'

Mia frowned. 'He's called Hugh Howey. It's the third part of a post-apocalyptic sci-fi trilogy.'

'She reads a lot,' Diane explained after Mia had left the room. 'She's a proper bookworm, like you were at that age. A different kind of book, mind. She's definitely not into the girly stuff. And it's not only the arts that she does well in at school. She's also really good at maths, computing and the sciences. She's quite the all-rounder.'

'Really?' Mark said. 'That's interesting.'

Hannah said nothing. She knew the 'girly stuff' comment was a dig at the kinds of novels she used to tear through as a youngster: mainly love stories and classics by the likes of Jane Austen and the Brontë sisters, which Diane had regularly branded a waste of time. Such disparaging remarks were precisely the reason she didn't want to mention her own book. Hannah was fiercely proud of her achievement; while a part of her wanted to boast about it, she also didn't want to give her sister the chance to pooh-pooh it.

Diane had barely read at all as a child, so it was definitely interesting that Mia was a keen reader, especially with all the other distractions on offer these days.

Mark, obviously thinking along the same lines, continued: 'I thought kids didn't read books any more. That's what you always hear in the news. They're supposed to be permanently glued to their smartphones, right?' He laughed, pulling his own phone out of his shirt pocket and giving it a little shake. 'Just like the rest of us.'

'Good point,' Hannah added. 'I haven't seen Mia on a phone once. Doesn't she have one?'

'Oh, she has one all right,' Diane replied. 'She usually spends more than her fair share of time on it, believe me. She hasn't today because I confiscated it.'

Hannah and Mark both looked at her expectantly after this, the implication being that she should elaborate, but no further explanation came.

Anyway, now Mia was on her way to bed – a move quite possibly pre-orchestrated by her mother – Hannah assumed the reason for their journey up north was soon to be revealed.

Part of her dreaded what was about to come. And yet, anticipating it would almost certainly involve Diane eating humble pie and asking for her help in some way, the competitive-sister streak in her was, in a warped way, slightly looking forward to it.

Deciding to let them stay the night had been similar. If Hannah was totally honest with herself, the fact that Diane had seemed so desperate – like she had no other option – had appealed to her sense of one-upmanship, as well as her compassion.

It was hard to feel anything approaching love or affection for Diane now when Hannah considered the awful state she'd been left in by her departure and the resulting loss of contact with her niece. Gradually, with a lot of patience and support from Mark, she'd learned to cope. She'd grown numb. Once warm emotions had run colder and colder until they'd frozen solid; she'd finally accepted the harsh reality that, for all manners and purposes, she no longer had a sister.

Except suddenly here she was again . . . dining and soon to be sleeping in her home.

How was Hannah supposed to deal with that? No wonder she felt so confused and conflicted.

'Well, who wants some coffee?' Mark asked, clapping his hands together as he stood up from the table.

'Good idea,' Hannah added, also getting to her feet and

starting to clear the plates. 'I'll give you a hand.' She looked at her sister as she added: 'Then we can all sit down and have a good chat, right?'

Diane nodded, her face looking very pale all of a sudden. 'Of course. But could I be awkward and ask for tea instead of coffee?'

'No problem,' Mark replied.

She also made a move to get up and help clear the dishes, but Hannah told her it wasn't necessary. 'You go and grab a seat in the lounge,' she said, keen to have a few moments alone with her husband before the big discussion.

'So what do you think she's going to say?' Hannah asked Mark a few minutes later. She spoke in a low voice but was glad of the noise of the kettle and coffee maker to ensure they weren't overheard.

He shook his head. 'I really have no idea. She's played her cards very close to her chest so far. It could well be money she's after, I suppose. What kind of car has she got?'

'I've not got a clue. I didn't ask. Why would I? And I didn't see them arrive in it. I don't even know where she's left it. A nearby car park, I suppose, although that won't be cheap.'

'Didn't she ask if we had a space?'

'Yes, when she first arrived, but I explained it was taken up with our own car and we didn't discuss it further. I was too shell-shocked by her arrival at that point to even think about it. What's her car got to do with anything anyway?'

Digging out some chocolates from the cupboard to serve with the drinks, Mark replied: 'I thought if it was a battered old thing, that might be an indicator of money issues. Never mind. Most people buy cars on credit anyway.'

'And if she does ask us for cash? She can see we've got plenty to spare, based on the apartment. So do we help her out or not?'

'She's your sister, darling. What do you think?'

Hannah peered at the coffee machine but saw it wasn't quite finished yet. 'Well, my first reaction would be to say no. She can't just waltz in here after everything that's happened and pretend like we're still close. I'd send her to Dad, although I guess she's already tried him first—'

'Whoa, slow down, Han. You're making a lot of assumptions here. Why don't we wait and see what she has to say? It may not be what we think at all. And we don't have to say yes or no to anything straight away. We can say we need a little time to discuss it with each other and think it over.'

Hannah let out a sigh. 'The problem is Mia. I wouldn't want her to suffer in any way, even though she doesn't seem to like me very much.'

Standing behind his wife, Mark reached around and encircled her waist with a strong arm, planting a tender kiss on her neck. 'What do you mean? Why do you think she doesn't like you? You barely know each other. She's a teenager, that's all. They're supposed to be grumpy. It's in the job description.'

Mia popped her head into the lounge to say goodnight as they were serving up the hot drinks.

'Sorry, you don't want a tea or coffee at all, do you?' Hannah asked her, feeling bad for not offering earlier, even though she was keen to get on with their adults-only conversation.

'No, she's fine,' Diane answered. 'You've already brushed your teeth, haven't you, love?'

Mia nodded.

'Enjoy *Dust*,' Hannah added, immediately wishing she hadn't, for fear of sounding like she was trying too hard.

Mia nodded again and, before disappearing off to her room, whispered something to her mum.

'No, not now,' Diane replied. 'You can have it back in the morning, like we discussed. And don't go rooting through my stuff for it, because you won't find it.'

Hannah realised they were talking about Mia's confiscated mobile and, although she left without saying anything more, it was clear from the stamp of the teenager's feet that she wasn't happy with the outcome.

They'd put her and Diane together in the larger of their two spare bedrooms, which contained twin singles. There was also a double bed in the third room, but it wasn't made up and Hannah hadn't felt like making the extra effort to do it.

Once they heard the bedroom door shut, Mark walked over to the lounge door and shut that too, signalling it was time to get down to business – whatever that meant.

Hannah was really glad he was here. Mark was her rock and she wouldn't have wanted to do this without him. It helped that he knew all the ins and outs of what had gone on between the two sisters, having witnessed first-hand the detrimental effect it had had on his wife.

Mark could see her sister for what she was: an adept manipulator, who knew exactly how to wrap unsuspecting people – particularly men – around her little finger. Not that she'd shown much sign of that skill so far today. But why would she in the company of people already wise to her tricks?

Hannah was actually surprised how accommodating Mark was being. He'd made it clear long before the sisters' falling-out that he neither liked nor trusted Diane – and the way things had ended up, he'd been proved right. Not that he'd ever said so. He wasn't that kind of man. As for what was going through his head right now, she couldn't be sure. Hannah didn't even know what she thought about this weird, uncomfortable situation. It all hinged on what her sister was about to say.

'So,' Mark said, sitting back down next to Hannah on the couch and pouring some milk into his coffee.

From the armchair opposite, Diane cleared her throat before finally beginning to talk.

'Right,' she said. 'I'm sorry it's taken so long for me to get to the point, but, as I mentioned earlier, I really wanted to wait for Mia to be out of the way. This isn't a conversation for her ears.'

She paused to take a sip of her tea as the others watched in silence.

'So you're probably wondering what I'm doing here after all this time. You must think I have a right nerve turning up like this – I get that. But here I am anyway and, as you've probably guessed, I need to ask for your help.'

28

Diane stood up and walked over to the window. She stared out over the city and gave a dramatic sigh, leading Hannah and Mark to flash each other a confused sideways glance.

'I've missed this place,' she went on, continuing to gaze outside with her back to the others. 'I didn't think I would, but it's true what they say: home *is* where the heart is. It's been far too long . . .'

Diane paused again, running a hand through her short hair. Hannah could feel Mark getting edgy, his knee jumping up and down next to her. She was on the verge of saying something herself – telling Diane to stop messing around and get to the point – when her sister turned back to face them with tears running down her face.

Despite everything, seeing this instantly made Hannah want to jump up and give her a hug. It was instinctive, particularly because crying wasn't something she'd witnessed Diane do many times as an adult. But Mark must have sensed what she was feeling; he pressed a firm hand on to her knee and whispered in the tiniest of voices: 'Don't.'

So she didn't. She stayed put and told herself, even though her heart said otherwise, that they were probably crocodile tears. She waited for Diane to carry on, which, after taking a deep breath and wiping her eyes with one hand, she did.

'So the reason I've come here isn't to ask you to do something for me. Not directly anyway . . . It's for Mia.'

These words sent Hannah's mind racing, because they

29

weren't at all what she'd expected to hear. Maybe the visit wouldn't turn out to be about money after all, she thought. Unless Diane wanted to enrol Mia in a private school or something and she needed help paying the fees. Was she being bullied perhaps? Gosh, it would be hard to say no if that was the case.

'Would you like a tissue?' Mark asked, as Diane's emotions got the better of her again. He reached into a drawer under the coffee table, pulling out a box and handing it over.

'Thank you,' Diane replied, accepting it, then wiping her eyes and blowing her nose. 'I'm sorry. I didn't mean for this to happen.'

Was this all for show? Hannah wondered. She knew what her sister was capable of, but this was very convincing. If it wasn't for Mark's hand, clamped back on her knee after getting the tissues, she'd have definitely got up to comfort her by now. 'It's okay, take your time,' she said instead, not wanting to appear totally cold-hearted.

'Right,' Diane said, sitting back down after a long moment, placing a hand on each arm of the chair and slowly exhaling. 'I can do this.'

Hannah wasn't sure whether this was meant for herself or for them, but either way it appeared to work. Speaking slowly and steadily, her eyes darting between her two-strong audience and occasionally into the distance, Diane finally got to the point.

'I'm in a big mess,' she said. 'As you can probably see. I'm afraid I'm not in a position to tell you why right now, for reasons that will become apparent later, but I've got some things I need to sort out: really important things. I can't emphasise that enough.

'Both of you must know deep down that I wouldn't be here if that wasn't the case. I mean, I could totally understand you thinking this to be some kind of bullshit, but it's not. Honestly, from the bottom of my heart, it's not. I'm backed into a corner and I've literally nowhere else to turn.

'So what I'm here to ask you, to get to the point, is whether you could possibly look after Mia while I get this mess fixed. Above all else, I want her to be safe and, well, I can't think of a safer place for her to be than here. I realise you hardly know her, or her you. I take full responsibility for that. But . . . you're family.'

Diane continued talking, but Hannah didn't listen to the rest. She was too busy trying to absorb what she'd just heard. It was almost an anticlimax after what she'd been expecting, and yet it was also huge.

Her long-lost sister was essentially begging them to take in her pride and joy: the child Hannah had always secretly envied her having; the niece she'd mourned the loss of; the teenager with whom she'd so far struggled to bond. Wow. She really hadn't seen this coming.

It was actually flattering that Diane found this the safest place to leave her. But why here and not with their father or one of the friends she must have made during her time in self-imposed exile? And what was this trouble she'd got herself into that she couldn't discuss?

'You're both very quiet,' Diane said, pulling Hannah back into the moment. 'What do you think?'

31

'Um.' She looked over at her husband. 'I think it's something we'll need to discuss privately, right, Mark?'

He nodded. 'Definitely. And I'm sure you have a few questions, Hannah, because I know I do. This has obviously come as quite a surprise.'

'Sure,' Hannah replied, her mind already a whirr of thoughts, examining the ins and outs of having her niece coming to holiday with them.

Although some of the practicalities were of concern, such as how she'd find a way to bond with Mia and whether it would affect her writing schedule, on balance she actually felt pretty excited about the idea.

Mark was staring at her, an expectant look upon his face, so she indicated that he should fire away with his own questions first.

'Well,' he said, appearing a bit thrown by this, 'for a start I was wondering when you were thinking of. We were considering taking a couple of last-minute trips away this summer, so there's that to bear in mind. Also, how long are we talking about: a few days; a week? Obviously, it would be nice to have some kind of idea about that.'

Mark cleared his throat. 'And as for this mess you say you've got yourself into, it's all very vague. It's not going to result in any, er, problems landing at our door, is it?' He blushed, hesitating before adding: 'Um, don't get me wrong, I'm not referring to Mia as a problem. What I mean is . . . I'm simply concerned one or both of you might be in some kind of danger.'

Mark nudged Hannah at this point – a gesture obviously

meant as a request for her support. But all she could manage was to nod her head and say: 'Yes, quite.'

Hannah wasn't surprised by his questions. They were very practical and a far better reflection of his views on children than his successful chat with Mia earlier might have indicated. Clearly the idea of their niece staying alone with them for any amount of time concerned him. This was no surprise to Hannah. Mark wasn't into kids. He'd been that way for as long as she'd known him. He wasn't particularly interested in them and he'd never wanted one of his own.

To be fair, this was something he'd made clear to Hannah from an early stage in their relationship. At that point she had hoped to have a family one day and, naively perhaps, thought she'd eventually be able to persuade him otherwise. But as they'd got to know each other better and moved from dating to living together, with marriage becoming a possibility, Mark had re-emphasised that having children wasn't something he ever wanted.

She still remembered what he'd said to her during one particularly intense conversation, which had proved to be a crossroads event in her life. She'd been twenty-four at the time. It was a frosty January night in Didsbury, south Manchester, where they'd been living then. They'd been out for dinner at an unremarkable Italian restaurant that no longer existed and, having shared a couple of bottles of red, their talk on the way home had turned serious.

'You know how much I love you, don't you?' Mark had said, squeezing her hand through her leather glove.

'Of course,' she'd replied, leaning over to plant a kiss on his cheek. 'Me too.'

'Well, because of that I need to say something, before it's too late.'

These words had made Hannah's heart stand still. She'd felt a sudden sense of panic rise up in her chest. 'That sounds scary,' she'd replied in a small voice, fearing that Mark was about to break up with her.

'Sorry. It's about kids. It's been on my mind for a while. I've told you already I don't want to have them, but before we take things to the next level, I need you to understand that I absolutely mean it. It's just . . . I don't really get children and I don't want to be responsible for bringing another life into this world. I'm one hundred per cent serious – and I'm afraid that's never going to change.

'The thing is, Han, that I know you would like a family. And because I love you so much, I can't let you stay with me thinking I'll be able to give you that. I won't. So as much as it would break my heart to lose you, I'm giving you a get-out-of-jail-free card. I don't want to be the one who stops you getting what you want out of life.'

The conversation had continued for a while, and much soul-searching on Hannah's part had followed it. During this difficult period, she focused on the fact that she'd never felt anything close to the love she did for Mark for anyone else before. She simply couldn't imagine a life without him, as her recent panic at the prospect of being dumped had demonstrated. Plus there were solid reasons for Mark's standpoint, rooted in his past and a tragedy that had ripped his family apart. So ultimately

Hannah had decided their relationship was worth the sacrifice.

A few days after she'd told him this, he proposed, and the following year they were married.

Since then, there had been a few private regrets along the way – particularly when, out of the blue and with no father on the scene, Diane had announced she was pregnant with Mia. However, for the most part, Hannah hadn't looked back. She and Mark still had a wonderful relationship; they enjoyed the kind of varied, glamorous, spontaneous lifestyle that only a childless couple of their age could.

It was this her husband was keen to protect, she assumed, with his queries about the details of Diane's request. But despite her antagonism towards her sister, Hannah was feeling increasingly excited at the prospect of Mia coming to stay. What could be the harm in it?

Diane was just about holding things together. In answer to Mark's questions, after wiping her eyes again and then blowing her nose, she said: 'I, um, was hoping you might be able to take Mia right away. It shouldn't be too long until I get things sorted: hopefully only a few days. And, no, there's no chance of any danger, as you put it, following us here. You've nothing to be concerned about.'

'What about you?' Hannah asked her. 'Are you going to be all right?'

'I'm a big girl. I can take care of myself, but please don't push for any details because I can't provide them. It's better that you don't know anyway.'

'And Dad? Why did you come to us rather than him?

Or did you try him first and we were second choice?'

'Dad's about to go away on a cruise around the Med. But even if he wasn't, I couldn't bear the idea of bloody Joan getting her claws into Mia. Believe it or not, you two were always first choice.'

Well, at least we still agree on something, Hannah thought. Joan was their father's second wife, who'd appeared on the scene far too soon after their mother's death for her liking. Hannah had always thought of Joan, who was nine years younger than sixty-seven-year-old Frank, as a gold-digger. And despite the fact they'd been together for a long time now, she'd never taken to her. Joan had been a widowed neighbour of her parents, who'd rather quickly turned into something else after Maggie's death. Once she and Frank had got married, she'd convinced him to move to a village near Cambridge to be close to her family yet far from his northern roots. That said, he was at least living much closer to Diane and Mia in Bournemouth than he had been previously.

Hannah could understand why Diane wouldn't want Joan manipulating her daughter like she had their father, who was a different man now than he had been with their mother. He was henpecked, basically, living the life she wanted him to lead and never daring to contradict her.

After a few more quickfire questions and answers, Diane said she'd give them some time alone to discuss the situation and followed Mia off to bed.

'So,' Hannah said to Mark once it was just the two of them in the lounge, 'what do you think?'

CHAPTER 3

Mark Cook knew his wife well enough to see she was already sold on the idea of having Mia come to stay.

When Diane had finally got round to explaining the reason for her visit, there had been a distinct change in Hannah's attitude towards the situation. He'd sensed it immediately – and he even understood why. Her problem was with her sister, who under this proposal wasn't going to be around. Hannah had been expecting a plea for cash, but instead she'd been offered the chance to bond with her long-lost niece.

Of course she was keen on the idea, even though Mia hadn't exactly been friendly to her earlier. His wife had been devastated by what had gone on between her and her sister all those years ago. It had nearly broken her beyond repair. It surely would have, had she known the whole truth. And losing access to her niece – who she'd doted on, like a surrogate child of her own – had been especially hard.

The toddler Hannah had loved to spoil rotten was long gone, replaced by a fourteen-year-old stranger. But despite Mark's major reservations about the request – based on a deep-seated distrust of Diane and his knowledge of her full potential to wreak havoc – he had little confidence in his ability to convince his wife. Despite what he felt, he couldn't risk sounding more negative about her sister than she was, nor could he be seen as the one to put his foot down and say no. It was too risky. Diane was too much of a wildcard, especially after all these years. It had been such a relief to have her out of their lives for so long. Now she was back, he had no idea what was going through her mind – and the more he thought about this, the more it terrified him.

Sure enough, as soon as her sister had left the room, Hannah's eyes lit up. 'Well, that was unexpected,' she said in a low voice. 'What do you think, love? I have to admit I'm pretty excited by the idea. It would be amazing to get the chance to reconnect with Mia.'

Mark smiled. 'I had a feeling that's what you were thinking. It is all a little bit odd, though. And what about this mysterious mess Diane's got herself into? Any idea what it might be?'

'I don't know,' Hannah whispered. 'I'm not too inter-ested in that, to be honest. I'm mainly relieved she's not asking us for money or planning to stick around herself. The last thing I expected was that I'd want to agree to anything Diane asked of me. But I do really like the pros-pect of having Mia here for a bit. What's the harm if it's only for a few days? She's changed so much from the little girl I remember. I'd love to get to know her again. What do you think?'

'You seem quite set on the idea. Diane's your sister, so I think it should be your decision.'

'That's nice of you,' Hannah replied, squeezing his hand, kissing him on the cheek and gazing into his eyes. 'But this is your home too; I won't agree to anything you're not happy about.'

A big part of Mark wanted to say no at this point. He had a bad feeling about the whole business, but as this wasn't based on anything he could communicate to Hannah, he bit his tongue. 'If it's what you really want, then you have my blessing. But I'd sleep on it, rather than saying anything to Diane tonight while she's still awake. That way you can be sure.'

'Of course,' she replied. 'You know I love you, don't you?'

'I do. And I love you too, which is why I want you to be careful.'

'I will.'

Hannah made the announcement at breakfast the next morning, when all four of them were again sitting around the dining table.

'So, Mia,' she said, after taking a long sip from her coffee. 'Your mother asked us last night whether you might be able to stay here for a short holiday. Of course we'd be only too delighted to have you.'

'Both of us, you mean?' Mia asked, the frown on her forehead revealing she clearly didn't know anything about this.

39

'Um, no. Just you, love,' a flustered Diane replied, clearing her throat several times. 'I have a few things I need to sort out. I thought this might be a nice break for you.'

'What kind of things? You said we were only going on a quick trip. I have plans with my friends.'

'We'll talk about this in private after breakfast,' Diane said. 'I was waiting to see if it was possible before mentioning it to you.'

Mia raised her voice. 'But this is so not fair. I—'

'Do you want your phone back this morning or not?' Diane snapped. 'I can take it with me if you like.'

'No, Mum, please—'

'Eat your breakfast then and drop it.'

Mark was as surprised to see this work as he was about Diane not telling Mia in advance about the request she'd made of him and Hannah. Mia barely said another word for the rest of the meal and looked on the verge of tears.

Hannah's move to announce their decision this way, rather than speaking to Diane privately first, was – Mark assumed, even though they hadn't discussed it – designed to unsettle her. He had to admit it was a decent way of emphasising the fact that Hannah was no pushover, despite agreeing to help. And yet seeing Diane baited in this way made him feel uncomfortable, as of course did Mia's less than ecstatic reaction to the news.

Later, after the pair had had their private discussion, from which mum and daughter had both emerged red-eyed but reconciled, the teenager seemed to have accepted what was happening. She still didn't look over the moon about it, but why would she? She was essentially being left with two strangers. At least he and Hannah both remembered spending time with her as a toddler; she was unlikely to recall that now.

Meanwhile, Diane hadn't wasted any time in packing her things ready to leave. It was almost like she was keen to get out of there before they changed their minds. There was a stilted goodbye with Hannah, which focused on practicalities like the swapping of mobile numbers in the absence of affection. Then, in sharp contrast, Diane gave her daughter a tender, lingering hug with whispered final words and tears.

As for Mark, he'd been tasked with accompanying his sister-in-law down to her car to pick up some further things for Mia and to give her directions on how best to drive out of the city.

It started to feel awkward as soon as the metal doors slid shut and the two of them were standing next to each other in the lift. Staring at the red LED level indicator, Mark willed it to move faster or even to stop at another floor so someone else could get in and break the tension. Neither of these things happened and not a word passed between them.

It was Diane who'd suggested he should be the one to accompany her to the car, and this bothered him. She'd conveyed it as being down to his strength and a presumed familiarity with the best routes in and out of the city centre, which looked very different to the last time she'd been here. However, Mark suspected it was more to do with her wanting a word with him in private, which was precisely the reason why he wasn't facilitating a conversation by making small talk.

There was only one subject he and Diane had ever needed to talk about in private – and just thinking about that made him very nervous, particularly after she'd been out of his and Hannah's lives for so long now.

Thankfully, she gave no indication of wanting to say anything as they left the apartment block and stepped out into a pleasant summer's morning: warm but with a fresh breeze. Mark was dressed in khaki shorts and a red polo shirt; Diane was in the same navy leggings as yesterday but with a fresh sky-blue T-shirt. Speaking only for functional purposes, such as to discuss which car park they were heading to and the quickest way to get there, they walked at a brisk pace. He had offered to carry her backpack for her, but she had politely declined, saying it weighed very little.

The multistorey NCP where Diane had parked was only a couple of streets away. When they got there, it was already chock-a-block with cars, presumably belonging to early-bird Saturday shoppers or, like Diane, people who'd spent the previous night staying nearby. Her car was a white Vauxhall Astra, a couple of years old and in decent nick. This didn't give much away about her financial status, although, as she hadn't asked them for money, that wasn't particularly relevant now.

Diane opened the boot to reveal two suitcases: one black, one navy. She indicated that the black one was Mia's, so Mark lifted it out. Feeling its considerable weight, he was relieved to note it had a set of wheels and a telescopic handle. He certainly wouldn't have fancied carrying it back to the apartment.

'Is this all Mia's stuff?' he asked.

'Yes.'

'It's heavy. Does she really need so much for a couple of days?'

'Teenage girls have a lot of stuff. Trust me: she'll be happier this way than not having enough.'

Trust her, Mark thought. That was something he would never do.

'Right, well, I'd better get going anyway,' Diane said, to Mark's considerable relief. 'What's the best way to the M60?'

He gave her quick directions back to the motorway ring road around Manchester, from which she claimed to know the way. 'It would be easiest with a satnav,' he said. 'Don't you have one?'

'I do, but it's a bit temperamental and several years out of date,' she replied. 'I prefer not to rely . . .'

At this point, standing at the side of the car next to him, looking at a map he'd printed out from the computer to help her, Diane's voice faded out.

'Are you okay?' he asked, looking over and seeing she'd closed her eyes and that her hands were tightly gripping the roof of the car. It was hard to tell for sure in the artificial light, but he could swear she looked paler than before. 'Is there anything I can—'

'I'm fine,' she replied through gritted teeth. 'It's just stomach cramps: time of the month. It'll pass in a minute.'

43

'Oh, right.' Mark felt more awkward than ever now. He didn't know whether to look at her or away from her, so instead he found himself staring at the map and hoping his face hadn't turned bright red.

Sure enough, a few moments later Diane declared that she was 'all right now'. She unlocked the driver's door and sat down behind the wheel, accepting the map as Mark handed it to her. To his relief, she made no effort to kiss or hug him or shake his hand as they said their goodbyes, with her remaining seated and him stooped at her side, peering into the car through the open window.

'Thank you for taking in Mia,' his sister-in-law said. 'She really means everything to me.'

Mark was surprised to hear her voice waver as the words came out. There were fresh tears in the corners of her eyes too.

'No problem,' he said, wondering for the umpteenth time what kind of trouble she'd got herself into. 'Take care. We'll keep her safe for you, so no need to worry. You concentrate on sorting out whatever it is you need to do and get yourself back here in one piece. See you in a few days.'

He stood back from the vehicle, wheeling Mia's case with him. As Diane pulled the Astra out of the parking space, he thought he must have misjudged her reason for bringing him here. Perhaps she'd changed over the years she'd been away. But it would take much more than this to convince him – and he really struggled to picture a future in which the sisters got along again and were back in regular contact. However, there was a reason time was said to be a great healer. A couple of days ago he could hardly have imagined the possibility of her and Mia staying the night at their flat. Never mind Mia staying on alone for a short while.

Before driving off, Diane called him over. He assumed she wanted to check something to do with the directions he'd given her, but instead she reached out and handed him a white envelope with his name handwritten on the front.

'What's this?' he asked.

'I'm sorry,' she replied, driving off without saying another word.

Mark was dumbstruck. He wanted to shout after her. He even considered chasing her on foot to the exit. But instead he stood there, open-mouthed, alone in the middle of the car park, one hand on Mia's suitcase and the other holding the letter-sized envelope.

What the hell was this all about? What was Diane up to? Why bother to get him alone only to hand him this message, or whatever it was? Surely she could have slipped it to him at some point while they were in the apartment?

He was torn between ripping the envelope open immediately to find out what it contained, or waiting until later. The truth was that it scared him to think what he might find within.

He remained there, contemplating this, for several minutes until eventually a large SUV came along, wanting to drive by, forcing him to move out of the way. So he stuck the unopened envelope into the side pocket of his shorts and wheeled the hefty case to the nearest lift.

He made it halfway home before curiosity got the better of him. He stopped at a vacant bench, sat down and pulled the envelope out of his pocket.

He took it in both hands, one holding each side like he was watching a video on his mobile, and raised it to eye level. The quivering of his limbs made the flimsy paper jiggle backwards and forwards. He told himself this was down to the breeze, but his raised heartbeat and shallow breathing were dead giveaways of the real reason.

Mark scrutinised the four letters of his name, which were scrawled in a large, loose hand using blue biro. The writing style wasn't dissimilar from Hannah's; if there was any other information to be gained from examining it, Mark wasn't the person to do so. He had absolutely no clue whether it had been written in haste, anger or whatever. As for what it contained: not much, by the feel of things; probably one or two sheets of paper.

The only way forward was to open it, of course. He knew that, but it took a few more minutes of staring at the envelope – building up to it – before he felt ready to do so.

His heart raced faster still as he finally ran a finger under the seal and pulled out the contents: a single sheet of plain A4 paper, folded three times and with writing on both sides.

Taking a deep breath and then slowly exhaling, he unfolded the letter and read what Diane had to say to him, penned in the same blue ink as the envelope.

Dear Mark,

If you're reading this, that means I've chickened out of speaking to you in person. I apologise. In my defence, my head's all over the place right now.

I'm writing this in the spare room of your lovely apartment. It's after three in the morning. Mia is asleep in the bed next to me and, apart from the city noises that float in through the open window behind me, everything here is calm and still.

Everything except me, that is. I can't sleep tonight. I wonder if you and Hannah can after what I've asked of you.

I really hope you'll say yes. If you're reading this, then you must have, so thank you for that, from the bottom of my heart.

I don't deserve your help – but Mia does. She's an innocent party in everything that's happened to bring us to this moment and I honestly believe there's no better or safer place for her to be right now than here with you. Please don't blame her for my mistakes.

Now to get to the point. There's no easy way to say this, which is why I've been waffling and, of course, why I'm writing this letter in the first place. I already know there's a good chance I won't dare to tell you in person tomorrow.

I know you suspected this previously. I know you came right out with it and asked me, yet I denied it to your face. Honestly, I thought I was doing the best thing by everyone in telling you that. But it was a lie – and now it's time for the truth.

Your suspicions were right: Mia is your daughter.

I know. That must be a shock to read. You probably don't even believe me. I can totally understand why you'd think it's yet another lie.

But it's not. I swear it on my own life, for what that's worth.

I'm afraid I can't bring myself to swear anything on Mia's life. She's too precious to me. Look at her, though, and then look in your heart. Spend some time with her, like you did before, and I think you'll see that what I'm saying is true.

Why am I telling you this now? Well, for one thing, because it's the right thing to do. Secrets and lies are no good. They eat you up inside.

There's more to it than that, of course, but I think I've given you quite enough to digest for now.

For what it's worth, I'm truly sorry for everything I've put you through.

Diane

Mark read the letter three times in total, one immediately after the other. Even then he didn't feel like he'd truly absorbed its contents.

It was worse than he'd expected. Much worse. He'd been pretty sure it would be something to do with that one night they'd spent together. That huge mistake he'd made around fifteen years ago and regretted ever since. But not this. Not Mia.

He'd feared maybe Diane was looking for money after all; that she'd been planning to blackmail him by threatening to tell Hannah unless he coughed up some cash.

That was the most likely scenario he'd been able to come up with after she'd handed him the envelope.

But not this.

How could he be Mia's father?

He knew it was technically possible, but . . . if he actually was, how could Diane have kept that from him for so many years? Naturally he'd been suspicious once, because the dates were too close for comfort. He'd asked her outright on several occasions and, as her letter specified, she'd always been adamant that Mia wasn't his child. Eventually, he'd believed her. It had been a relief, to be honest.

He'd never forgotten their night of passion – and not in a good way. It was still a regular source of nightmares, which usually ended with Hannah walking in and discovering them in bed together. But in recent years, with so much water under the bridge, he'd barely thought about the possibility they might have conceived a child together. Had Mia been around and in his life, it may well have been a different story. He could have seen things in her to make him wonder, as had happened when she was younger.

Having kids had never been on Mark's agenda. He'd ruled it out long ago, thanks in no small part to a devastating experience he and his family had been through when he was still a child himself. It was something he avoided discussing or even thinking about to this day. He preferred to tell people he simply wasn't a paternal kind of man, which was also true. It wound him up when parents fussed on social media over things like their child's first day at school or the outfit they'd dressed up in to go trick-or-treating on Halloween.

So after more than a decade of not seeing Mia – a girl Mark had been assured was only his niece by marriage – she'd been pushed far from his thoughts.

Until now.

At this moment Mia was right at the heart of his thoughts. He had no idea what he was going to say to her when he returned to the flat. How could he look at her or Hannah without giving away what he'd just read? What if Diane had already told Mia or given her some kind of hint? And how was he supposed to know for sure she wasn't making it up?

Mark's mind leapt frantically from one thought to another. This was a potential disaster. No wonder Diane hadn't wanted to tell him in person, although how he wished she had. There were a million questions he wanted to ask her. Not least, he needed to know if she'd told anyone else so far or planned to do so in the near future. Frank, his father-in-law, was a terrifying possibility. But even that paled into insignificance compared to the prospect of Hannah finding out.

He knew how heartbroken she would be to discover he and Diane had slept together. He'd already imagined that scene countless times. And for Hannah to find out now, all these years later, knowing they'd kept it from her and lied to her face. It would be truly awful.

But this was so much worse. The very idea of him

fathering Mia – giving Hannah's hated sister a child while denying his wife the same – that would devastate her.

He'd have to get Diane's mobile number from Hannah's phone, preferably without her realising, and contact her directly. More secrets and lies, in other words; digging himself deeper. But what choice did he have?

Mark read the letter through a fourth time. He was hoping to miraculously uncover some further answers or explanation: a little detail perhaps, which he might have missed on the previous occasions due to shock. But he found nothing of the sort.

Letting out a long, frustrated sigh, he folded the paper up, slid it back into the envelope, folded that in half and shoved it firmly into his pocket. Destroying it would probably be the wisest thing to do, but Mark knew he'd want to read it again. No, he'd have to hide it somewhere that Hannah, and Mia for that matter, wouldn't find it. His work briefcase would probably be the safest option. As usual, it was full of business-related paperwork he'd brought home in the hope of finding a spare moment over the weekend to catch up on a few things. Hannah was extremely unlikely to look in there and, for extra peace of mind, he could also lock it with a small key. Then on Monday he could stash the letter somewhere in his desk at work.

So there was one tiny problem solved. If only that was all he had to worry about.

Mark held his head in his hands and fought to clear his thoughts.

He knew there was no point in feeling sorry for himself,

or wishing none of this was happening, because it was. Fact of life.

His only option at this moment was to put on a brave face and pretend everything was all right. He had to do his utmost not to give the slightest indication to Hannah or Mia of there being a problem. Otherwise he was finished.

'Come on!' he said under his breath, slapping both cheeks with his hands to shock himself into action. Keeping a cool head in a crisis was the kind of thing he did at work all the time. He could manage this. It was the only way.

So Mark jumped to his feet.

Standing tall, willing his mind to follow his body's example, he paced purposefully in the direction of home.

CHAPTER 4

Hannah was standing outside the spare bedroom, or Mia's room as it had now temporarily become, with her right ear to the closed door.

She was listening to see if she could hear any sound from within; trying to work out whether her niece was awake yet. It was 10.05 a.m. on Monday: two days since Diane had left Mia in her and Mark's care.

Hannah had been awake since just before 7 a.m. when Mark had kissed her goodbye as he left for the office. She always found it hard to sleep in when it got light so early during the summer months. Blackout curtains or blinds would fix that. But she actually quite liked to be up early: to gaze out of the window and watch the city below move through its own morning routines while she did the same from the comfort of the apartment.

Off her and Mark's bedroom, as well as an en-suite bathroom, was a small balcony with a table and two chairs. Sometimes she liked to drink a cup of tea or coffee there and enjoy the sounds as well as the sights of Manchester. There was a communal garden on the roof, which had sounded wonderful when they'd moved in, although in practice they rarely ever used it.

If Hannah was going properly outside – actually leaving the apartment – she preferred to do so at street level. There was so much more to see close up: not least a bottomless supply of characters and dialogue to feed her fiction.

Unfortunately, the weather today didn't make her want to go outside at all. Not even on to the balcony. The sunshine of the past few days had vanished, replaced by grey skies and incessant drizzle. Typical Manchester weather.

It made Hannah feel sorry for all the schoolkids, like Mia, who were finally free from the constraints of education and deserved better. It was the end of July, for goodness' sake. Mind you, if Mia was planning to stay in bed all day, the weather didn't really matter.

Hannah tiptoed away from her position in front of the bedroom door, having stayed there for at least a minute without hearing any sign of life whatsoever. She walked through to the lounge, shutting the door behind her and finally feeling like she could make some noise again. Just as well this wasn't one of the typical open-plan apartments that were so prevalent nowadays. Hannah and Mark had specifically sought out one like this, with separate rooms around a central hallway, which they both preferred. In the last few days, thanks to their unexpected visitors, it had proved useful.

But what was she doing, creeping around her own home? It was ridiculous when she thought about it. And in doing so, rather than making the noises she normally would at this time on a Monday morning, she was only increasing the likelihood of Mia staying in bed longer.

So what should she do: start hoovering? No, that would be a bit over the top. She hadn't had breakfast yet, thinking it rude to do so without her guest; how much longer was she going to have to wait? Until what time did fourteen-year-olds usually sleep? Mia had been up of her own accord by 9 a.m. yesterday, although the sound of Hannah and Mark moving around and chatting had probably roused her.

What if the poor thing was lying awake in her bed, waiting to hear Hannah moving around, and, because she'd been so quiet, still hadn't got up?

Wow. Who would have guessed how awkward this was going to be?

Hannah made a decision: she'd switch the radio on here in the lounge, not too loud but enough to make it obvious she was up and about. If that hadn't worked by 10.30 a.m., she'd start making breakfast and knock on Mia's door to let her know.

Meanwhile, after tuning the hi-fi in to Radio 2, she looked over at the desk in the corner of the room. Her eyes were immediately drawn to the laptop lying there on top of it, gathering dust next to the printer. That was where she ought to have been for the last couple of hours. Instead of worrying about what time her niece would get up and how they would spend the day together, she could have used this quiet period to get some writing done.

Hannah's first novel was due to be published next

January. Although that was still a way off, she'd finished working on it now, at least in terms of writing and editing. However, from what her editor and publicist had told her, there would be plenty more to do promotion-wise near to release. She didn't even want to think about that yet. It made her nervous. Meanwhile, her mind was on the next novel: the second part of the two-book deal she'd signed, which she was due to deliver next March.

She hadn't even got halfway through her first draft yet and, although her editor had been enthusiastic about the synopsis she'd written initially, Hannah was far from happy with how it was going. There was still plenty of time, but she wanted to get ahead of the game, particularly as she feared not being able to produce something as good as her debut release.

Chatting in bed last night, Mark had asked her how she was getting on with it.

'Um, okay, I guess.'

'That doesn't sound too convincing, Han. What's up? Anything I can help with?'

'Not really, unless you want to write it for me.'

Mark had crossed his eyes at this and pulled a wonky face. 'Hmm. Maybe not. Don't think I've got that in me like you, darling. I could read what you've got so far, if that would help.'

'No, thanks,' she'd replied, somehow finding a way to grin despite her frustration. 'It's not fit for human consumption yet.'

'Hey, I never said I wanted to eat it,' Mark had replied, deadpan. 'I love you a lot – but not that much.'

'You know what I mean. I'm just not very happy with it at the moment. I suppose I'm anxious the publishers will be disappointed. And that March deadline somehow doesn't feel very far away.'

Mark had reassured her, as he was always so good at doing, that such doubts were only normal in the circumstances. He'd recommended she have a chat with her literary agent, Bruce Wilks, about them.

'Yeah, maybe,' she'd replied. 'But I don't want him to start doubting me too. Plus he's on holiday at the moment. I'm not going to bother him while he's away.'

Hannah was embarrassed by her doubts and fears. She still struggled to refer to herself as an author, although she hoped that would change soon. Once she'd held a physical copy of one of her books in her hand – seen it on the shelves in stores – surely that would change.

As for her second novel, pushing on with it was all she could realistically do. She considered writing a few words now. There wouldn't be time to do much before she had breakfast with Mia, one way or another. But something was better than nothing.

Hannah sat down at the desk and opened up her laptop, buoyed by a wave of optimism. Then she proceeded to spend the next ten minutes on the Internet looking up the sleeping patterns of teenagers. She read that most tended to fall asleep and wake up later than they had as children, with their sleep patterns varying from one day to another. Teens usually required eight to ten hours of sleep per night to function at their best, apparently.

Well, that's interesting, Hannah thought. However, she

wasn't sure what to do with the information and felt annoyed she'd looked at it rather than write.

'Stuff it,' she said, slamming the laptop shut and striding over to Mia's bedroom.

She knocked on the door three times before announcing: 'I'm making us some breakfast, Mia. See you in the kitchen in ten minutes?'

There was a slight pause before a gravelly voice replied: 'Right.'

'Would you like tea or coffee?'

'Um, coffee.'

'A boiled egg?'

'Sure.'

'Great. See you soon.'

Hannah smiled to herself, pleased with how her wake-up call had gone. Mia's replies could have been a bit more polite: a please or thank-you wouldn't have gone amiss. But in her niece's defence, it had sounded like she'd just woken up.

As Hannah walked to the kitchen, she wondered how to keep Mia occupied for the rest of the day. She and Mark had spent much of the previous forty-eight hours trying to make their visitor feel welcome and at ease. They'd told her to call them both by their first names, rather than Aunt Hannah and Uncle Mark. Considering her age and the fact that they'd not been in her life for such a long time, it seemed more sensible – less forced – than the alternative; hopefully it would help her to feel comfortable in their presence.

They'd also spent a good amount of time showing Mia

58

around Manchester. On Saturday they'd strolled around the city centre, pointing out the location of the main shops and so on, before grabbing some food at a new pizza restaurant that had recently opened near Deansgate.

Yesterday, they'd gone out in the BMW to give Mia a flavour of some of the countryside around Manchester. They'd walked around Hollingworth Lake in Littleborough, a short drive out of the city, although Mia hadn't given much away in terms of whether she'd enjoyed it or not. She hadn't spoken a great deal on either day, mainly responding to their questions rather than making conversation.

This wasn't a huge surprise, considering her age and the fact she was only now getting to know her aunt and uncle. But it did mean Hannah was feeling apprehensive about being alone with her today. She really hoped to avoid a return to the awkward silences of last Friday, when Mia and her mum had first turned up.

Mind you, over the weekend, Hannah had done much more of the talking than Mark. He'd seemed more reserved than usual – not quite himself – but she guessed that made sense, considering his views on children. He probably needed time to adapt to Mia's presence.

As she put two eggs on the hob to boil, Hannah's mind turned to her sister, wondering when she was likely to contact them. Surely she'd phone or text today, having so far remained quiet since her departure on Saturday morning. If not, Hannah decided she probably ought to make contact herself soon.

She switched on the kitchen radio and laid two places at

the small table. This was where she and Mark usually ate when they didn't have company. She had considered using the dining room again, as they always had with Mia so far, but it seemed silly when there were only the two of them.

After a couple of reminder calls that breakfast was ready, Mia eventually appeared. Bleary-eyed and with her dark hair tied up in a messy bun, she was wearing grey jogging pants and a creased pink crop top.

'Good morning,' Hannah said. She smiled despite feeling annoyed at how long it had taken Mia to emerge. 'Grab a seat and I'll pour you some coffee.'

Mia stifled a yawn as she sat down on one of the two chairs.

'Did you sleep well?'

'I woke up a few times.'

'Oh dear. Did you hear Mark getting ready for work?'

Mia shrugged. 'Maybe.'

'He left just before seven, so . . .'

Hannah thought Mia might respond to this information, but instead there was a long silence.

As Hannah poured some coffee into her niece's cup, it occurred to her that maybe this wasn't an appropriate drink to serve a fourteen-year-old. How was she supposed to know? She struggled to remember at what age she'd started drinking coffee, and it wasn't like Diane had left her with an instruction manual.

She'd definitely had coffee with them yesterday morning, but Hannah couldn't recall what she'd had on Saturday morning when Diane was still around.

'Sorry, is coffee what you usually drink for breakfast

at home?' Hannah asked as Mia added milk to her cup. 'It occurred to me that . . . well, I've no idea what the norm is for someone your age.'

'Coffee's fine,' Mia replied.

Hannah nodded. She handed Mia a boiled egg, instructing her to help herself to some of the toast she'd already placed on the table. 'There's cereal too, if you'd like some,' she added without getting a response.

'So, um, your mum's all right with you drinking coffee? It's just that . . . I wouldn't want to step on any toes.'

'Uh-huh.'

Hannah, feeling awkward at the lack of interaction, took a slow sip from her own cup of coffee, which she enjoyed black as usual. Once upon a time she used to be able to knock back coffee all day long, but nowadays she had to be careful not to drink too much, for fear of the caffeine making her edgy.

She heard an unfamiliar pinging sound all of a sudden, which had her looking around the kitchen, wondering where the noise had come from.

Then she saw Mia pull her mobile phone out of her trouser pocket; she realised it must have been the sound of her receiving a message.

'Oh, would you mind not using your phone at the table, please?' Hannah asked before she had the chance to look at it.

Mia turned bright red and shoved the mobile back into her pocket without a word, staring down at her plate. A moment later Hannah noticed tears trickling down her cheeks, which made her feel awful.

'There's no need to get upset, Mia,' she said in a gentle voice. Part of her wanted to reach out and squeeze her niece's hand or similar, but it felt like the wrong thing to do in the circumstances, like she would be overstepping boundaries. 'I'm sorry if I sounded like I was snapping at you. If it makes you feel any better, I'd have said exactly the same thing to Mark, had he taken his mobile out during a meal. It's a pet hate of mine. Everyone's glued to their phones enough as it is, rather than talking to the people around them. So under this roof mealtimes are a phone-free zone, I'm afraid.'

Mia continued to look down at the table in silence. She refused to meet her aunt's eye while painstakingly peeling the shell off her egg. Finally she placed it on her buttered toast, slicing it up and spreading it out.

The sight tickled Hannah, who recalled Diane switching to eating a boiled egg like this in her late teens, having picked up the method from a boyfriend. Previously, she'd always cut off the top and dipped soldiers inside or scooped out the contents, as they'd learned at home. As far back as Hannah could remember, if a chance had ever presented itself to do things differently – particularly from the rest of the family – her sister had always jumped at it. Classic Diane.

Hannah wondered if Mia was the same way. She'd not known her long enough yet to be able to tell.

After a short period of listening to the radio and eating in silence, allowing Mia time to get over the phone incident, Hannah decided to try to make fresh conversation. 'So is there anything you particularly fancy doing today, Mia?'

'Not really.'

'Well, as you must have noticed, it's not very nice weather this morning. And according to the forecast, there's little chance of any improvement later on. In other words, we're probably best doing something indoors.'

Mia nodded, keeping her eyes on her plate and the food she'd been poking and prodding with her cutlery more than eating.

'There are several nice art galleries and museums nearby, but . . . well, I've honestly got no idea whether that's the kind of thing you would enjoy doing or not. I wouldn't want to drag you around somewhere you'd find boring.'

There was a long pause before Mia replied. 'I, er, I'm not actually feeling that well. My stomach hurts. I think I might be starting my period.'

This threw Hannah somewhat, as it was a long way from the response she'd expected. Despite the evidence right in front of her, she still hadn't got used to Mia being fourteen. Mind you, it wasn't like she'd had any preparation for this. Until a few days ago, the only Mia she knew – apart from the odd photo she'd spotted at her dad's house over the years – was the pre-schooler she'd been when Diane moved her away.

'I see,' she replied. 'Sorry to hear that. Do you, um, have everything you need: tampons, pads, paracetamol, perhaps? Because if not, I can always—'

'I'm fine,' Mia said. 'But can I chill in my room for a bit and read my book?'

'Of course. That's fine. I thought you'd want to be out and about, rather than stuck here with me, but if that's how you're feeling, I understand. I've had my fair share of period pains over the years. Why not take it easy this morning and then see how you feel later on?'

Mia nodded, looking teary again all of a sudden.

Oh dear, Hannah thought. Surely she wasn't still upset about the mobile phone reprimand. Unless she was afraid Hannah might confiscate it, as her mum had the other day. She could understand how that might be a scary prospect for a young teenager staying with people she barely knew, miles away from home.

'Are you all right?' she asked. 'You're not still upset about what I said earlier, are you? There's no need to be. I'm not cross, particularly as you put it away so quickly.'

'It's just . . . I thought it might be Mum at last.'

'Oh, right. I see. Haven't you heard from her today?'

Mia shook her head. 'Not since Saturday evening when she sent me a text to say she'd got home.'

'Oh dear.'

I've sent her a few messages since then and I've tried to call her, but she's not answered.'

'Right. Well, I'm sure there's a good explanation. She's probably busy. She said she had a few things to do while you were staying with us, so that's most likely it.'

Hannah eyed the food in front of her niece, which she'd barely touched, and then looked down at her own plate, which was empty save for a few crumbs. She helped herself to another piece of toast, which was cold now, and slapped on some butter and marmalade. This was as much about giving her something to do with her hands as it was about still being hungry.

She cut the toast into two triangles and, before taking a bite, asked: 'Aren't you feeling hungry?'

Mia said not, sliding her plate forward on the table to emphasise she was done and then nursing her coffee.

Seeing her niece so downhearted proved too much for Hannah. 'Listen,' she said. 'I can waive the no-phones rule this once, seeing as it's obviously upsetting you not knowing if it's your mum or not. Go ahead and have a look.'

Mia's face instantly brightened, only to sour again after she pulled out her mobile and read the message.

'What's wrong?' Hannah asked.

Mia shook her head, slipping the phone back into her pocket. 'It's not from Mum. It's one of my friends.'

'Never mind. I'll try and get hold of her later, if you like. Is there anything in particular you need to ask her?'

She hesitated, frowning and scratching her head before continuing. 'I, um, was wondering when she was coming back for me. She did say it would only be a few days.'

Hannah couldn't help feeling dismayed by this, although she did her best to hide the fact by smiling and nodding. 'Of course. I totally understand. I was your age once. It's only normal that you'd rather be at home with your friends and so on than here with us.'

Later, when Mia had returned to her bedroom and Hannah was in the lounge, glad of a break from struggling to make conversation, she pondered Diane's lack of contact with her daughter.

It was odd she hadn't been returning Mia's calls and

messages, especially after leaving her alone here with a strange aunt and uncle. What was Diane up to?

Hannah stared at her number: the latest entry in her smartphone's long list of contacts. The last time Diane had featured would have been on a much simpler device – something clunky by modern standards, with a rubbish camera. The world of technology had moved on a lot in the years they'd been apart, as had Hannah. She could only assume the same applied to her estranged sister.

Her thumb hovered above Diane's name on the touch-screen. She knew all she had to do to call the number was press down. And yet, for some reason, she couldn't bring herself to do it. Was this because she dreaded having to talk one-to-one with her again? Or was she afraid of not getting an answer?

Hannah decided it was probably a combination of the two, although the latter was of particular concern in light of Mia not being able to reach her. It was strange they'd not heard anything yet about when she was coming back for Mia.

God, what if something had happened to her? What would they do then?

No sooner had she decided to stop dithering and call the number than her mobile began to ring of its own accord.

CHAPTER 5

'Hello?' Hannah said, answering the phone in a clipped tone, as if Mark had caught her in the middle of something. 'Is everything all right?'

'Hi,' he replied. 'Yes, I'm fine, thanks. What about you? You sound busy.'

'Oh? I'm not really.'

'How's everything going with Mia? Are you finding it okay on your own with her?'

Hannah brought Mark up to date about Mia sleeping in, their stilted breakfast chat, and lastly her niece's claim to have period pains.

'I see,' he replied, glad not to have had that particular conversation with their guest. He knew it would have embarrassed him, even though modern men were supposed to be able to talk comfortably about the time of the month. Dads in particular, he thought, feeling the knot in his stomach tighten. The knot that had been there since he'd read Diane's letter.

But it was Hannah's next comment that really got Mark's attention. Lowering her voice, she said: 'I think the real reason Mia's feeling off this morning is because of her mum. Diane's not been replying to her calls or messages, apparently.'

'What? Not at all?'

'She sent her one message on Saturday to say she'd got home; nothing since.'

This surprised Mark, who'd assumed mother and daughter had been in regular contact. He'd certainly seen Mia typing and receiving various messages on her phone while she'd been staying with them. These must have been to and from her friends at home.

Unbeknown to Hannah or Mia, he'd also tried and failed to get hold of Diane several times yesterday.

He'd grabbed her number from Hannah's mobile. When Diane hadn't answered, his mind had gone into overdrive, reading all kinds of potential meanings into this. Now he had a new perspective on the situation.

'That's a bit odd,' he said into his phone, which was tucked between his chin and right shoulder as he made a brew for himself and a handful of colleagues in the kitchen at work. He couldn't remember the last time he'd done this, but judging by the shocked looks on his co-workers' faces when he'd offered, it was long overdue. In truth, he'd wanted an excuse to make this call away from prying ears in the open-plan office, since all the meeting rooms were occupied. Mark wasn't one for sharing personal information with colleagues; the last thing he wanted this morning was to face nosy queries about who Mia was and why she was staying with them.

At times like this he'd have appreciated having his own private office, but that was far too traditional to fit in with the firm's modern, open ethos.

'What's that noise?' Hannah asked.

'I'm brewing up. It's probably the kettle you can hear.'

'What? I thought you said you never had time for that. Are you feeling all right?'

'Very funny. So where's Mia now?'

'In her bedroom, reading. I mentioned the art galleries and museums, but she said she didn't feel up to going.'

'Look on the bright side: at least you might get the chance to do some writing.' Mark bent down to get the milk out of the fridge as he spoke, cricking his neck in the process, forcing him to switch the phone back into his hand with a groan.

'What was that?' Hannah asked. 'Are you all right?'

'It's nothing. I'm just trying to do too many things at once. So what do you think is going on with Diane?'

He heard the sound of his wife sighing down the line. 'Who knows?'

'It certainly seems strange for her to go silent like this . . . assuming Mia's telling the truth.'

'What do you mean?'

Yes, good point. What did he mean? The idea that Mia might be fibbing had only occurred to Mark as he'd said it. It was based solely on a paranoid, unsupported fear that she might be working against him – in cahoots with her mother.

'Never mind,' he said. 'Ignore me. I'm, er, just thinking out loud.'

'Why would she make such a thing up? You weren't here. You didn't see how upset she was. I felt so sorry for her that I even let her check her mobile at the breakfast table.'

'You what?' Mark replied, grinning in spite of the guilt and fear that had been eating him up ever since Diane's flabbergasting revelation. 'That can't be right. You must be going soft in your old age. You'll be answering a call in the cinema next.'

Hannah had long had a bee in her bonnet about people using mobiles at mealtimes. She found it the height of rudeness and, although Mark wasn't quite as offended by it as she was, over the years she'd converted him to the cause. He hadn't spotted Mia doing it so far, perhaps because Diane had similar feelings to Hannah, which she'd instilled in her daughter.

That didn't sound like the Diane he remembered, who'd always been far better at breaking rules than following them. Maybe motherhood had changed her. She'd confiscated Mia's mobile for some reason when they'd first arrived, so there were obviously boundaries in place.

'And you've still not heard anything from Diane either?' Mark asked.

'No. I told Mia I'd try to get hold of her. She wants to know when her mum is coming back for her.'

'That's understandable. She is only fourteen. She's probably homesick. So are you going to try calling Diane yourself?'

She cleared her throat. 'I guess so.'

Hearing reluctance in Hannah's strained tone of voice,

Mark spotted an opportunity. 'You, er, don't sound very keen.' He held his breath for a moment before adding: 'Would you rather I tried to get hold of her instead?'

'You'd do that?' she asked, already sounding happier.

'Of course, if it makes life easier for you.'

'That would be amazing. You're the best.'

Mark winced at this, wishing it was true, before forcing himself to add: 'Could you text me her phone number?'

Once he'd dished out the brews to his bemused colleagues – one of whom actually took a photo of him handing over their cup 'to prove it really happened' – he returned to his desk and tried to distract himself with work.

When lunchtime came around, Mark popped out, having taken Diane's letter from his briefcase and stuffed it into a trouser pocket. He read the contents over again at a crumb-covered table in a quiet back-street sandwich shop where no one knew him.

Diane's words hadn't got any better or less terrifying with time. As Mark's eyes scanned the letter's contents, the cheese-and-pickle sandwich he'd ordered lying untouched next to his can of cola, he felt his heart pounding at the prospect of what he might say if he managed to reach her by phone.

He didn't have the slightest clue what Diane was up to, but he was desperate to know. He needed to discover whether she was definitely telling the truth in her letter and, if so, why she'd chosen to tell him now. Something specific must have sparked her recent actions – and Mark was determined to get to the bottom of it.

Meanwhile, he'd done as she'd asked. He'd looked at Mia to see if he could see himself in her. He'd scrutinised the girl, as surreptitiously as possible, over the last couple of days. He'd examined her physical appearance, from her eyes and smile right down to the shape of her feet. He'd considered the way she walked and talked; her gestures; the type of things she said and did; what made her laugh; what made her frown.

At certain moments, he'd thought he'd seen hints of himself or other family members, such as his mother. At other times, he'd become convinced these were mere projections and there was nothing concrete at all.

There was plenty of Diane, though. Over the years, particularly before the big falling-out, Mark had seen loads of old snaps of Diane and Hannah together as girls. Fourteen-year-old Mia could easily pass for their sister.

But could she pass for his child?

Could she really, truly be his daughter?

And if so, why had Diane lied to his face about it when he'd asked her previously?

His mind jumped back to one particular conversation. It had been in 2008 during those awful, raw days following the death of her and Hannah's mother, Maggie, and before the disintegration of the sisters' relationship. Little had he known at that point how much was about to change, and how drastically it would affect all of their lives.

The sisters had spent a couple of days at their parents' home. They'd both wanted to be there to console and support their dad, who was so devastated he could barely function, and to start planning the funeral. To make things easier for them, Mark had agreed to move into Diane's house, a small terraced property in Withington, to look after Mia while they were away. This was despite him being pretty clueless when it came to children.

Mia had recently turned three and had at least stopped wearing nappies during the daytime. With the help of a list of instructions left by her mum, detailing mealtimes, toilet habits and other daily routines, he'd just about managed, thankful she had a placid temperament for a young child.

However, unbeknown to Diane, there had been several phone calls to his mother, Alma, along the way. Having no grandchildren of her own, she'd been only too happy to give him tips and advice. She'd even offered to come over and lend a hand, but he'd said that wasn't necessary.

That afternoon there had also been a minor incident in his car. He'd taken Mia out to the park and, while stuck in traffic on the way back, she'd announced she needed a wee 'right now'.

'You can wait a few minutes, can't you?' Mark had asked.

Her only reply had been to shake her head vigorously, turn bright red and do it there and then in her car seat before starting to cry.

Luckily, he'd managed to keep a cool head and, somehow, to juggle cleaning the car and putting Mia in the bath and then bed before Diane arrived home.

'Thanks so much for looking after her,' she said after

popping up to give her a kiss goodnight. 'She's zonked. You must have kept her busy.'

'I did my best. I'm pretty shattered too. Maybe I should text Hannah and ask her to run me a bath.'

Diane smiled. 'She's probably in there herself. It's been a tough couple of days.'

'I bet. How's Frank managing?'

'He's not. He's in a mess. Mum might have been ill for ages, but it's like Dad never faced up to the fact this would happen one day. I mean, it's not something you can really prepare yourself for, is it? But the way he's acting, you'd think she'd been fighting fit and her death was a total shock. He's all over the place. He's even said things like there's no point in him carrying on without her.'

'How's he going to cope now you and Hannah are no longer there with him? Do you think he'll want to move back to Manchester?'

Frank and Maggie Wells had lived in the Altrincham area for most of their lives, where the sisters had grown up in a large Victorian family home in a leafy, well-heeled street. But two years ago, after both taking early retirement, they'd sold up and moved to a bungalow close to the sea in Southport. Although this had always been a shared dream of theirs, it had come as a surprise to the rest of the family, particularly in light of them recently becoming grandparents. However, soon after the move, they'd revealed the devastating news that Maggie had been diagnosed with stage four breast cancer; she'd effectively relocated there to die.

Mark knew how hard it had been for Hannah to watch

her mother gradually fade away, slowly getting more frail and less like her old self; increasingly reliant on the various drugs she'd been prescribed. He assumed Diane's experience had also been tough, although he knew Hannah thought her sister hadn't been as supportive or visited as often as she had when Maggie had got closer to the end.

Ultimately, her death had been a release, for Maggie, but also for her family. As painful as it was to lose her, at least they no longer had to watch her suffer, losing a little more of herself every day. Now they could finally move on to grieve for the strong woman she'd once been, rather than the dying patient she'd become.

'Dad will have to manage,' Diane replied, 'like the rest of us. As to whether he'll stay there or not, that's up to him. It's way too early to talk about that yet. At least he seems to know plenty of people around there now. One of the neighbours, a woman called Joan, even brought him a lasagne over this afternoon.'

While they spoke about this and the funeral plans, Mark's mind wandered. Spending so much one-to-one time with Mia over the past couple of days had affected him in ways he hadn't predicted.

Despite usually feeling disconnected and indifferent towards children, Mark had been surprised to find he really enjoyed spending time with Mia. Okay, the weeing in the car hadn't been much fun, but apart from that she'd been consistently cute. There hadn't been the slightest hint of a toddler tantrum.

Little Mia, who was usually too busy with Hannah to notice him, had hung on his every word. She'd made him feel special in a way he hadn't experienced before. At certain moments she'd unexpectedly planted a kiss on his cheek or climbed on his knee for a 'huggle buggle', as she called it, melting his heart.

Occasionally she'd pulled an exaggerated sad face and mentioned her late grandmother, clearly trying to process what Diane had told her before leaving. 'Granny's gone, Uncle Mark. I miss her,' she'd said several times, shaking her head and shrugging in a way that made her look far older than her years.

When he'd tucked her up in bed that evening, having read her the same story three times – about a cat who was scared of going to the vet – a very earnest Mia had told him: 'I love you, Uncle Mark.'

'Thank you, Mia,' he'd replied, overwhelmed. 'That's nice of you to say. I, um . . . I love you too.'

And even though he'd only said so because she'd said it first, there had been a certain truth in his words that had got Mark thinking.

It was this he was still mulling over as he and Diane spoke in the kitchen later. He felt a fondness for Mia unlike anything he'd experienced towards a child before; he wondered if it might in fact be something biological.

Despite falling pregnant alarmingly soon after that awful night – the one Mark wished he could banish from his memory forever – Diane had always fervently denied any chance of his being Mia's father. Of course he'd asked her. As much as it pained him to dig up what had happened between them and despite having no desire to be a dad, Mark wasn't the kind of person to bury his head in the sand. He was a man who faced up to his responsibilities. Ironically, this had been ingrained in Mark by the same tragedy from his past that had shaped his desire not to be a father, having been badly let down as a child by someone who should have watched over him.

But Diane had always seemed so dismissive, like it was a ridiculous suggestion. Eventually, he'd accepted it and moved on. The fact it was easier this way had been an added bonus.

And yet, as far as he knew, Diane had never told anyone the father's identity, not even Hannah or their parents, which was weird. She'd not been in a relationship around that time – not publicly anyway – and had taken the stance that it was no one's business but hers.

'Would you like a drink before you head off?' Diane asked, having described to Mark the type of coffin they'd agreed on for Maggie's funeral. 'I've got plenty of wine and beer,' she added, gesturing towards the fridge, 'unless you've drunk it all while you've been here.'

Normally he'd have said no and headed home. He usually avoided being alone with Diane at all costs, in light of their chequered past. But he needed to address his thoughts about Mia.

'Go on then,' he replied. 'I'll have a quick beer. And don't worry: there's plenty left. I've not had a drop while I've been responsible for Mia.'

Diane raised an eyebrow. 'Great.' She walked over to the fridge and pulled out two bottles of Grolsch.

Mark fought to keep his breathing steady.

As his sister-in-law opened a kitchen drawer and pulled

out a bottle opener, he noticed she was wearing a green top very like one his wife had.

'You and Hannah must have similar taste,' he said, making small talk in a bid to calm himself down.

'Oh?' she replied, turning around and pouting in a way that made him uncomfortable. 'How so?'

Mark cleared his throat, wishing he'd chosen his words more carefully. 'I, er, just mean what you're wearing. That, um, top. I think she might have the same one.'

Diane laughed. 'Oh, okay, I get you. Well spotted. She does have exactly the same top – this one, in fact. I borrowed it from her this morning. Nice, isn't it?'

Mark managed an awkward laugh, shuffling his feet on the tiled kitchen floor.

'So you managed all right with Mia?' Diane asked after they'd moved through into the small lounge. 'Everything seems in good order. Hannah and I were surprised not to get more phone calls from you.'

'Yes, we muddled through. The instructions you left were a big help.' He paused before adding: 'She's a lovely little girl.'

Mark's mind skipped into overdrive. He asked himself repeatedly why exactly he thought Mia might be his child, apart from the obvious fact that he and her mother had slept together soon before Diane fell pregnant.

Did he see himself in her? God, that was a hard question to answer. She had green eyes, like he did, but a lighter shade. They were piercing in a way that reminded him more of the pale blue eyes that Hannah and Diane shared. Her hair was dark brown, like his. But that was also her mother's natural colour and Mia's hair was straighter than either of theirs. Just like some other man's hair, perhaps.

As for the rest . . . who could say?

Maybe he was being stupid, delusional. Could spending time with only a three-year-old for company mess with your mind? Plus there was the fact that Diane had just lost her mother, which probably made this an inappropriate moment to raise such a sensitive issue. He was tempted not to say anything after all.

Then he remembered how it had felt to hear Mia say she loved him; to hold her cool little hand in his while walking through the park that afternoon. There was definitely a connection between the two of them. He felt it in his gut – and he had to know the truth. So he grabbed the bull by the horns.

'Listen, Diane. I need to ask you something about Mia. I've really enjoyed spending time with her. More than I ever imagined. I know you've said otherwise in the past, but . . . she's mine, isn't she? I know she is. I can feel it. Please tell me the truth.'

Diane stared at him for a long moment, poker-faced. She slowly began to nod her head and then, in a voice that sounded so calm it was almost menacing, she said: 'Well, this is a surprise. Your timing is lousy, but fine, I get it. I'll tell you the truth if that's what you really want, Mark.'

CLIENT SESSION TRANSCRIPT: HCOOK290719

S: How are you, Hannah? It's been a while since our last session, hasn't it?

H: Yes, it has. I didn't feel like I needed to see you again until now, Sally. Things have been going well. Really well, actually.

S: That's good. I'm glad to hear it. Such fantastic news about your book deal, by the way.

H: Thanks. I appreciate that.

S: So what's changed to bring you back to see me again?

H: Last Friday my sister Diane turned up out of the blue – without any warning at all – after all those years of no contact. It's totally messed my head up again. For a start, she left her fourteen-year-old daughter Mia behind when she left. The last time I saw her she was a toddler.

S: Your niece is staying with you?

H: Yes, I don't know for how long. Diane begged me and Mark to take her in for a few days while she sorted some things out, whatever that means. She wouldn't elaborate.

S: And how do you feel about it all?

H: I feel anxious. Seeing Diane again has brought back memories of how I became after we fell out and then she moved away. I'm afraid of having another breakdown; of losing everything I've rebuilt in her absence.

S: It's only normal to feel that way in the circumstances, Hannah, but it's an emotional response rather than a rational one. There's no foundation for such fears. You need to have confidence in the strong, successful, confident woman I see before me. You're not the person you once were. The past is gone and all that remains is who you are right now. Yes?

H: Yes.

S: And that is?

H: Someone strong, successful and confident.

S: Exactly. So tell me about Mia.

H: It's been good to see her. I spent a lot of time with her when she was little, before they moved to Bournemouth, and I missed her terribly afterwards. But she's so different now. She might as well be another person altogether. I remember reading bedtime stories to her, taking her for walks in her buggy and feeding the ducks. But she has no memory of me at all. I don't know where to begin with her. I'm not sure she even likes me much. The two of us were alone in the apartment today for the first time and she spent most of that shut in her bedroom.

S: Where's Mia now?

81

H: At home with Mark. I didn't want to leave her alone yet, which was why this late appointment was ideal. Thank goodness you had a cancellation.

S: I'm glad this has worked out for you. And Diane? What was your initial reaction when she turned up on your doorstep unannounced? Was any part of you glad to see her?

H: Glad? Not really. Shocked, perplexed, anxious: those are more suitable words to describe how I felt. I knew she'd want something, because that's Diane all over. I guessed it would be money, but instead it was about us looking after Mia. I doubt I'd have agreed to much else; I think Diane knew Mia would be my weak spot, based on how much I doted on her when she was a young child.

S: I recall from our previous chats that you never expected Diane to reach out to you. Now that she has, do you think this could be the start of a healing process?

H: Hmm. She may have made contact after all these years, but I don't think it was with a view to patching things up between us. I got the impression she was out of other options. As soon as we'd agreed to look after Mia, she was gone: off to deal with whatever mess she's got herself into.

S: And what do you think that mess might be?

H: After more than a decade apart, I honestly don't know. She got very upset when she asked for our help – tears and everything. They seemed genuine, although Diane's always been good at manipulating people and

82

situations. I found out earlier that she's barely been in contact with Mia since leaving her here in Manchester, which seems totally strange to me.

S: I see. So in what ways was Diane manipulative in the past, Hannah?

H: There were several occasions, before our falling-out, when I felt like she used my affection for Mia to her advantage, as she has now really. I used to act as a free babysitter all the time, for instance, usually while she went out partying. Mostly I didn't mind, because I loved being with my niece, particularly since I've never had any children of my own. But sometimes it did feel like she was abusing that bond.

S: Can you be more specific?

H: Sure. The example that springs to mind was on my wedding anniversary one year. Mark and I both had the day off work and were planning a walk in the Peak District followed by a slap-up meal in the city centre. Then I received a call from Diane first thing that morning, saying Mia had diarrhoea and couldn't go to nursery. She was in a panic, since she had some important course on at work that day, which she didn't feel like she could miss. I agreed that Mark and I would step in to look after Mia, which wasn't much fun, since she pretty much cried and pooed the whole time. It definitely wasn't the special day we'd planned. Anyway, at least we still had the meal out to look forward to, until Diane managed to ruin that. Rather than getting home on time, as you'd expect, she didn't roll up until nearly seven-thirty that evening, by which point we'd missed our reservation and were too worn out to bother doing anything else. She'd been to the pub with her colleagues, believe it or not, and blamed not being in touch on her phone battery having died.

S: She was drunk when she got back, despite her daughter being ill?

H: Oh no, she hadn't been drinking. She was in the car. But I couldn't believe she'd gone at all, knowing Mia was unwell and it was our anniversary. Not much of a thank-you for our help, was it? She claimed to have been pressured into it by her boss, but I didn't believe a word. What kind of manager would insist a mum went to the pub in that situation? Plus she could've called us from the office or someone else's phone to at least give us a heads-up. No, she went to the pub because she wanted to; because she's selfish. Mark and I were both fuming. But somehow, a few weeks later, she had me babysitting again. I loved spending time with Mia. I figured she was the closest thing I'd ever have to a daughter, which was why it hit me so hard when Diane took her away from me and moved down south.

S: Why do you think Diane turned to you rather than someone else on that particular occasion? Why not your parents, for example?

H: They weren't living locally by that point. They'd moved to Southport and had enough on their plates dealing with Mum's cancer. Since Mia's father has never been in the picture, I was the only other family

Diane could ask to help. She manipulated our parents too, though, just in different ways.

S: Perhaps you could expand on that last point, Hannah. It sounds like something that's bothered you.

H: Um, yeah. I guess so. I don't know what Diane's relationship with our father is like nowadays, but after she had Mia I felt like she relied on Mum and Dad giving her cash handouts far more than she ought to have done. She was excellent at playing the struggling single mum card. Then she'd think nothing of going out and splurging however much on a load of new outfits for herself. Growing up, Diane was the one always getting in trouble – receiving detentions and poor grades at school; staying out past curfew – while I worked hard and did what I was told. Because of this, Diane used to tell me I was Mum and Dad's favourite, which I probably started to believe. But as adults, things seemed to switch around for us. It was assumed, since both Mark and I had decent jobs, that I was fine on my own, while Diane needed their support: financially and emotionally. And then she gave them their only grandchild, which reinforced the situation.

S: Would you say you were jealous of this?

H: I suppose so. It felt unfair, like she was being rewarded for getting herself into a mess. It was never really about money. Mark and I have always been fortunate enough not to need help. It was the principle of the matter. I felt Diane was manipulating Mum and Dad: taking advantage of their kindness and generosity;

85

their blind love for their granddaughter. Meanwhile, she refused to tell anyone who Mia's father was or to ask him to do his bit. Plus, when Mum got really ill, Diane would use Mia as an excuse for why she couldn't go over and help out, leaving me and Dad to do the heavy lifting. But the way she talked after Mum died, you'd have thought it was her always driving over there, helping with the shopping and cleaning; tending to Mum's needs; teaching Dad how to cook. She had the big advantage of being able to show up with Mia, which always trumped anything I could do. Sorry, I sound like a jealous idiot now. I'm probably making the situation out to be worse than it was, but I guess her reappearance has dug it all up again.

S: So you felt unappreciated?

H: Sometimes, yes. I'd be over there in Southport, helping out however I could, and all they'd talk about would be whatever issue Diane had at that particular moment: how there was a leak in her roof, for example, or an issue with one of the staff at Mia's nursery. There was always something. Poor Mum was dying. The last thing she needed was to be worrying about Diane. My sister has always been perfectly capable of looking after herself. She's also incredibly adept at making herself the centre of attention. It was the same after our mother died. Diane made a big play of her grief, particularly at the funeral, as if to suggest she had a closer bond with her than anyone else. She wouldn't stop telling people how awful it was to have to watch a parent die such a slow and painful death; how she wouldn't wish that on her worst enemy. She kept recounting a conversation they'd had near the end, where Mum had apparently said she would have done anything to spare her the pain of watching her fade away. To me it felt like Diane trying to give people the impression she was always the one there at Mum's side, which simply wasn't true.

S: Is there any chance that the reason Diane avoided visiting near the end was because she found it so difficult to watch your mother die?

H: Hmm. That's not how it felt at the time.

S: Everyone deals with death differently, Hannah. Don't take this the wrong way – I'm playing devil's advocate – but is it possible that your view of the situation might be coloured by your subsequent falling-out with your sister?

H: I honestly don't know. Maybe.

S: In terms of each of your relationships with your parents, do you think Diane remembers things the same way as you do? With pairs of siblings, it's not uncommon for both to consider the other to be the parents' favourite. I'm not saying this is true in your case, but some parents deliberately play their children off against one another.

H: Possibly, I guess. Like I said, she definitely thought of me being favoured when we were children. She often used to call me a goody two-shoes or a swat; she'd moan to Mum and Dad that they were tougher

87

on her than me. Once we were adults, I've no idea what they told her out of my earshot, but I suppose they might have bugged her about following my example and settling down with a nice man. They certainly used to bother me about giving them another grandchild, although Mark and I had made it very clear this wasn't on the cards.

S: Did that upset you?

H: What? That it wasn't on the cards or that Mum and Dad nagged me about it?

S: This is your session, Hannah. You should focus on whatever you feel to be most relevant.

H: Um, I'm not sure. We've spoken before about me and Mark not having children, haven't we? It wasn't my initial preference, but I accepted it a long time ago. I chose my husband. I suppose it did grate a bit when Mum and Dad used to bring it up though, like rubbing salt into a wound.

S: Wound. That's an interesting word choice. It suggests you hadn't fully come to terms with your decision at that point.

H: Well, no. I can't disagree with that. There were times when it was hard, especially after Mia was born; even when Diane was pregnant. It reminded me what could have been. What I was missing out on.

S: And now, having Mia back in your life as a teenager? Do you have those feelings again?

H: Um, it's not quite the same as when she was little. Being around babies often seems to trigger something, I don't know . . . biological? That broody feeling.

Whatever, it's different with a fourteen-year-old. When I've looked at my niece these last few days, I've often found myself feeling sad; regretting all those years of her life I've missed out on. It's most of her childhood. That's not something I'll ever get back.

S: Does that make you angry at Diane for taking her away?

H: Definitely.

CHAPTER 6

Hannah read her sister's text message for about the thirtieth time since receiving it yesterday lunchtime.

Please don't call the police. There's really no need. I'm fine. Just busy sorting things out. Taking longer than expected, but I'll be in touch soon.

That was the sum total of Diane's communication with her since leaving Mia in her care last Saturday morning. It was Thursday now; tomorrow it would be a week on from when the two of them had rolled back into her life, like a travelling circus taking over an empty field. And still Hannah had no idea when Diane would be coming back to get Mia.

Both she and Mark had tried phoning and texting her countless times since learning she hadn't even been in touch with her daughter. But until this message had arrived, following hot on the heels of Hannah's threat to call the police in an emotional voicemail plea, none of them had heard anything.

In fact, soon after the arrival of the text, Mia had burst out of her bedroom, announcing that she too had heard from her mother. But in her case it had been a short phone call.

'Excellent,' Hannah had replied, thinking it was about damn time. 'What did she say?'

'That she was sorry for not being in touch earlier. She's been really busy, apparently. Oh, and for us not to worry.'

'Did she mention anything about when she'll be coming back?'

Mia's face had fallen at this question, the rare glint of happiness fading from her eyes. 'Um, only that she wasn't sure yet when that would be. But it didn't sound like it would take too long. Is that . . . okay?'

'Of course,' Hannah had replied. 'You're welcome here for as long as you need. You're family, Mia, and family sticks together at times like this. Besides, we love having you staying with us.'

Hannah hadn't mentioned the fact that, prior to Mia's arrival, she and Mark had discussed the possibility of jetting away for a last-minute city break to somewhere like Madrid or Lisbon this weekend. Equally she hadn't told her niece about the dinner reservation for two she'd had to cancel the other night in one of Manchester's most exclusive new restaurants. Such things could always be rescheduled. And the last thing Hannah wanted was for Mia to feel like she was getting in the way.

Back in the present, sitting at her desk in the lounge, looking at her phone when she ought to have been writing, Hannah wondered whether to try calling Diane again now.

91

She and Mark had discussed this before he left for work and they'd agreed it was best to wait for a few more days. But every time she read that damn message over again or even thought about it, she felt herself itching to do something on the spot.

If only she knew what Diane was up to and why it was taking so long. But after not seeing her for more than a decade, Hannah didn't have a clue. She knew next to nothing about her sister's life nowadays and wasn't comfortable asking Mia many questions, for fear of worrying her or making her feel awkward. The teenager had mentioned in passing that Diane now worked in some kind of recruitment role, but despite some gentle nudging, she hadn't elaborated. Was this because she knew her mum wouldn't want her aunt to know more?

Ever since her niece had come to stay, Hannah had wondered what kind of things Diane had said to her over the years about the sister with whom she'd fallen out. Had she bitched about her, slowly poisoning Mia's mind, or had she avoided all mention of her? Hannah doubted she would have had anything nice to say – not after the awful way things had ended between them – which was why she still couldn't get her head around her choosing this as the best place to leave her only child.

And what would happen once Diane did return? Would she whisk Mia away down south again, not to be seen for another decade, or would this be the start of a healing process? Hannah wasn't even sure if she wanted that. She'd got used to things as they were now and she'd never been very good at dealing with change. If she did allow her sister back into her life, it could blow up in her face. Hannah couldn't bear to have to go through all of that anguish again, which was why she'd returned to counselling on Monday to keep herself on an even keel.

Over the past week she'd given some thought to what kind of mess Diane had got herself into. The three most likely possibilities she'd come up with were: drugs/alcohol issues, a boyfriend turned nasty, and/or money problems. None of these theories were rooted in solid facts, though; they were pure speculation, based on what she knew about her sister before they fell out.

For instance, Diane used to like a drink and, unlike Hannah, had dabbled in recreational drugs when she was younger. She'd gone out with some dodgy blokes in her time, having always had a thing for bad boys. Plus she'd always been better at spending money than saving it.

'Don't you think she'd have asked us for help by now if the issue was financial?' That had been Mark's take on the money theory when they'd discussed it the other night, out of Mia's earshot. He'd also pointed out: 'Remember you thought she was going to ask for cash when she first turned up.'

'Yes, but maybe she's too proud to do that. I'd probably be the last person she'd want to come begging to, don't you think?'

Mark had snorted at this. 'Well, she pretty much did that when she asked us to look after Mia for her, didn't she?'

'True. But I don't think that's quite the same as asking for money.'

Hannah hadn't suggested any of these things directly to Mia – but she had tried a little fishing. For a start, she'd asked how things were with her mum generally, to which she'd got a very informative 'fine', accompanied by a shrug. She'd also queried whether Diane had a boyfriend, to which Mia had replied: 'Not that I know of. She goes out on dates occasionally, but not recently. She's always said she won't bring a man home to meet me unless she's really serious about him. I guess that means there's not been anyone serious so far.'

That didn't rule out a dodgy boyfriend, mind: the kind she wouldn't ever want to meet her daughter. Perhaps that was why she'd hidden her away up north, to keep her out of his reach. Maybe he was a drug dealer who'd got her hooked on something nasty and, because she owed him so much money, had threatened to pimp Mia out to his sleazy, disgusting friends. They could have had a fight during which she'd killed him and now she was busy chopping up the body and disposing of the parts.

Hmm, Hannah thought, frowning at the black computer screen facing her. The machine was on, but it had gone into standby due to lack of use. Great. She was able to dream up all kinds of outlandish scenarios when it came to imagining what the hell her sister was up to, but could she get any work done on her actual book? Not so much.

'Come on, Hannah,' she told herself. 'Stop procrastinating and get on with it.'

She activated the screen of her laptop and peered at the time: 8.41 a.m. Dammit. That meant she'd been sitting here for nearly an hour and hadn't written a single word, despite that being the sole reason she'd plonked herself down at her desk so early.

First she'd wasted far too long browsing news websites to read that morning's headlines. Then she'd opened her emails and seen a request for a meter reading from their electricity provider, which of course she'd had to do immediately rather than sometime later. And finally there had been all that time she'd spent wondering about bloody Diane.

Having done next to no writing since Mia's arrival, Hannah had made a decision in bed late last night. She'd been kept awake by a combination of Mark's on-off snoring and puffing noises as he breathed, together with her own restless brain. And as her mind wandered from one worry to another, she'd determined early morning was the best time of day for her to crack on with book two. So she'd planned on rising bang on 7 a.m. today, as soon as Mark had left for work, and getting a good shift in before her house guest even got up. However, the plan had gone awry from the off when, still tired from her lack of sleep, she hadn't managed to drag herself out of bed until 7.30 a.m.

She'd fallen into the habit of waking Mia at around 10.30 a.m. and then making breakfast. It did seem a little lazy to Hannah that her niece needed to lie in for so long every day, but she'd decided to let it slide on the grounds that she was, after all, a teenager on holiday from school.

Anyway, at 8.45 a.m. Hannah finally wrote her first fresh sentence in nearly a week. Then she deleted it, stared at the screen for a while and rewrote it as it had been the first time. She sighed, dragged a hand through her uncombed hair, and typed some more.

She was finally starting to find something approaching her flow, around twenty-five minutes later, when she heard the sound of a door opening in the hall.

'Morning,' came Mia's voice a second later.

Hannah twisted around in the desk chair and saw her niece standing in the open doorway of the lounge in her dressing gown, hair all over the place like she'd been backcombing it. 'Oh, hello there,' she said, doing her best to hide the frustration she felt at being interrupted. 'You're awake earlier than usual.'

Mia yawned. 'I guess I am. What are you doing?'

'Um, just catching up on some things,' Hannah replied, a strange, self-conscious feeling washing over her. Fearful that Mia might walk over and start reading what she'd written, she fought off the urge to shut the laptop. But she needn't have worried. The teenager merely nodded and announced she was going for a shower.

'No problem,' Hannah said. 'I'll make us some breakfast when you get out. Oh, and please remember to put the extractor fan on in the bathroom.'

'Will do,' Mia replied, although when Hannah walked past a few minutes later, she saw the switch for the fan was still off and, with a sigh, turned it on herself. The last thing Hannah wanted to be was a nag, but she knew from experience how long her niece's showers tended to last – and all that steam needed somewhere to escape.

'Um, you forgot to put the fan on again when you were

in the shower,' she said later over breakfast. 'Please try to remember. Otherwise the bathroom will get mouldy.'

'Did I?' Mia replied. 'I'm sure it was on.'

'Well, it was, but that's because I turned it on when I saw you hadn't.'

'Oh, okay.'

Hannah hesitated before adding: 'And would you mind terribly not hanging your wet towel over the bedroom door? There's plenty of room on the rail in the bathroom.'

'Sure,' Mia replied, like it was the first time her aunt had asked her this rather than the fourth or fifth.

Moving the conversation on to less awkward matters, Hannah asked how she was getting on with the book she was reading.

'Oh, yeah. I finished it last night.'

'Good ending?'

'It was, actually, but now I feel a bit sad to have finished it,' Mia replied, in between mouthfuls of toast, 'especially as it was the last part of a trilogy.'

'I know what you mean. I think it sometimes feels like losing a friend when you finish a good book. Have you got something to read next?'

Mia nodded and said she had some things on her Kindle. After a slight hesitation, she added that she'd noticed some interesting novels on the large bookshelf in the lounge. 'Would it be okay if I, um—'

'Of course,' Hannah said, almost too enthusiastically. 'Help yourself. Read anything you like.'

She had to stop herself from grinning at this point, enjoying having something to bond over with Mia. So far, despite the fact that Mark had been out at work a lot for the last few days, he seemed to be the one Mia preferred. She was usually more animated and engaged when he was around, spending less time cooped up in her bedroom than when it was just the two of them.

Hannah had been getting a bit paranoid about this, even though she told herself it was probably down to the novelty of having a man around – a potential father figure even – which had apparently never been the case at home.

She'd also considered the fact that perhaps she reminded Mia a bit too much of her own mother – and that was weird for her.

Since books seemed to be the thing they had most in common, Hannah was itching to ask which ones in particular Mia had her eye on. Maybe now was also the right time to mention her own soon-to-be-released novel: a subject that hadn't arisen so far and which Mark was still under orders not to bring up without her approval.

But a voice in her head told her to stop. It warned her that now was a good time to sit back, play it cool, and let Mia continue to be chatty, rather than taking over the conversation with her own agenda. She'd read somewhere that teenagers were like cats; if you tried too hard with them, they wouldn't warm to you. Whether that was true or not, she had no idea. But it felt like the best course of action here, so she went with it.

'Is there anything you fancy doing today?' Hannah asked instead.

So far that week they'd been out for several short trips around the city together, including visits to Manchester

Art Gallery, the Museum of Science and Industry and the Whitworth. Mia hadn't seemed to enjoy any of these places as much as Hannah, though. She'd walked around with her, smiling and nodding in the right places, but there hadn't been any genuine spark of interest so far as Hannah could tell.

Apart from the Whitworth, an art gallery where she sometimes went to think or write in its glass-walled café overlooking the park and all its squirrels, she hadn't been to these attractions for ages. It was all too easy to forget about what was on your own doorstep.

Mind you, they were all the kinds of locations kids went on school trips, because they were educational. Mia was a teenager on holiday from school, so maybe they weren't good choices in the first place.

But what else was Hannah supposed to do to entertain her niece? She could barely remember what kind of thing she was into at fourteen – and that was pretty much her only frame of reference.

Mia shuffled in her chair and cleared her throat before replying. 'Um, I was wondering if it might be okay for me to go out for a bit by myself today.' Her eyes darted all around the room, looking everywhere apart from at Hannah, while her fingers grasped at each other on the surface of the kitchen table.

'Right,' Hannah replied, trying to disguise her surprise. 'I see. Is that, er, something you're allowed to do at home in Bournemouth?'

'Yes, definitely.' Mia nodded, finally meeting her aunt's gaze with an earnest look. 'I go out by myself all the time.

99

I walk twenty minutes to school and back every day during termtime.'

Hannah found herself in unchartered waters. Diane hadn't given her any guidelines about this kind of thing, so she guessed it was up to her to decide. But what if something happened to Mia while she was out alone? She'd never forgive herself. It was all well and good Mia saying she was allowed to do this kind of thing at home. But teenagers couldn't always be relied on to tell the truth, could they? And if she was anything like her mother . . . Diane had told fibs all the time when they were growing up. How often had Hannah had to cover for her less well-behaved sister?

And yet her niece was fourteen. She'd seen plenty of kids her age wandering around the city centre without adult supervision. Plus she was fast running out of ideas about how to keep her entertained; if Mia was able to do things by herself, Hannah would get more time to write.

'What were you thinking of doing?' she asked.

'Well, I was reading online that Central Library is pretty modern and fun. I was thinking about going there for a bit.'

Hannah was taken aback by this, which was a million miles away from what she'd expected to hear. She wanted to kick herself for not thinking of it, knowing Mia's fondness for reading. How could she say no?

'That sounds like a good idea,' she said. 'Do you know where it is? It's only a short walk. We passed it the other day when we went to Manchester Art Gallery, which is very nearby.'

'I remember,' Mia replied. 'So you're okay with it, then?'

'I guess so, as long as you're careful and take your phone with you. Do call me if you have any problems whatsoever. Manchester is a lot bigger than Bournemouth, remember, and there are plenty of unsavoury types about, so you need to keep your wits about you and your hands on your purse at all times, okay?'

'Sure.' Mia was grinning now, obviously excited at the prospect of enjoying some freedom.

'You can take my library card, if you like. That way if you see any books you fancy, you can always borrow them.'

'Thanks. That would be great.'

'If libraries are your thing,' Hannah added, 'there's also a place called the John Rylands that you should visit. It's on Deansgate, if you remember where that is. I'm sure you could get directions from your phone. It's more than a hundred years old and very atmospheric. Somehow it always reminds me of Harry Potter's school, Hogwarts.'

'Really? That sounds good. Maybe I'll go there too.'

'Good. But before you go anywhere, I want you to let me have any dirty clothes that need washing and I'll sort them out for you. I can't have you running out now, can I?'

'Okay, will do. Thanks.'

Forty-five minutes or so later, Mia had delivered her pile of washing to Hannah and was ready to head out on her first solo expedition.

'Do you have any money?' Hannah asked her at the

front door of the apartment. She reached for her purse, which was in her handbag on the coat rack. 'Because I can always—'

'No,' Mia replied. 'I'm fine, thanks. Mum left me with a bit and, when I spoke to her the other day, she said she'd put some in my bank account. I have a cash card, so . . .'

'Okay, if you're sure,' Hannah replied, impressed. 'You've got my number saved in your phone, right? And you'll keep it on in case I need to get hold of you?'

'Yes.'

Hannah stepped forward and gave Mia a kiss on the cheek. 'Have fun and be careful.'

'I will. Bye.'

'Goodbye.'

And with that, Hannah suddenly had the apartment to herself again.

Bizarrely, the first thing she chose to do with this freedom was peek in Mia's bedroom. She didn't want to pry, but rather to see what state it was in and whether it needed cleaning.

It was a bit of a mess, unfortunately. The bed was unmade and, although Mia's wet towel wasn't hanging over the bedroom door, it was balled up in one corner of the floor, which was arguably worse. At least that explained the musty smell.

The curtains were still closed, so Hannah opened them and then the window to let in some fresh air. She saw that Mia was using the spare single bed as a general dumping ground for her stuff. This made Hannah twitchy, but she

102

resisted the temptation to tidy up, other than to move the wet towel to its correct location on the rail in the bathroom. She did allow herself to give the room a quick once-over with the hoover and duster, being careful not to move any of Mia's personal items, for fear of looking like she'd been snooping. For the same reason, she resisted making the bed or changing the sheets, but she made a mental note to do the latter in her niece's presence once she returned.

As Hannah finished up in Mia's room, shutting the window again to make it less obvious she'd been there, she heard a knock at the door.

Surely that couldn't be her back already, she thought.

It wasn't. It was Kathy from down the hall.

'Hello, stranger,' Hannah said, beaming at her closest friend from the apartment complex: a chirpy widow in her early seventies who'd always reminded her of her late mother. They often had a brew and a chat together, but Kathy had been away for the past three weeks on a coach trip around America with an old friend. 'So how was the holiday?' she asked after giving Kathy a big hug and inviting her inside.

'Oh, it was wonderful,' Kathy replied, running a hand through her short, curly white hair. 'But I've got terrible jetlag now. My poor old body's got literally no idea what time it is any more. And all that food they made me eat . . . goodness me.' She patted her ample stomach, shaking her head and wearing a wry grin.

'Would a cuppa help?'

'What do you think?' Kathy giggled, following Hannah

through to the kitchen and helping herself to a seat at the table. 'It always helps, doesn't it?'

'Tea or coffee?'

'Definitely tea, please. Honestly, those Americans: they're lovely and all, but no one managed to make me a proper brew the whole time I was over there. That was one of the things I missed most.'

'Tell me all about it, then,' Hannah said as she filled the kettle.

A while later, after Kathy had provided her neighbour with a thorough and often hilarious summary of the trip and the various characters she'd met along the way, she turned the conversation back to Hannah.

'So enough about me,' she said. 'How are things with you and Mark? What's new? Any gossip?'

'Well, it's not just the two of us at the moment, Kathy. We have a house guest.'

She spent the next few minutes bringing her neighbour up to speed on the situation.

'Well, you won't believe this,' Kathy replied. 'But I've got a visitor arriving on Sunday too. Do you remember my grandson, Todd?'

'Of course. How old is he now?'

'Thirteen. And he's coming to stay for a fortnight while his mum and dad get a new kitchen and bathroom fitted at their home in Lancaster. The place will be a building site while the work's underway. Goodness knows why they decided to get it all done in one go, but they were keen for him to be out of the way, so I offered to have him stay here.'

After pausing to take a big sip from the large mug of tea Hannah had made for her, Kathy added: 'I was actually a bit worried about how I would keep him occupied for two weeks. Perhaps he and . . . sorry, what did you say your niece was called again?'

'Mia.'

'Perhaps he and Mia could keep each other company some of the time. You know, assuming they get along okay and they want to do that.'

Hannah, who'd met Todd several times and remembered him as a quiet but polite boy, nodded and smiled. 'Do you know what, Kathy? That sounds fantastic. I've no idea how long Mia's going to be with us for, but I'd be more than happy to introduce them and see what happens. She's just gone out on her own for the first time, which I'm not entirely comfortable with; I'd be much happier if she had someone with her. I'll run it by her later on, but I can't see why she'd mind. I get the impression she's dying for some company her own age.'

Pleased by this unexpected turn of events, Hannah raised her mug and chinked it against Kathy's. 'Cheers,' she said. 'It's good to have you back.'

CHAPTER 7

Mark looked at the clock on the wall of his office: 3.36 p.m. Time seemed to be moving at a snail's pace this Thursday afternoon. He had plenty to do, as usual, but he couldn't get his mind into gear.

Having that pint of lager at lunchtime had been a mistake. A few of the senior staff had gone out for a bite to eat at the pub and Mark hadn't been able to resist. The Mia and Diane situation had been playing on his mind all morning and he'd hoped a little alcohol might take the edge off.

It had certainly helped him relax and put aside his problems for the hour or so they were out. But once back at his desk, he'd started to feel sleepy and maudlin. At one point he'd had to take himself off to the loos to splash cold water on his face and – in a low moment, staring at his reflection in the mirror and wondering where this would all end – he'd barely avoided bursting into tears.

Thankfully, he had no meetings scheduled for the rest

of the afternoon and the office was quieter than usual, due to it being peak holiday season. He was supposed to be concentrating on clearing the paperwork accumulating in his in-tray and catching up with all the unanswered emails in his inbox. But instead he found himself using his phone's web browser to research DNA paternity testing.

This was something he'd started thinking about after failing to make direct contact with Diane. He'd tried phoning her numerous times now, leaving her five voicemails as well as sending three texts. He'd been careful in terms of what he actually said or wrote, making no specific reference to the real reason he desperately wanted to speak to her, but he hadn't received any response at all.

She had at least phoned Mia eventually and sent Hannah a text. So where was his reply? How dare she ignore him after dropping that bombshell last Saturday! It was so out of order, particularly as it had left him fearful of what she was up to; fretting over whether she was on the brink of coming clean to Hannah too.

As for Mia, having spent some time with her now, he was pretty sure she had no knowledge about it so far. Whether or not that would remain the case depended on her mother. However, for all her faults, he couldn't see Diane wanting to mess with her daughter's head over such a sensitive issue.

She apparently had no such qualms about messing with his head, though. For the umpteenth time in the last few days, Mark's mind jumped back to that one-to-one discussion they'd around eleven years earlier in the aftermath of Maggie's death and the couple of days he'd spent looking after Mia.

'I'll tell you the truth if that's what you really want, Mark,' Diane had said to him.

And then, if what she was now claiming to be true was to be believed, she'd done the exact opposite and told him a pack of lies.

'Of course I want to know the truth,' Mark told his sister-in-law. 'You owe me that at least.'

He wished Diane wasn't wearing the green top she'd borrowed from Hannah, which almost made him feel like he was talking to his wife. This exacerbated his sense of guilt and brought back to mind the events of that damned night, when he was now convinced Mia had been conceived. He usually did his best to avoid thinking about it, especially around Diane, since doing so served no purpose. The fact was that he'd slept with his wife's sister and hidden it from Hannah ever since. Dwelling on the matter wouldn't change a thing.

It terrified Mark that, by pushing to discover the truth about Mia, he risked opening a can of worms that could devastate his marriage. But he couldn't stop himself.

'So is she my daughter?' he asked, sitting forward in his chair and taking a sip from his bottle of beer.

After a long pause that made Mark want to shout at her to stop playing games, Diane finally replied. 'No, she's not. It's nice that you bonded with her, though. She is still your niece and, seeing as her father isn't around, it's good for her to spend quality time with a close male relative.'

'What?' Mark snapped. 'I thought you said you were going to tell me the truth, Diane. How's this any different to what you've said to me before?'

'Give me a minute, will you? But you can't repeat what I tell you: not even to Hannah. If you do, well, you'll force me to deny it and reveal that we slept together.'

'Why would you threaten to do that?' he said in a raised voice, shaking his head in disbelief. 'If I'm not Mia's father, then what purpose would it serve other than to break your sister. Is that really what you want?'

'Keep it down, please,' Diane replied in little more than a whisper, 'or you'll wake Mia up. Is that what you want?'

Mark didn't reply, taking a minute to calm down while she glared at him. God, she was a piece of work. How could she and Hannah have such different temperaments, despite being raised in exactly the same environment?

'If I wanted to tell Hannah, I'd have already done so by now,' Diane said. 'But if I tell you this, I need to know you won't repeat it.'

'Fine,' Mark replied, sighing. 'But whoever this man is, how can you be so certain he's the father and I'm not?'

'For a start, I know when I took precautions and when I didn't. But I've also had a test carried out to be sure. The father paid for it and now we have an agreement whereby I keep quiet about his involvement and he does the right thing financially.'

'Doesn't he want to be involved in Mia's life?'

'We both agreed it wasn't a good idea.'

Mark shook his head and took another swig of his beer. 'So are you going to tell me or not?'

'Do I have your word you won't repeat this?'

'Yes.'

'Fine, it's a bloke I used to work for – an old boss of mine. He's quite a bit older than me and married with kids of his own. We had a short affair. There were no real feelings: it was just sex. Things were already over by the time I discovered I was pregnant. Neither of us wanted any more from the relationship. He was never going to leave his family and I didn't want him to, so we reached our agreement instead. He's kept up his side of the bargain – financially, I mean – and I'm happy with that.'

Mark paused, expecting Diane to elaborate, but instead she took a swig from her bottle of beer and stared at him, apparently waiting for a response.

'Seriously?' he asked. 'That's all you're going to tell me? And his name?'

'That's irrelevant. It's none of your business. I've already told you more than I've told anyone else.'

'What about Mia?' Mark asked. 'You're happy for her to grow up without a father?'

'I'm perfectly capable of deciding what's best for my daughter, thank you very much.'

Mark knew better than to push this any further. He finished his drink and made his excuses. Why stay? If he wasn't Mia's father, what more was there for the two of them to discuss? All in all he felt pretty stupid, wondering what had gone through his head to make him so sure Mia was his daughter. He was also uncomfortable about having discussed his and Diane's night of shame, which neither of them had mentioned in a long time. Doing so was like reopening an old wound; it felt more real as a result, sharpening his sense of guilt and increasing the negativity he felt towards his sister-in-law.

As for Mia, he couldn't simply switch off the powerful feelings he'd developed over the past couple of days. Whatever he felt about her mother, she was a lovely, sweet little girl. He'd have to settle for calling her his niece.

In the car on the way home, Mark gave himself a firm talking-to. 'Come on,' he said to his reflection in the rear-view mirror. 'Stop sulking. You should be glad about what you've learned. You never wanted kids anyway; especially not with Diane. And where would you be now if she'd told you otherwise? You'd be panicking about what to do next, terrified your marriage was doomed. Move on now, Mark. Get on with your life and forget about this.'

The sound of Mark's desk phone ringing snapped him out of his memories and back into the present. He shook his head to try to clear the fog and, stifling a yawn, picked up the receiver. 'Hello?'

'Hi, Mark. It's Sharon on reception. Sorry to bother you. I'm actually looking for Adam King, but he's not answering his line. Do you know if he's around?'

Mark looked up, glad it wasn't a call for him. He spotted Adam, who'd also been at the pub earlier, talking to another colleague on the far side of the office. 'Yes, I can see him. If you send the call back to his desk, I'll let him know to take it. Who's calling?'

'Joe Wilder.'

'Right. I'll tell him.'

Mark jumped to his feet and called over to Adam, the firm's commercial director, who flashed him a thumbs-up and dashed back to his desk to take the call.

Mark frowned at his busy in-tray and was about to start tackling it when he was overtaken by an urge to have another quick look on his phone about DNA testing. He recalled reading newspaper articles and seeing TV programmes about how easy it was to do these days: something his searches so far had confirmed. However, they'd also thrown a spanner in the works, in that his initial idea had been to do it secretly, without Mia or Diane's knowledge, and that no longer looked feasible.

He'd pictured being able to sneak some hairs from Mia's brush and post them off to a lab together with whatever sample was required from him. But the more he read online, the less likely an option that became. Apparently hairs were only useful if they included the root and up to ten could be required; even then, they were less reliable than the favoured option of an oral swab.

What's more, he'd also discovered it was illegal for DNA testing to be carried out in the UK without the consent of the person from whom the sample was taken or, in the case of minors, someone with parental responsibility for them. It was even illegal simply to collect a DNA sample from someone without their explicit consent.

In other words, there was little chance of him being able to get a paternity test done without involving Diane and Mia. Certainly not if he wanted to stay on the right side of the law anyway. He kept looking, though, in the vague hope he might somehow find a way.

It probably would have been quicker to look using his desktop, but he didn't want there to be a digital record of the sites he'd been visiting that one of the IT guys might come across. He also used his personal phone, rather than his work one, making sure to clear his browsing history afterwards.

All the actions of a guilty man, he thought. And he was inevitably digging himself deeper. Every new secret he kept from Hannah, every extra deception, was like a needle unpicking a crucial defence: that his mistake, horrendous as it was, had happened once, about fifteen years ago, and never been repeated.

He had never cheated on Hannah before or after that night. He loved her with all of his heart and had no interest in being with anyone else. But how could that ever excuse all of his lies?

He knew plenty of men who'd been spurred on by not getting caught having a one-night stand or even an affair; it had led to them doing it again. But that hadn't been his experience at all. He'd never stopped feeling guilty and, even with Diane out of the picture for so long, he still worried about his wife finding out.

Following the sisters' big quarrel, Mark's greatest fear had been that Diane might finally tell Hannah out of spite. That idea had terrified him – literally kept him up at night, running worst-case scenarios through his mind. This had eased with time, as he and Hannah had both started to accept they might never see Diane or Mia again.

Now he was terrified of being discovered afresh.

He had the feeling Diane's letter to him was only the

113

start. The fact that she wasn't responding to his attempts to contact her did nothing to ease that concern. So what was she going to do: return whenever she felt like it and make a big announcement to the others? He couldn't rule out that possibility. So, as things stood, if he wasn't able to arrange a DNA test, what options were there apart from waiting to find out, while rehearsing what – if anything – he might say to his wife to soften the blow?

After looking around the office to make sure no one was too close to see, he pulled Diane's letter out from where he'd stashed it, at the very back of the lockable drawer in his desk.

Her use of the words *now it's time for the truth* particularly bothered him, as did the bit about secrets and lies. *They eat you up inside*, she'd written, which he couldn't disagree with. But that didn't mean he was happy for her to do and say whatever she liked, regardless of the consequences. Surely the two of them ought to at least have a discussion first. Was that really too much for a guy in his situation to ask?

The one part of the letter that gave him a glimmer of hope was right at the end, where she apologised for everything she'd put him through. It would be a bit odd for her to write that, assuming she meant it, only to drop a grenade in his lap.

He let out a long, frustrated sigh. All this speculation was hurting his head, but what else could he do when speaking to Diane wasn't an option?

'Bloody hell, mate,' a voice from behind him said. 'It can't be that bad, can it?'

Mark froze. He recognised Adam's voice and did not want him to see the letter. Leaving it where it was on the desk, he slowly swivelled around in his chair, hoping his body would hide what he'd been looking at.

'Adam,' he said, forcing a smile on to his face. Apart from the odd pub lunch, like today, Mark wasn't much of one for socialising with people from work, unless there was a good business reason. He preferred to keep the two things separate, as in his experience it led to lots of talking shop when he'd rather be letting his hair down.

However, Adam King was an exception to the rule. The pair had started at the firm around the same time and, being on a similar level and both in their mid-forties, they'd naturally become friends. Adam, a portly, bald chap who loved his food and drink, was also married without kids.

The couples had tried socialising together on one occasion, but neither Mark nor Hannah had really clicked with Adam's wife, Mary: a brash barrister with a habit of rubbing people up the wrong way. Although the men had never discussed it, Mark suspected Mary hadn't taken to them either, since there had been no further such invitations from either side. Not that it had harmed the men's friendship. They'd carried on as they had before, both asking after each other's wives from time to time, but leaving it at that.

'That sounded like a Monday morning sigh to me,' Adam went on. 'What on earth's so bad that it's stressing you out on a Thursday afternoon?'

'Oh, nothing,' Mark lied, widening his smile. 'I'm just ready to go home, I think.'

Adam lowered his voice. 'You're not kidding. I've hardly been able to keep my eyes open since lunch. I don't know about you, but I'm thinking of knocking off soon.'

Mark laughed. 'Sounds like a plan. What did Wilder want?'

Joe Wilder, the man who'd phoned for Adam, was the boss of another firm they'd recently taken over down in Southampton. He was a moaner, always finding problems and looking for other people to solve them.

'Oh, the usual complaints. I think I'm going to have to go down there next week. You don't fancy coming along too, do you? Maybe you could crunch some numbers to make him look bad; get him off our case a bit.'

Mark was about to decline, since he knew it would probably involve an overnight stay and, with things as they were at home, it felt like bad timing. But then it occurred to him that Southampton wasn't too far from Bournemouth, where Diane lived.

'Possibly,' he replied. 'What day were you thinking of going down?'

'I'm fairly flexible, although not Monday, as I have meetings here that I need to attend. I can't be bothered trying to do it all in one day. We'd fly, obviously, but that still takes a while when you factor in all the messing around at the airport and the transfers.'

Mark nodded while his brain whirred, weighing up the options. He'd have to check how long it took to travel from Southampton to Bournemouth. Hopefully there would be a direct train; if so, it might be feasible for him to nip over there and try to find Diane. He'd have to get her address first, but Mia could provide that. The question was whether to do it on the quiet, which could get complicated, or tell everyone what he was doing, obviously without mentioning the reason he was so desperate to see Diane.

The latter made more sense, although he'd have to suggest it to Hannah in just the right way, so she thought it was a good idea. If she said not to bother, that would leave him in a tricky situation where going ahead regardless could reveal his own interest in making the trip. But telling her felt like the best move. It would also make life easier in terms of finding out the address from Mia.

'Can I have a word with Hannah and let you know tomorrow?'

'No sweat. It would be great to have you along, mate.'

Once Mark was alone again – as much as he ever could be in an open-plan office – he hid Diane's letter back in the drawer, which he immediately locked. He had to be more careful about where and when he looked at it in future. The idea of anyone else ever discovering its contents terrified him.

CHAPTER 8

'Are you ready, Mia?' Hannah asked, tapping on her bedroom door. 'We need to go soon.'

'Yes,' Mia replied. 'Almost ready.'

Nearly twenty minutes later she finally emerged, wearing a pair of faded denim shorts and a navy polo shirt. Her hair was tied neatly back in a ponytail and – to Hannah's surprise – there was none of the dark, dramatic make-up she usually favoured. Today's look was far more subtle, allowing her natural, fresh-faced beauty a chance to shine through.

Her lovely green eyes glistened in the sunlight as she knelt down to put her trainers on in the hall.

Hannah was tempted to tell her how nice she looked, but having once been a teenage girl herself she knew this might not be the right thing to say. There was a distinct change of appearance today from what she'd seen previously. What this was supposed to signal, Hannah couldn't be certain, but it surely had something to do with the fact that Mia was about to meet a boy of around her age. Perhaps dressing down was her way of signalling that she wasn't interested in impressing Todd. Or maybe it was exactly the opposite. Either way, Hannah kept quiet.

'Where's, um, Mark?' Mia asked, looking around for some sign of him. 'Isn't he coming too?'

'No, love. He's gone for a run and then a game of squash. He likes to keep fit.'

Mia's face fell. 'Oh, right. Who with?'

'I'm not sure, actually. He plays in a local league, so it depends who he's been drawn against this week. Do you ever play squash?'

Mia shook her head. 'I'm not really into sport.'

'You haven't left your wet towel in your bedroom, have you?' Hannah asked her, already knowing the answer.

'Oh, sorry. I think I have. Do you want me to move it?'

'Please,' Hannah replied. She almost said something sarcastic but managed to bite her tongue.

Once that was done, they left the apartment and made the short walk along the corridor to her neighbour's front door, with Hannah leading the way.

A moment later they were being greeted by an effusive Kathy and her red-faced grandson.

'Well, aren't you a pretty one,' Kathy told Mia, whose cheeks flushed to match Todd's. 'You look like a young version of your gorgeous aunt.' Grabbing her right hand and giving it a good squeeze, Kathy stared into her eyes before adding: 'Yep. Bright as a button too, I'd wager. Delighted to meet you, Mia. Do come in.'

Hannah greeted thirteen-year-old Todd, who'd grown a lot since she'd last seen him and now had that gangly look typical of kids his age, not yet comfortable in his ever-changing adolescent body.

'Hello,' he replied in a deep voice that sounded strange coming out of his mouth, like there was a male ventriloquist hidden somewhere nearby.

Hannah had to stifle a laugh, covering it up with a big smile and questions about how Todd was doing and the building work taking place at his home that had led to his visit.

Next she introduced her niece to him, leading the two teenagers to nod awkwardly at each other, both muttering some kind of greeting and then looking at the floor. Todd was slightly taller than Mia, despite being a year below her at school.

'Come on through to the lounge, everyone,' Kathy piped up at just the right moment. 'I hope you're hungry, because I've got plenty for you to dig into.'

Kathy had come up with the idea of inviting Hannah and Mia over for Sunday afternoon tea as a way to introduce the youngsters and break the ice.

Her apartment was a smaller, two-bedroom version of Hannah and Mark's place, although Kathy's more old-fashioned taste in furnishings, such as her preference for carpets over hard floors, meant it had a very different feel inside. She had a small balcony off the lounge, which was open when they entered, letting in warm air from outside as well as the sounds of the city.

'Lovely day today, isn't it?' Hannah said.

'It is,' Kathy replied. 'Not quite as nice as some of the weather I saw in the States, but it definitely feels like summer. I did wonder about sitting us on the balcony, but there's not a lot of room out there and I thought it might be a squeeze.'

'No, this is perfect.' Hannah's eyes fell on the coffee table in the middle of the room, which was packed full of cakes. 'Goodness me, Kathy. You're spoiling us.'

Her hostess giggled as she directed them all to sit down. 'I'll make a pot of tea. Would anyone like anything else to drink?'

'Tea for me, please,' Hannah said. Mia requested the same.

'Todd?' Kathy asked, already on her way to the kitchen. 'You're not big on tea, are you? I've got cola, lemonade or cordial instead, if you like.'

'Um, lemonade, please,' he replied in that booming new voice of his, which again made Hannah smile to herself.

Kathy had two floral patterned sofas arranged in an L-shape around the coffee table. Hannah sat on one and patted the space next to her, indicating that Mia should join her. Todd was called into the kitchen to give his grandmother a hand.

'Are you okay?' Hannah whispered to her niece, who looked far from comfortable, perched on the front of the sofa cushion like she was ready to spring to her feet at any moment.

'Fine.'

'These cakes look good, don't they? What do you fancy? I think I might go for a scone with jam and cream.'

'I'm not sure.'

A few minutes later Todd reappeared from the kitchen. He was carrying a tray of teacups and saucers, a jug of milk and his glass of lemonade in such a shaky, awkward manner that Hannah got up to help him, fearing a breakage otherwise.

'Thanks,' he said, his facial expression changing from one of wide-eyed, intense concentration to blissful relief. 'I'm, er, not very good at carrying things.' Giggling nervously, he added: 'I don't think I'll ever make much of a waiter, will I?'

Hannah gave him a reassuring smile. 'Not to worry. You got it all here in one piece.'

Kathy reappeared, carrying the pot of tea. She instructed Todd to grab a seat and for everyone to help themselves to the superb spread before them, which included donuts, chocolate eclairs, vanilla slices, jam tarts and a luscious-looking Victoria sponge.

'Are you expecting another six people, Kathy?' Hannah joked. 'I can't believe how much there is here.'

'Well, the sponge cake is homemade, but the rest is shop-bought, I'm afraid,' Kathy replied. 'I did wonder whether I ought to have made some sandwiches too.'

'Don't be silly. This is wonderful. Mark will be gutted when he finds out what he's missed.'

'You'll have to take something home for him. It'll be a nice reward for all that running around on the squash court. I don't envy him in this warm weather.'

Hannah asked Todd if he ever played squash.

'Um, not much,' he replied. 'My dad plays and I have

had a go a couple of times, but I'm not very good. Tennis is more my game.'

'Do you like to play tennis, Mia?' Kathy asked.

'No, not really,' she said.

Kathy popped back to the kitchen, returning with cake forks and serviettes, which she passed around before asking why no one was digging in yet. 'Come on, stop being polite. Let's start with you, Mia. What would you like?'

For the next thirty minutes or so, the four of them remained in the lounge, eating, drinking and chatting. Well, it was Hannah and Kathy who did most of the talking. They tried to involve the other two as much as possible, but it was an uphill battle getting them to open up, Mia in particular.

Just as Hannah was starting to think this might have been a bad idea, there was a breakthrough.

'How did you like Central Library?' Kathy asked Mia. 'Your aunt told me you'd paid a visit. It's not your typical library, is it?'

'No, I really liked it,' Mia said, her eyes lighting up as she placed her freshly drained teacup back on to its saucer. 'There are loads of things to do. They've got these cool viewing pods where you can access an archive of local film and video footage. There's also a media lounge with loads of iMacs and stuff – even gaming consoles. I've never seen that in a library before.'

Todd's ears pricked up at this. 'Do you like gaming?' he asked her.

'Sure.'

'I brought my PlayStation with me. It's all set up in my

123

bedroom, if you fancy having a go.' He turned to Kathy. 'Is that all right, Gran?'

'By all means,' she replied.

To Hannah's surprise, Mia, who'd barely said a word to Todd so far, seemed more than happy to disappear with him to play whatever games these machines were capable of running. Hannah had never used one – not a modern console anyway – and she had zero interest in changing that. Computer games had never been her thing, although apparently the same couldn't be said for her niece.

Once the teenagers were safely out of the way, having shut the bedroom door behind them, she and Kathy grinned at each other and shrugged.

'Well, I didn't see that coming,' Hannah said. 'I was about to give up and take Mia home.'

Kathy giggled. 'Kids today . . . What do we know, hey? I couldn't believe my eyes when Todd turned up with that thing – flatscreen TV and all – but it seems he'd be lost without it.'

She explained that Karen, her daughter and Todd's mother, thought it would keep him out of trouble while he was staying there and make her life easier as his host. 'And he's always on that mobile phone of his,' she added, shaking her head. 'All that time in front of a screen can't be good for them, if you ask me. But I'm not his mother, so I don't interfere. Is Mia the same?'

'She didn't show up with her own television, if that's what you mean.' Hannah smirked. 'She has a phone, of course, and a Kindle – but that's just for reading books, which she seems to do a lot. I get the impression she's quite easy to live with, compared to other teenagers, but it does seem like some things I tell her go in one ear and out the other. She never remembers to put the extractor fan on when she has a shower, for instance, which she really needs to, considering how long she spends in there. And don't get me started on wet towels. I'm convinced she'd collect a mountain of them in her room if I didn't get involved.'

Kathy laughed. 'My problem with Todd is usually getting him to shower at all. You're right, though: they're not always great at listening to instructions. I don't even think it's deliberate, to be honest. I think it's more a case of them being so distracted by other things – their mobiles, for instance – that what we say doesn't register.'

Kathy eyed the various cakes still spread out on the coffee table. She cut herself a sliver of the Victoria sponge after first offering her guest some more, which she politely declined. 'She seems like a mini version of you, Hannah, what with the way she looks, the library visit and the books. She must be proud as punch about you becoming a published author. How's all that going, by the way?'

'Yeah, about that,' Hannah said, running a hand through her hair and clearing her throat before continuing. 'I, er, haven't said anything to Mia yet regarding my book deal.'

'Oh? Why ever not? It's such a wonderful achievement. I was telling everyone I met on holiday that my friend was an author and they should look out for your book when it's released.'

This made Hannah smile. 'Really? That's so nice of you, Kathy. I am going to tell Mia soon. It hasn't come up yet.'

'Haven't you discussed what you do for work?'

'No. You know what kids are like. They're not interested in that stuff.' As she said this last sentence, words she'd not expected to hear herself utter, Hannah marvelled at how much she'd already learned from Mia's visit. Although everyone had been young once, as a childless adult it was easy to forget so much about that time; living with a minor was eye-opening.

'She must have seen you writing.'

'Not really. I haven't done much since she arrived. It's all been a bit hectic. I need to crack on soon or that deadline for book two is going to start looking scary. I'm already not as far on as I'd like to be.'

'You'll be fine,' Kathy said in that reassuring, motherly way of hers. 'Give yourself a break. Does your sister know about your book? What's her name again?'

'It's Diane – and no, not to my knowledge. I think that's part of the reason I haven't told Mia yet. My relationship with her mum has been off for so long now that I guess I'm guarded. I'm not even sure what Mia thinks of me. She seems to get on better with Mark.'

'I thought he didn't like kids. Wasn't that the reason you didn't—'

'Yes, exactly. And he's hardly even around most of the time. During the week he's working and now he's out playing squash. Next week it looks like he's going to be away for a night down south, visiting that place his firm recently took over. Mind you, I shouldn't complain about that, as he's offered to try to find Diane while he's down there.'

126

Kathy nodded, chewing on her last morsel of cake. 'So you still don't know when she's coming back for Mia?' she asked once her mouth was empty.

Hannah shook her head. 'But Bournemouth isn't that far from Southampton, where Mark's heading, so he thinks it's feasible.'

'Don't take this the wrong way, love, but it seems quite extreme to have to go and search for her like that. Is there something I'm missing?'

'You don't know my sister like Mark and I do.' She lowered her voice, mindful of her niece's proximity, even though Todd's bedroom door was still shut. 'There's definitely something strange going on; I've no idea what that is, but it's unlikely to be anything good.

'She's not answering our calls; the only one who's spoken to her since she left here last weekend is Mia, during one very brief and vague phone chat. I've had a single text from her – and that was only after I left a voicemail threatening to call the police because I was so worried. I mean, who turns up out of the blue after all that time of no contact, only to dump her daughter and go AWOL? It's not normal behaviour, is it?'

'Right, I see. No, that definitely doesn't sound good.'

'It's not. But please don't say anything to anyone, Kathy; especially not Todd, in case those two do end up friends.'

Kathy reached forward and touched her hand, looking her in the eye. 'Of course I won't. Poor Mia. How's she coping with it all?'

'She seems to be all right, considering. But it's hard to say for sure, since I'm only just getting to know her. I should probably try to have a chat with her about it, but I'm also mindful of not worrying her. I've nothing to compare her behaviour with, apart from what she was like as a toddler – and that's hardly helpful.'

'No, I suppose not. If there's anything I can do to help, please let me know.'

'Thank you. I appreciate that. You're a good friend, Kathy.'

CHAPTER 9

Hannah had just got off the phone to her literary agent, who was back in the office this Tuesday morning after a fortnight's holiday in the South of France with his wife and two young daughters.

A big, bald chap in his early fifties with a booming voice and a laugh to match, Bruce Wilks had an imposing but affable personality ideally suited to his job. He also appeared to know everyone who mattered in the publishing industry and to have read every book of note that Hannah could think to mention. He was part of a prestigious, long-established London literary agency and had a wealth of experience that Hannah felt made him an ideal match for her clueless novice. Bruce had been at her side every step of the way so far – a reliable source of guidance and reassurance – and she really appreciated having his firm but friendly hand on the tiller.

After the usual pleasantries about Bruce's trip to the Côte d'Azur, where Hannah and Mark had also holidayed several times, the conversation had turned towards literary matters.

Pippa, Hannah's editor at the large, London-based publisher with whom she'd been lucky enough to sign a deal, had sent them both an email relating to *The Boy at the Window*, Hannah's debut novel.

A petite, softly spoken, pensive type in her mid-twenties, Pippa had an impressive grasp of the publishing industry and its latest trends, plus a great eye for detail. She'd contacted Hannah and Bruce on this occasion to show them an amended version of the cover, which she and her colleagues were keen to use.

Hannah liked the new version, but she'd wanted Bruce's feedback before replying. Fortunately, he liked it too, which made things nice and easy. Now all Hannah had to do was draft a quick email reply to Pippa.

At times like this she often felt like she needed to pinch herself. Her dream of being a published author was coming true. She pulled up the attachment of the tweaked cover design her editor had sent over and stared at it for a while on her laptop screen.

It did look good. Like . . . well, a real book.

Slipping into a daydream, she imagined walking along a Metrolink carriage and happening upon someone with their head buried in a copy of her novel. She pictured herself standing silently behind them in the aisle of the tram, watching them engage in her fictional world and wondering whether or not to tap their shoulder; to reveal herself as the author and offer to sign it.

And then the fantasy came to a crashing halt as the

reader morphed into a sneering Diane, who threw the book to the floor, declaring it to be 'utter rubbish'.

Hannah shook her head and placed her palms over her face, her fingertips running across her closed eyelids like erasers trying to delete the horrible image she'd conjured up. What was wrong with her? Why couldn't she just enjoy the run-up to her first novel being published, like a normal person? Instead, here she was, worrying what her stupid sister would think of it. Why did she even care? Bloody Diane. It was so typical of her to reappear now to spoil things; to get inside Hannah's head again and make her doubt herself just as her life was getting back on track.

'So don't let her!' Hannah shouted at the empty room, slamming both fists on to the desk, jumping to her feet and walking over to the window in a bid to change the direction of her thought process. 'Screw Diane,' she said to her faint reflection in the glass. 'Who cares what she thinks? I've managed perfectly well without her for years now. I'm the one who should be judging her; not the other way round. What kind of mother dumps her daughter in a strange city, miles from home, only to go incommunicado? So what if she spurns my book when she finds out about it. It'll only be because she's jealous.'

Hannah realised that speaking her thoughts out loud in this way would probably make her look unbalanced to most people. However, it was something she did from time to time as a way of pulling herself together when she felt like she was losing it; giving herself a stern talking-to when no one else was around to do so.

At Hannah's lowest ebb, when her then very fragile mental state had forced her to leave her old job as an advertising copywriter, she'd had to adapt to spending a lot of time home alone. During this difficult, traumatic period, she'd discovered that vocalising her thoughts could be a helpful way of addressing their less logical, anxiety-fuelled elements. They somehow sounded less convincing when spoken out loud than they did niggling away in her mind. So actually, as far as Hannah was concerned, talking to herself didn't make her unhinged; it helped her to stay sane, just as her counselling did. She'd even mentioned the habit to Sally during one of their early sessions, and she'd encouraged it, telling Hannah to stick with this coping method if she found it helpful.

All the same, Hannah knew it wasn't something to do in company: at least not in front of anyone other than Mark, who'd seen it all before. She certainly wouldn't have said any of these things out loud in front of Mia, not least because they involved her mother. But her niece wasn't home. She'd gone out with Todd about half an hour ago to show him around Central Library, with its fancy computers and games, and then to 'hang out around town', as she'd put it.

Hannah was delighted that the kids, who'd also spent several hours together on Todd's PlayStation yesterday, were getting along. Things hadn't looked promising initially, but that must have been down to shyness. It was nice to see them going out and doing something together. Knowing Mia wasn't wandering the city centre alone was a weight off Hannah's mind.

What did bother her, though, was the fact that she still hadn't told Mia about being a writer and having her novel published. She knew this was weird, particularly in light of her niece being a keen reader. Hannah recognised it for what it was: a protection mechanism designed to stop Diane from finding out and potentially spoiling her achievement. And yet Hannah also knew she couldn't continue to keep it a secret from Mia.

Mark had warned her of this as they'd chatted in bed on Sunday night. He'd started off by telling her how he'd bumped into her friend Laura on his way home from playing squash that afternoon.

Laura was a former colleague of Hannah's from her copywriting days. At one time she and Mark had frequently socialised with her and her husband, Ralph. One reason for this was that they also didn't have any kids – although not out of choice. They'd been down the IVF route without any success: a harrowing experience that had played some part in the fading of their friendship. Hannah's own experiences had played a more significant role, though, thanks to everything she'd been through following the death of her mother and the falling-out with Diane. Of particular significance was the major public breakdown Hannah had eventually had at work, culminating in her departure.

She and Laura were still in touch. They occasionally met up for a coffee, but it wasn't like it used to be between them.

'I almost didn't recognise Laura,' Mark had said. 'It's been so long and you never mentioned she'd cut her hair short. Anyway, she said she'd give you a call to arrange another coffee soon. And she seemed very excited about reading your book.'

'Right,' Hannah had replied. She'd tried to ignore the wave of panic she felt at the idea of any of her old work mates reading the start of the book: a section inspired by her office meltdown. The issue was that several of them, including Laura, had witnessed the real-life incident and were bound to spot the similarities between that and the one in the story.

Somehow Hannah had transformed the most difficult part of her life so far into a positive: turning the negative experience on itself as a way to regain her confidence and recover. After first going off on stress and then quitting the job altogether, she'd been through an awful period in which – due to crippling anxiety – she'd barely left home. Then Hannah had started to see Sally, her counsellor, who'd encouraged her to take ownership of the situation in order to turn it around. This had led to Hannah pursuing her lifelong dream of writing a novel. Following a couple of false starts, she'd eventually found her flow by writing about a character in a similar predicament to her own. And so her book – about a housebound woman who grows suspicious after spotting a child alone in a nearby apartment – had taken shape.

But happy as she was with her resulting book deal, the idea of people who knew her reading something so personal gave her the willies as much as it excited her.

'Have you told Mia about it yet?' Mark had asked.

Hannah had frowned. 'No. It hasn't come up.'

'What does she think you do for work?'

'I don't know. We've not discussed it.'

Mark had run his palms across the cotton-encased summer quilt that covered them both in bed, smoothing the fabric over his lower body. 'Hasn't she seen you doing any writing?'

'Possibly,' Hannah had replied. 'But I haven't done much since she's been here. I've found it hard to concentrate and, when I've had some free time, there have always been other things to do.'

'Maybe if you told her about it, you'd also find it easier to make time to write. It'll end up being awkward, if you're not careful.'

Hannah's only reply had been a grunt, followed by a declaration that she was too tired for further conversation. However, after sleeping on the matter, she'd accepted that her husband was right.

In the meantime, she now had a great opportunity to get some writing done, since she wasn't expecting Mia back until late afternoon. At 2 p.m. Hannah had a counselling session scheduled with Sally, who she was glad to have started seeing again in light of Diane and Mia's reappearance, desperate to avoid this triggering a setback in her mental state. However, that appointment was still a while off.

'Come on, Hannah,' she told herself, sitting down in front of her laptop. 'Crack on. No excuses.'

Progress was slow initially as she fought off self-doubt. But as she let herself be drawn back into her fictional world, letting the real one and its various problems fade away, she found her rhythm.

By the time she stopped typing, she'd reached the end of a chapter. She saved the document and leaned back in her chair, looking up at the ceiling and letting out a long sigh as she stretched her arms out on either side and wiggled her fingers around. Thank goodness for that, she thought. All her doubts and fears were still lurking in the background, but the act of writing had muted them.

Was she totally happy with what she'd just written? No. She could easily read back through it and tear it to pieces. But she knew from experience not to do that, and she felt good about having made some progress.

Hannah picked up her mobile and finally allowed herself to read the text message that had arrived while she'd been busy – from Laura.

She'd been tempted to open it straight away but hadn't wanted to interrupt her flow. She had a good idea what it was about anyway, in light of Mark bumping into Laura the other day.

It was a shame how things had drifted between the two couples, considering how well they'd always got along with one another. Maybe it was still fixable. It would only take her inviting Laura and Ralph over for a meal. It wasn't like she was inundated with female friends of her own age. She couldn't think of any she was closer to than kind, lovely Laura.

And yet Hannah still felt embarrassed about the cringe-worthy way she'd crashed out of her old job. Seeing Laura never failed to bring it all back, when she'd rather just forget about it and move forward.

Hi, Han. How are you? Saw Mark on Sunday. Got me thinking. Why don't the four of us meet up soon like we used to? Maybe a nice meal somewhere swanky to celebrate your book deal? Can't wait to read it! Already pre-ordered online. X

Hannah read Laura's message over twice and felt her heart race. The suggestion of a meal out together was timely and easier than cooking at home. But again the idea of her friend reading her novel, packed full of her personal angst, made her nervous.

Much had been changed and exaggerated from her real-life mental collapse, but still. Anyone who knew her as well as Laura did could read all sorts into the book that wasn't there, seeing themselves in characters and so on.

The same applied to Diane, plus her dad and his second wife, Joan. They'd all contributed one way or another to Hannah's descent and, as a result, there were bound to be parts of the narrative that rang true, despite how much she'd altered.

As for Mark, he'd already read the story at an early stage. He was also the one person in her life who already knew everything about her – good and bad – and who she could trust without question. They had no secrets. They told each other everything, which was why their marriage was still as strong today, if not stronger, than it had been when they'd first tied the knot. Mark had been her rock throughout, for better for worse, just as he'd pledged during their wedding vows. Without his help, she very much doubted she'd be where she was today.

So why did she care what anyone else thought? She had her husband; he was all she needed.

'Calm down,' she told herself. 'You wanted to write a book. Of course people who know you are going to read it. What did you expect? If they can't understand that it's fiction, that's their problem.'

CLIENT SESSION TRANSCRIPT:
HCOOK060819

S: Hello, Hannah. How are you today?

H: Not too bad, thanks. I got some work done on my next book this morning, so I'm in a good mood about that. It's been difficult getting down to it since Mia's been staying with us.

S: She must be impressed that her aunt will soon be a published author.

H: Hmm. This is going to sound strange, Sally, but I haven't actually told her yet.

S: I see. Why's that?

H: It just hasn't come up, although Mark and I have already discussed this and I'm going to tell her really soon – before it gets weird.

S: Has something been holding you back?

H: Yes, although it's less about Mia and more about Diane, I think. I was a big reader when we were growing up and she wasn't. She used to make fun of me for constantly having my nose in a book. It was another excuse to call me a swat. Plus she'd make comments about how I ought to get some real friends rather than the imaginary ones I read about. That kind of thing. She saw reading as a waste of time.

S: What about your dream of becoming a writer?

H: Hmm. I tried to avoid discussing that with Diane, knowing it would be something else for her to make fun of me about. I remember we both went on a school trip to London once. I must have been thirteen or fourteen. In the coach on the way down, I discovered she'd stolen a short story I'd written at home and was passing it around her friends, getting them all to laugh at it. It was a typical soppy teenage effort about unrequited love, inspired by some of the romantic novels I'd been reading at the time. Of course that made it – and me – an easy target for ridicule. I was mortified. It ruined my whole trip. I couldn't believe my own sister would do something so mean. I didn't speak to her for nearly a week after that.

S: I see. So Diane doesn't know about your book deal either?

H: Not to my knowledge.

S: And you're hesitant to tell Mia because you know that will lead to Diane finding out about it?

H: I suppose so. Part of me wants her to know – to prove her wrong for mocking my early writing attempts. But I'm also afraid she'll find a way to ruin it for me, or at least take the shine off my achievement. The big irony is that Mia's a bookworm. She's mad keen on reading, just like I was at her age. Loving books is something we share, which we can talk about together. It's not like we have much else. Mia has no memory whatsoever of all the times we spent together when she was little. We do have Diane in common, of course, but that's a can of worms I'd rather not open, bearing in mind the dilapidated state of my relationship with my sister. Anyway, I'm going to tell Mia. Mark's away tonight, so I'm planning to take her out for dinner. That should provide us with a good opportunity to have a decent chat.

S: How's having Mia as a guest working out in practical terms?

H: Well, I'm far from an expert on modern teenagers. However, I can now tell you that this particular fourteen-year-old sleeps a lot, spends an awfully long time in the bathroom, keeps a messy bedroom, and has a selective memory when it comes to domestic dos and don'ts, like remembering to hang up her wet towel after showering. I have Mark pretty well trained, so my niece's less disciplined ways can be a challenge to my sense of order. But I could probably do with learning to be more flexible anyway. Plus living with us is a big change for Mia too. Overall, it's great to have the chance to get to know her again. My main worry at the beginning was that she'd be bored with only adults for company, but she's made a friend: Todd, the grandson of my neighbour Kathy. I feel that's taken the pressure off a bit. I don't need to worry so much about entertaining her, and I get more time to work, like this morning. Still, it's hard not to worry when she goes out and about without me or Mark to watch over her, knowing she's our responsibility at the moment. I guess this is how it feels to be a parent.

S: What about Mark? As someone who's never wanted children, how's he finding it?

H: Good question. You know what men are like. They don't tend to give much away about their feelings – and Mark's no exception. Obviously he's out at work a lot of the time, but when he is around, he's pretty good with her. They're into some of the same films and TV shows – mainly sci-fi and superhero stuff that doesn't really appeal to me – but it gives them something to talk about. I actually think Mia's more comfortable around him than me. I worry that she doesn't like me; that Diane's poisoned her mind against me.

S: Has Mia said anything to give you that impression?

H: No, but . . . she plays her cards close to her chest. Our relationship now is so different from when I last knew her. As a toddler, her eyes used to light up when I paid a visit. She'd run over to me and wrap her arms tight around my legs, telling me how much she'd missed me. And then she'd cry when I had to go home, begging me to stay just for a few more minutes. I loved playing with her and her dolls and toys. She was always so creative, allocating character roles even when we played hide and seek. So one of us would be the princess and the other the wicked witch. Or

142

a fluffy bunny and a hungry crocodile. We had so much fun together. I felt like we had a wonderful bond and . . . it's hard sometimes that she doesn't recall any of that.

S: I understand. But don't forget that Diane chose to leave her in your care, which can't have been an easy decision considering the state of your relationship. Don't you think that might be because you once had that strong bond with Mia? It's not something your sister will have forgotten, is it?

H: Maybe. I'd not thought of it that way. I just don't know what to make of the whole visit, because – typical Diane – it's all so vague and up in the air. I still don't know the real reason why she's left Mia here or for how long it's going to be. And if I'm totally honest, part of me is scared to get too close to Mia for fear that my sister will eventually take her away again and stop me seeing her. You know what that did to me on the last occasion. I don't think I could cope with it a second time.

S: There you go, underestimating yourself again. Remember: strong, successful, confident. What are you?

H: Strong, successful and confident.

S: Good. Look what you've achieved with your writing, Hannah. There was a time when you didn't believe yourself capable of that, remember. But you proved you can achieve anything you put your mind to, didn't you?

H: I guess so.

S: I know so. Have you tried contacting Diane to get some specifics about Mia's stay?

H: Yes, but she's not making it easy. Even Mia is struggling to get hold of her. I don't know what's going on. That's one of the reasons Mark is away tonight. He's flown to Southampton for work and this evening he's going to take the train to Bournemouth to try to speak to her.

S: I see. That sounds like a positive step. Hopefully you'll get some answers.

H: I'm not holding my breath.

S: Maybe you should consider giving your sister a chance. I was looking back through some transcripts of our earlier sessions. When I asked you why you weren't prepared to reach out to Diane to try to resolve your conflict, you said: 'It's always me who gives in. It's never her, because she thinks she's always in the right. Well, I'm not doing that any more. Diane can be the one to reach out this time. Otherwise, we're done.' Do you remember saying that?

H: Vaguely. It's true what I said about Diane anyway. She's never been one for apologising or holding out an olive branch. Even after she humiliated me on that school trip to London, I don't recall her ever saying sorry. She didn't see what she'd done wrong. It was just having a laugh, as far as she was concerned; I needed to lighten up. On that occasion, it was me who decided to start speaking to her again eventually, mainly because it was easier than staying angry.

S: Didn't your parents have anything to say about it?

H: I don't think I told them what had happened. It would have just given Diane another excuse to call me a goody-goody and moan about how Mum and Dad always took my side.

S: Would you say there's ever been a time when the pair of you got on well?

H: Good question. We've always had our differences – our rivalries and jealousies – and I wouldn't claim we've ever been best friends. That definitely wasn't the case at secondary school, when we seemed to go from one spat to another. Not long after the London trip incident, for example, she stole a boy from me. It was a guy she'd never shown any interest in previously, who she suddenly pursued and then went out with for a few weeks after I'd happened to mention that I liked him. It was clearly just to get one up on me, like in sixth form when she heard I was auditioning for a school production of *Romeo and Juliet*, so she became interested too. And guess what? She ended up bagging the lead role, while I had to settle for playing her mother. Diane had never displayed any affection for Shakespeare or acting before that show – and she never did again, which says enough. Things did improve as we got older, though, and were no longer living and spending so much time together. After Mia was born, I'd go so far as to say we got on pretty well for a while. That was probably us at our best before Mum got really ill and things started to go the opposite way.

S: Interesting, particularly in light of what you said in

our last session about Diane taking advantage of your fondness for your niece and relying too heavily on your parents' generosity around that period.

H: Yes, those feelings came later. Initially, after I got over my jealousy that she had a child and I didn't, there was a kind of honeymoon period. If I couldn't be a mother, I decided to make the absolute most of being an aunt, so the three of us spent a lot of time together, especially while Diane was on maternity leave.

S: Could that perhaps be something to work towards again?

H: Not likely. It was a fleeting period of harmony. I can't see us ever getting back to that now. We've been out of each other's lives for well over a decade. But . . . I must admit that you do have a point about Diane making the first move towards reconciliation. Even if it was to ask a big favour of me, I ought to recognise the fact that she reached out. It must have been hard for her. For so long now I've hardened my heart to the idea of us ever making up. I've basically written her out of my life. But maybe I ought to at least rethink that. Perhaps I should give my sister a chance, for Mia's sake if nothing else. The idea terrifies me, though, because it leaves me vulnerable. Diane hurt me so badly last time. How do I know she won't do it again?

S: You don't. Not for sure. But if you close yourself off to new possibilities due to fear, then fear wins. Why not try instead to believe in yourself and your ability to deal with whatever life throws at you, including the bad stuff? That way you get to remain open to opportunities that might really improve your quality of life. It's okay to be afraid. It's normal and healthy. But allowing your fear to control you will never make you happy.

H: The thing is, Sally, I was happy with my life before Diane came back into it.

S: Great. But that doesn't mean you couldn't be even happier, does it? And even if things don't work out with her, she can't take that happiness you've already achieved away from you – not if you don't let her. You're the one who controls that, right?

H: I suppose I am.

CHAPTER 10

Mark jumped into a taxi outside Bournemouth railway station and told the cheery cabbie Diane's address. It was in a suburb a couple of miles away from the main town centre. Mia had given him the details.

He had wavered about whether or not to tell her why he needed to know. His chief concern had been that she might speak to her mother in the meantime and tip her off. But Hannah had felt it best to be upfront and honest with her, so that's what they'd done. The pair of them had sat Mia down over the weekend to discuss the matter.

'What's going on?' she'd asked them, her face pale and lined with concern. 'Is everything okay? Is it about Mum?'

'Yes, it is,' Mark had said. 'But there's no news, as such: nothing to be concerned about. It's just that we've not heard anything from her since that single text message she sent to Hannah.'

'No, neither have I,' Mia had replied, letting out a long sigh. 'Not since the one time she phoned me.'

'Have you tried messaging her?'

'No, she said not to; that she'd probably be too busy to reply.' Reaching for her phone, she'd added: 'I can do, though, if you want me to.'

'No, no, that's fine,' Hannah had said, perhaps a little too quickly. 'You'd best do as your mother asked.'

Clearing his throat, Mark had gone on to explain about his business trip to Southampton and how he was planning to call in and see Diane while he was down there. But he'd carefully framed this as a friendly visit to see if there was anything he could do to help, rather than checking up on her.

'Southampton?' Mia had replied. 'That's not around the corner.'

'Well, it's a lot closer than Manchester; it'll only take me half an hour by train.'

'Oh, okay. Mum and I hardly ever take the train. She prefers to drive.'

Back in the present, Mark glanced at his watch. It was 6.03 p.m. on Tuesday. Thankfully, he'd managed to escape the office – and Joe Wilder's moaning – in good time. Although Adam had been disappointed to be left alone with a dinner invite from Wilder, meaning an evening of yet more ear-bending, he'd graciously accepted the situation after Mark had brought him up to speed with what was going on. Mark had at least helped Adam out earlier by knocking Wilder down a peg or two, thanks to his downbeat analysis of the taken-over firm's current financials.

'Lovely warm evening, isn't it?' the taxi driver said,

turning around to wink at his fare as he added: 'Anyone would think it was summer.'

Mark laughed. 'Definitely.'

'In town on business, mate?'

'No, I'm visiting, um . . . a relative,' Mark replied, smiling at the man's reflection in the rear-view mirror and loosening the tie he'd put on that morning at Adam's request 'to power dress the shite out of Wilder'. He hadn't had time to change before taking the train and now he felt overdressed. Oh well. At least it would support his story that he was in the area on business, assuming he actually managed to find Diane to tell it to her.

'Not from round here?' the cabbie asked.

'No,' Mark replied.

'I didn't think so.'

'That obvious?'

'Well, the accent's a bit of a giveaway. Where are you from? Somewhere up north?'

'Manchester.'

'Oh yeah? Red or blue?'

'Blue.'

Mark expected some football banter to follow, but instead the vehicle jerked to a sudden halt, making Mark glad he'd put on his seatbelt. Next thing, Mr Cheery turned into Mr Sweary and stuck his head out of the window, effing and jeffing at the van driver in front, accusing him of driving like an imbecile, only to get a mouthful back in return.

He thought for a moment that his driver might actually get out of the taxi and start scrapping in the street, but luckily a police car drove past in the other direction at just the right moment, pouring cold water on the dispute.

'What a bloody idiot,' the cabbie said, shaking his head. 'They give a driving licence to anyone these days.'

'Mmm,' Mark replied through pursed lips, feeling awkward as hell and wishing the journey over as soon as possible.

There was little conversation after that. Just a lot of tutting and more headshaking from behind the wheel as they made their way along a road that gradually turned from leafy suburban affluence to a tired commercial zone of discount shops, fast food takeaways, To Let signs and vape stores.

'Nearly there now,' Mark was told as they took a speedy sharp left turn, which had him clawing his fingers into the spongy material of his seat in a bid to stay vertical.

Sure enough, about thirty seconds later, the taxi drew to a halt on a narrow side road in front of a row of tatty terraced houses. Each property appeared to be a slightly different shade of off-white, and none of them had been painted any time recently. Their paved front yards were filled with wheelie bins that stared up at an assortment of damaged drainpipes, misted double glazing and rickety roofs.

'Are you sure this is it?' Mark asked.

'It's the address you gave me.'

'Right. Great. Thanks for that.'

Mark settled up, leaving a small tip out of habit rather than desire, and a moment later the cab was gone.

He stood still on the pavement for a moment, wondering

how best to announce himself to Diane if and when she answered the door. It really was a balmy evening, he thought: significantly warmer than it had been when he'd left the apartment that morning. He loosened his tie some more and removed his suit jacket, throwing it over his right forearm and then finally biting the bullet and walking up to Diane's front door.

He rang on the bell once for a couple of seconds and then waited. There was no answer; after a minute or two, he rang again, immediately following it up with a firm rap on the privacy glass in the black wooden door. He waited for another moment, but again there was no reply.

Great. Mark let out a frustrated sigh and took a few steps away from the house so he had a view of all the windows at the front, upstairs and down. Unfortunately, they were each fitted with vertical blinds, which were closed; since it was still broad daylight, there was little chance of being able to ascertain whether there were any lights on inside.

He walked back up to the house and held his face close enough to the white uPVC bay window to smell the layer of salt coating its grimy outer surface. He guessed there was probably a lounge or dining area on the other side. Not that he could tell. Even that close up, he couldn't make out anything through the blinds.

Mark's next move was to kneel down and flip up the letterbox, which he was glad to find didn't have a draught excluder on the inside. He saw an empty hallway with exposed, polished floorboards, a busy coat stand and a cream carpeted staircase leading upstairs. The house looked much smarter inside than out, with fresh, teal-coloured walls and a large framed print of an L.S. Lowry painting just along from the door, depicting dozens of the artist's distinctive matchstick people against a backdrop of sooty industrial buildings.

There was no obvious sign of anyone being home, but he decided to call out regardless. What else was he supposed to do: turn around and find another taxi back to the railway station?

'Hello?' he bellowed, his voice echoing through the empty space. 'Diane? It's Mark. I was working nearby, so I thought I'd call in and check everything was all right. Hello? Can you hear me? Anyone home?'

He waited there after speaking, scouring the visible space for any sign of movement, only to be disappointed. It genuinely looked like no one was home, so what now?

Mark stood back up, brushing off the knees of his suit trousers. He reached into his pocket for his phone, having decided that calling Diane's mobile was probably the most sensible next move. Recent experience told him it was unlikely she'd answer, but it was definitely worth a try. Perhaps he'd even hear it ringing if she was hiding inside somewhere.

As he was locating the number, Mark heard a deep male voice address him from behind, from the direction of the road. 'Can I help you?'

The unexpected sound startled him, almost causing his phone to jump out of his hand. Luckily, he managed to keep hold of it, pocketing it again as he turned around to see who was talking to him.

'Oh, hello,' he said to a barrel-chested man, who looked to be somewhere in his late fifties or early sixties. He was a little shorter than Mark but stood ramrod straight in jeans and a tight black T-shirt that emphasised his soaring broad shoulders and a set of biceps like cannons. There was a sizeable gut there too, but he carried it well, oozing strength and self-confidence. What little remained of his balding white hair was shaved short; his skin had the kind of brown, leathery hue that spoke of years spent outside in the sun.

'I'm looking for Diane Wells,' Mark said after his initial greeting failed to elicit any further response. Realising that his smart business attire might be giving the wrong impression about his reason for calling by, particularly if Diane was in financial trouble, he added: 'I'm her brother-in-law, Mark Cook. Mia's currently saying with me and my wife, Hannah, in Manchester.'

The explanation appeared to work, as the man's face softened before Mark's eyes. 'Oh, right,' he said, his lips rising very slightly on one side in an almost-smile. 'Hello, in that case. I'm Rod. I live next door.'

Seizing the moment, Mark held out his right hand. 'Pleased to meet you, Rod,' he said.

With a subtle nod of his head, Rod reached out and accepted the handshake, almost crushing Mark's fingers in the process. 'You too. Matt, did you say?'

'Mark.'

'Right. Diane mentioned that Mia was staying with relatives up in Manchester for a bit.' He squinted at Mark as he continued: 'She didn't say anything about anyone coming to visit, though.'

'No, she wouldn't have. I happened to be working nearby as a last-minute thing, so I thought I'd surprise her. It doesn't look like she's home, though. I don't suppose you have any idea where she is, do you? I was about to phone her mobile . . .'

Rod shrugged. 'Sorry, no idea.' He turned around and scanned up and down the street for a moment. 'Nope. Can't see her car.'

Of course, Mark thought. Why hadn't he checked for the white Astra? He could picture Diane in it now, driving away from him in that Manchester car park, having handed over her incendiary letter.

'Is she usually out at this time, or—'

Rod frowned. 'I'm her neighbour, not her keeper, son. I have better things to do than monitor her every move.'

'What about work?' Mark was on treacherous ground here, since all he'd gleaned about her job these days was that it involved recruitment; knowing so little might sound odd to Rod's ears.

Diane had had various roles during the time he'd known her up north – mainly office-based – but none had lasted particularly long. The only occasion he could remember her staying in one place for any significant period had been the job she'd been doing when she fell pregnant, which had been something to do with insurance. She'd timed that just right to get her maternity entitlement and then, thanks to the office being relocated, had picked up a redundancy payment only a few weeks after returning to work. Otherwise, she'd flitted from one job to another, quickly growing bored of whatever she was doing and moving on. Whether that was still the case today or she'd found herself a proper career, he had no idea.

'What about it?' Rod asked, helpfully.

'Could she be there now?'

'Possibly. I don't think she's been at work much recently, though. When we bumped into each other the other day, she said she hadn't been feeling well. She looked under the weather too. I assumed that was why Mia was staying with you, to be honest.'

'Right,' Mark said, nodding his head like he knew what Rod was talking about.

Realising this conversation wasn't getting him anywhere, he reached for his mobile. 'I'd probably best try calling her again, then.'

But before he had a chance to do so, he heard the sound of a car and looked up to see Diane's Vauxhall pulling into a spare space on the street. For a long moment she stared at him wide-eyed from behind the wheel, barely moving; then she stepped out of the car and found a smile to paint over her confusion.

'Mark!' she said, approaching him and his new acquaintance while slowly shaking her head. 'Well, this is a surprise.' Her smile vanished as quickly as it had arrived when she asked him, frowning: 'Is everything okay in Manchester? Is Mia all right?'

'Yes, she's absolutely fine,' Mark replied. 'There's nothing to worry about. That's not why I'm here.'

Relief washed over her face. 'Good. You had me worried for a moment.'

Turning to her neighbour, she said: 'Hello, Rod. I see

you've met my, um, brother-in-law. I would have mentioned to you that he was coming, but er—'

'It's okay,' Rod replied. 'He already told me you weren't expecting him. I actually thought he was up to no good when I spotted him poking around, but – well – I'm glad to see his story holds up. Anyway, I'll leave you both to it. I'm on my way to the offie for some beers. Feeling any better today, love?'

Diane, dressed in skinny jeans and a green tank top, smiled at him. 'Yes, not too bad, thanks.'

On the contrary, Mark thought she looked pretty rough: pasty-skinned in the absence of make-up, noticeably thinner than her sister and with dark bags under eyes that spoke of several sleepless nights.

'I suppose you'd better come in,' she told Mark in a quiet, monotone voice once Rod had strode off along the pavement. 'Then you can explain what the hell you're doing here.'

CHAPTER 11

Mia Wells looked across the table of the restaurant at her aunt and smiled. She was so like her mum and yet, at the same time, so very different. This thought seemed to bob to the surface every time she found herself alone with her, like an obstacle to them getting along: a constant reminder her mum wasn't there.

Maybe this was why she'd found it easier to click with her uncle so far, even though he was around a lot less and was generally less chatty. There was also the fact that, until recently, Hannah and her mum hadn't spoken for such a long time. Mia had no idea what had gone on between them. Her mum had refused to say. But it must have been something pretty major to last all these years – and for this reason part of her felt like getting too close would be a betrayal.

Her mum had specifically told her not to think this way, mind. 'Don't you worry about what went on between us,' she'd said in the car on the way up to Manchester from

Bournemouth. 'It's ancient history and not something you should think about.'

'But I don't know her,' Mia had replied. 'She's never even sent me a birthday or Christmas present. As far as I'm concerned, I don't have an aunt.'

'That's not fair,' her mum had retaliated, much to Mia's surprise. It was the first time she'd ever heard her defend her sister. 'Hannah and Mark both spent a lot of time with you when you were little. I'm the one who ended that by moving away and cutting off all ties with them. They don't even know where we live to send you a present.'

'Well, Grandad does. They could have gone via him, couldn't they?'

'No, they couldn't actually. He's always refused to get involved or to be any kind of middleman. He's so determined to stay neutral, he avoids even talking about either of us to the other.'

Remembering this conversation, Mia realised she really ought to give her aunt more of a chance. Since she'd been in Manchester – effectively thrust upon her without warning – Hannah had shown her nothing but kindness and hospitality. She'd even helped her to find a friend around her own age in Todd. This evening, with Mark away down south, she'd offered to take Mia out for tea at a restaurant of her choice in the city centre.

She'd picked a burger place in the Northern Quarter that Todd had mentioned eating at once on a previous visit. Hannah hadn't looked particularly thrilled at this outcome, but she'd gone along with it nonetheless and now here they were, each staring at a menu, trying to make up their minds what to eat.

'So what are you going to have, Mia?' Hannah asked her. 'There's certainly a good choice of burgers, isn't there?'

'There are other things too, on the back of the menu,' Mia replied, pointing her aunt in the right direction. 'You know, if a burger isn't your thing. But I think I'll go for one with cheese and bacon.'

After the waiter had taken their order, with Hannah opting for fish and chips, Mia felt her mobile vibrate in her pocket. She almost reached for it, keen to see who was contacting her, but managed to resist, adhering to her aunt's rule of no mobiles at the table. The last thing she wanted was to have it confiscated again, as her mum had done on the way up here when she'd answered her back one too many times, sulking about being taken away from her friends back home.

But now she wondered if the message actually was from her mother, perhaps in response to Mark's visit. It wouldn't be before time, if so. She'd barely been in touch at all since leaving her here alone so unexpectedly. Mia hadn't heard a peep from her since that one brief phone call last week. She had 'really important things to sort out' apparently, whatever that meant. It was all very weird – not least the part about her staying with her estranged aunt and uncle. But Mia preferred not to think about it, because doing so only made her anxious. She'd been there, done that too many times already over the past week or so. It led to her coming up with all kinds of scary potential explanations – and she didn't want to go there any more.

Her mum, who'd uncharacteristically burst into tears when they'd first spoken about it in private, had made it abundantly clear she didn't want to share the details with her daughter. She obviously had her reasons for this. From what Mia had gathered during her time with them so far, Hannah and Mark were similarly in the dark.

As much as she wanted to get home to her friends, her bedroom and all her stuff, Mia now figured the best thing she could do was bide her time here until her mum had got herself sorted. For a while, mainly at the beginning of her stay in Manchester, she had secretly been considering running back home. The desire to do so had been particularly strong during Diane's initial period of silence, before she'd eventually phoned her and apologised for not being in touch sooner.

Even after that, Mia hadn't ruled out heading home under her own steam, largely due to worrying about her mum and feeling lonely. That first time she'd gone to Central Library alone, she'd even made a detour to the bus and train stations in order to familiarise herself with them just in case. The money her mum had put into her bank account could fund a ticket if necessary. However, she'd knocked this plan on the head, at least for the time being, after finding a friend in Todd and learning of her uncle's own trip down to Bournemouth to check on Diane.

'Have you heard anything from, er, Mark?' she asked, stirring the straw in her lemonade so the ice made a clinking sound in her glass. She was glad her aunt and uncle had told her to call them by their first names, but it still felt a bit unnatural, particularly having known them for such a short time. At school she was used to having to call her teachers 'Sir' and 'Miss'. The only other adults she tended to call by their first names were far more familiar, such as parents of her close friends.

Hannah shook her head as she took a sip from her glass of white wine. 'No,' she replied with a satellite delay. 'Not yet. I'm sure he'll call later on, though. He should be in Bournemouth by now. Hopefully he's with your mum.'

Imagining her uncle down there, Mia was struck by an unexpected wave of homesickness: a longing for familiar surroundings; a desire not to miss any more of the beach parties her pals kept messaging her about; all of her pent-up concerns about her mum.

'Sorry, I need the toilet,' she told Hannah, disappearing before she said or did something embarrassing and, once there, locking herself in a cubicle and having a little cry.

It wasn't the first time this had happened since her mum had left her in Manchester, but previously she'd always been alone, usually in the privacy of her bedroom, late at night. After a couple of minutes, she pulled herself together, wiped away her tears with a tissue and strode out towards the sinks to splash some cold water on her reddened cheeks.

Fortunately, none of the others in there asked if she was okay, which would have probably set her off again. She spent a few moments in front of the mirror tidying herself up. It was an easier job than it might have been, since she'd recently stopped wearing her dark make-up, having decided to take a break from all that while in Manchester. She'd been thinking of making a change to a more natural look for a little while. Doing so here, where she didn't have to face the inevitable comments from her friends and her mum, was the perfect opportunity. It had always wound Mia up when her mum had disapprovingly referred to it as her 'war paint', like she had to Hannah when they'd first arrived here. How patronising was that? If anything, such comments had encouraged her to slap it on even thicker and darker. But her mum wasn't around at the moment and Mia missed her more than she wanted to annoy her right now. Apparently it was true what they said about absence making the heart grow fonder.

Mia and Diane had always been really close until the last few years, when they'd increasingly started to clash about things such as bedtimes and curfews, household chores, 'respectful behaviour' (one of her mum's pet phrases), and not treating their home 'like a hotel' (another favourite). However, since Diane's departure and subsequent lack of contact, Mia had increasingly found herself focusing on the countless good times they'd spent together over the years, rather than the negative stuff.

There were so many happy memories: strolls and running races along the beach, plus the times they flew – and crashed – kites there on gusty days; watching the latest Pixar movies at the cinema while sharing a huge box of popcorn; that camping holiday in Cornwall where it rained so much one night that they had to abandon their tent and cuddle in the car.

For some reason, Mia also kept thinking back to when she was eleven and, for months on end, the pair of them had become hooked on the feel-good American TV show

Gilmore Girls. The appeal was obvious, since it was about a single mum and daughter with the perfect relationship. They were basically best friends. Diane had come home with the box set one day, saying she'd heard good things about it, and watching several episodes back-to-back on a Friday night had soon become their little ritual, often extending to Saturdays and Sundays. Mia remembered those times so fondly. And how she wished she and her mum had that same perfect relationship as the central characters, Lorelai and Rory. She'd settle for them being as close now as they had been when they'd watched it. Was it her fault things between them had changed? Was that why her mum had left her here in Manchester with her aunt and uncle?

Mia shook her head clear of such thoughts and headed back to the table, but only after checking her phone to see who the message she'd received earlier was from. It turned out to be Todd, saying he hoped she liked the restaurant. She fired off a quick reply: *So far, so good! :-)*

'Oh, there you are,' Hannah said when she returned. 'I was about to send out a search party.' She smiled at Mia, but this quickly morphed into a look of concern. 'Is everything all right, love? You look like—'

'I'm fine,' Mia snapped, more abruptly than intended. 'I had something in my eye. It's out now.'

'Okay,' Hannah replied. Her mouth opened a little, as if she was about to say something else. But instead she reached for her drink and took a slow sip, no longer meeting Mia's gaze.

Thankfully, a few seconds later their waiter returned with a plate of nachos smothered in melted cheese, sour cream and guacamole, which they'd ordered to share as a starter.

'Wow, this looks good, doesn't it?' Hannah said, her wide smile giving away her relief at having something else to talk about other than her niece's red eyes.

'Definitely,' Mia replied, smiling back in a bid to ease the tension.

Digging into the large plate together, and both getting rather messy in the process, did wonders for the mood at the table. Soon they were chatting away more comfortably than they had at any other time previously, discussing all sorts, from her day-to-day life in Bournemouth to places they'd both been or wanted to go on holiday. Somehow being there, just the two of them in a public space, rather than Hannah's home, made all the difference. So much so that at certain moments it reminded Mia of being out with her mum – in a good way, when they were getting along well together – which in turn led to a few flashes of guilt. She did her best to ignore these, though, by focusing on the conversation.

'So is Manchester like you expected?' Hannah asked her after their mains arrived, to which she replied – honestly – that it was much nicer than she'd thought it would be.

'Don't get me wrong,' she added, 'I'd prefer it if there was a beach and it was a little warmer. But no, it's a nice, friendly city – and there's loads going on. I might even prefer it to London. I've only been there a few times with Mum, but it's so big and impersonal, I don't think I could ever feel at home there.'

'So you could feel at home in Manchester, then?' Hannah asked, grinning. 'There are some excellent university options here . . . Just saying.'

Mia was shocked to hear this. 'University?' she said. 'I am only fourteen, you know. I'm not sure if I'm even . . . I don't know. It's so expensive too.'

'I'm only pulling your leg, Mia. There are good universities all over the country. But you should definitely start thinking about it. I'm not saying it would be the right thing for you or not. What do I know? But you seem like a bright girl to me and getting a degree opens a lot of doors. It is expensive, I agree. I don't approve of the tuition fees young people have to pay nowadays. It wasn't like that for my generation, so I don't see why it should be for yours. Do you have any idea what you'd like to do in terms of a job or is it too early for that?'

Mia felt her face flush as she replied: 'Um, I do, but you'll probably think it's silly.'

'Why do you say that? Of course I won't.'

'Well, you know how I like to read a lot?'

'I do.'

'I know it's hard to get into and that . . . but, er, I'd really like to try to become an author one day: to write my own novels.'

Mia had been looking down at her plate as she'd said this, partly out of embarrassment and partly wondering how she was going to get through the giant burger and huge portion of chips without bursting. When she looked up, her aunt was staring at her in a completely unexpected way. She almost looked like she was about to laugh – but

166

surely not. How cruel would that be, to crush her dreams in such a way?

Hannah explained: 'Um, sorry. I'm not smiling at what you just said, Mia. Well, not in the way you might imagine. I actually think that's a fantastic ambition to have. The thing is, um, there's something I've been meaning to tell you about me. I'm not really sure why I haven't said anything already. It's . . . oh, I don't know. I'll just come out with it, shall I? I'm an author. Not published yet, but I will be soon. My debut novel's due to be released next January.'

Mia couldn't believe what she was hearing. How had neither Hannah nor Mark mentioned this to her before? And what about her mum? Surely she'd have told her if she'd known about it.

'Hold on a minute,' she said after lifting her jaw back up off the ground. 'You're an actual author . . . of novels . . . with a publishing deal and everything?'

Hannah smiled, her cheeks radiating a pink glow. 'Um, yes. I suppose I am, although it doesn't feel quite that way yet since my book isn't actually out for a while.'

'What's it called?'

'*The Boy at the Window*.'

'Okay. Is it a children's book?'

'No, no. It's aimed at adults. It's kind of a psychological thriller. I like to think of it as a bit Hitchcockian.' She paused before adding: 'You know Alfred Hitchcock, right? I don't mean that in a patronising way – not at all – but as someone without children, it's hard for me to gauge what's on the radar of a modern teenager.'

Mia nodded at her aunt, still too shocked by her revelation to be offended. 'I've heard of him, but I haven't seen any of his films. Aren't they a bit creepy? I remember one of our English teachers at school telling us about one where all these birds start attacking people. Is that right?'

'Yes, exactly. They're probably not scary in the sense of modern horror films, but he was known as a master of suspense and a lot of his films have dated pretty well, considering. You should try one. I'd suggest *Rear Window* rather than *The Birds*, though.' She giggled. 'That's the one I'm thinking of really when I say my book is Hitchcockian.'

'So what's it about exactly: your book, I mean?'

Hannah gave her a brief synopsis of the plot before adding: 'But that's really all I can tell you without giving too much away. Hopefully you might like to read it one day.'

'Totally,' Mia replied. 'I've just found out my aunt is an author – my dream job. Of course I want to read your book. Do you have any copies yet?'

'No, although I'm hoping it won't be long now. They've been making a few adjustments to the cover recently.'

'What about an ebook I could read on my Kindle?'

'I've not had that yet either, to be honest. I've got several versions on my computer, but they're all word processor documents from various different stages in the editorial process. The most up-to-date version I have is a typeset printout they sent me to proofread, but that's covered in my scribble.'

'Oh, okay,' Mia replied, trying to hide her disappointment,

but not doing a very good job, judging by her aunt's reply.

'Sorry, Mia,' she said, wincing. 'It probably sounds like I'm being evasive, but honestly I'm not. I'd love for you to read it – and I'll be delighted to let you have a copy just as soon as I get some. Apparently the first thing they'll produce will be a proof version for reviewers and so on, which might be slightly different from the final one. But it'll be an actual book. I can't wait to get my hands on it.'

'I bet you can't,' Mia replied. 'It must be so exciting.'

'Definitely.' Hannah hesitated before adding: 'It is a book aimed at people my age, so there is a chance it might not be your cup of tea, but—'

'I'm sure I'll love it.' Mia gave her aunt a big smile and then turned her attention back to her food.

They both ate in silence for a while: Mia still trying to get her head around the fact that her aunt was the very thing she aspired to become one day. Seriously, how had she not known this until now? Her mum, who spent more of her free time buying and selling things on eBay than reading, had never seemed to understand this ambition of hers, despite the various encouraging comments from her English teachers about her creative writing. She preferred the fact that Mia was good at maths and science too, which she said were much better subjects for finding a decent job. She never seemed too interested in reading her daughter's compositions; whenever Mia mentioned becoming an author, she tended to smile and nod. Hence it had always felt like her mum humoured her, yet secretly considered it an impossible dream she'd soon leave behind.

Now Mia knew it was something a close family member had done, it made the dream feel so much more achievable.

'How's the burger?' Hannah asked her.

'Delicious,' she said in between mouthfuls, 'although I wish I hadn't eaten quite so many nachos now. How's your fish and chips?'

Hannah nodded, holding her hand in front of her mouth as she finished chewing, and then replying. 'Also really nice – but what you said about the nachos . . . I'm never going to get through all of this.' She giggled. 'Maybe we should ask for a doggie bag to take home what we can't manage.'

Later, as they were walking back to the apartment, both totally stuffed, Hannah brought the conversation back to literary matters. 'So what kind of book do you think you'd like to write, Mia?'

'I'm not actually sure yet,' she said, opting for honesty over trying to say something clever. 'A good one, hopefully. This might sound weird – especially to you – but I don't actually feel ready to write a novel yet. I'm not sure I have enough experience of life to know what I want to say. I have written quite a few short stories, though: some for school and others, well, just for myself.'

'Fantastic. That's as good a place as any to start.' She paused before adding: 'I don't pretend to be any kind of expert, Mia. If anything, I think I just got lucky. But I'd, um, be more than happy to cast an eye over anything you've written – you know, if you ever want me to.'

'Really? Thanks.' Mia meant it. She'd even hoped her

aunt might make such a suggestion. And yet now she had, Mia felt a little daunted. What if Hannah thought her writing was awful? 'I don't actually have anything with me at the moment,' she added hastily. 'It's all at home. But yeah, definitely. That could be, er, a big help. Thanks.'

Hannah, walking alongside her as they passed in front of the now familiar, imposing structure of Central Library, scratched her nose. 'So what was it you thought I did for a living before today?'

'I wasn't really sure.' Mia left it at that, although if she'd been pushed to continue, she'd have had to admit to not giving the matter much thought. The vast majority of adults' jobs were mundane and uninteresting: a depressing reminder of what real life held for all but a lucky few young dreamers like herself.

The truth was that Mia didn't even know the exact nature of Mark's job, even though he'd disappeared to do it every weekday while she'd been staying with her aunt and uncle. It was something office-based involving finances and technology, as far as she understood. Yawntastic, in other words, although it obviously paid the bills and some, based on the swanky apartment and so on.

'What's Todd up to this evening?' Hannah asked her next.

'He's probably busy gaming.'

'I think it's fantastic that you two have been, um, hanging out together. Kathy and I hoped you'd get along when we introduced you, but you never know with these things, do you? Are you planning to see each other again tomorrow?'

'Probably. If that's okay?'

'Of course.' Hannah smiled. 'It will give me a chance to get some work done on my next novel.'

'You're writing that already?'

'No rest for the wicked. My publishing deal is for two books.'

'Really? How far have you got?'

Hannah chuckled. 'Never ask a writer that question – well, not this one anyway – because the answer will always be "not far enough".'

Mia hoped this wasn't a disguised dig at her for turning up out of the blue and occupying so much of her aunt's time. It didn't seem so from the light-hearted way Hannah had said it. She was probably being paranoid. But the fact was that Mia didn't know her anywhere near well enough to be able to say for sure.

She'd worried enough already about getting in the way at her aunt and uncle's place: about the old saying that two's company, three's a crowd. If they'd wanted a child or children in their lives, they'd have had them. But they didn't. They obviously liked it being just the two of them – and this was something that had been in her head ever since her mum had left her there.

She wasn't stupid. She'd paid attention in science class. She understood that some people couldn't have children, even if they wanted them. However, from what her mum had told her on the journey up here, that wasn't the reason in this case.

'How come they don't have any kids?' she'd asked.

'I don't think there's any, er, medical obstacle, if that's what you mean,' her mum had replied, keeping her eyes on the road as they sped northbound up the M6. 'Although obviously I haven't spoken to them in a very long time. The subject did come up after you were born and Hannah told me they'd decided against it – that being parents wasn't for them. People are often very private about such matters, but I'm pretty sure that if there was any kind of infertility issue, I'd have known about it. Believe it or not, Hannah and I were pretty close before we fell out.'

It wasn't like Hannah or Mark had actually said or done anything to support her fears that they didn't want her there. They'd both been amazingly hospitable. And despite the fact that Mia had no memory of spending time with them as a tot, it was clear they did. Hannah in particular had dropped in several references to what she'd been like as a wide-eyed young child – and things they'd done together, like feeding the ducks or watching panto-mimes.

Mia was never sure how to react when she heard such things, because they could well have been made up, for all she knew; smiling and nodding had become her default response.

As she and Hannah walked into the lobby of the apart-ment block, Mia felt her phone buzz with another message. She pulled it out to have a look and saw that it was Todd again.

So? What did you have? Bet it was delicious, right?

She slipped the phone back into her pocket. She'd reply later.

It was great to have a friend nearby – someone around her own age. And she did already consider Todd a friend, even though they'd only known each other for a couple of days. He was good fun, although at times she really noticed he was a year younger than her. He'd say or do the odd immature thing that made her cringe. Like when she'd taken him to Central Library – since he couldn't believe what she'd told him about being able to play games there – and he'd found it hilarious to let out a big noisy burp in the quiet reading section. She'd thumped him hard in the arm for that and, although he'd kept on giggling, she was pretty sure he'd got the message.

She had to be careful with him, though. She'd been around boys long enough to know that he almost certainly fancied her. She'd seen the way he stared at her, all dreamy-eyed, when he thought she wasn't looking. And she knew from past experience, with other friends who were boys, that it was important not to give the wrong signals, or he'd probably end up trying to plant a kiss on her, which would ruin things.

She definitely wasn't interested in him in that way. He was nice-looking, with floppy ash-blond hair, deep blue eyes and a wonky grin she found cute. But despite being taller than Mia, he still looked too young for her and a bit gangly. Maybe in a few years, when he'd grown into himself a bit more, but not now. She already found the boys in her own year at school too immature. She preferred older lads, like her last boyfriend, Ant, who'd recently turned sixteen. Mind you, look how that had worked out. It had been great for a while until she'd realised he'd wanted to take things further way quicker than she was ready for. And then he'd showed his true colours, dumping her by text and telling his mates she was a 'prick-tease'. Bastard.

You live and learn, she thought. And if there was one thing she'd learned from growing up as an only child with a single mum and no father on the scene, it was this: she did not want to get pregnant unless she was in a long-term, steady relationship with someone she loved; a man who loved her back and would be a father to their child.

So, unlike some of her friends at school, Mia was in no rush whatsoever to have sex. Because abstinence was the only contraceptive that worked one hundred per cent of the time, right?

'Thanks again for the meal,' she told her aunt once they were back inside the apartment. 'Still no message or anything from Mark?'

Hannah shook her head. 'Not yet. Would you like a tea or coffee?'

'No, thanks. I think I'll read in my room for a bit.'

Hannah's face fell a little on hearing this, Mia thought, although her aunt's actual reply made her wonder if she'd imagined it. 'No problem,' she said. 'If you need anything, give me a shout.'

CHAPTER 12

Diane led Mark into the house, shutting the door to the front room as she passed it and continuing to the rear of the property. She entered a decent-sized kitchen – light wood-effect worktops with white gloss painted cupboards – that looked on to a small backyard.

Mark stood in the doorway for a minute, feeling like a spare part, not knowing whether to take a seat at the circular pine table or just to keep standing. He opted for the latter, figuring it would be rude to sit down without being invited to do so. He stared at the back of Diane's head as, without speaking, she rooted around in one of the cupboards. He still couldn't get used to seeing her with such short hair; never mind the burgundy colour. It made her skin look so pale; gave her a totally different look to Hannah, which could only be a good thing as far as he was concerned.

Before getting there, Mark had expected to find the place in a total mess. He wasn't sure why exactly. It just fitted in with the idea of Diane being in trouble. In fact, the opposite was true. The kitchen looked like it had barely been used in the past few days, with no dirty or recently washed-up cutlery or crockery in sight. Everything he'd seen so far of the inside of the house looked clean and tidy.

After continuing to hunt through the cupboard for a little while longer, Diane let out a loud sigh, shut the door and turned around to face Mark.

'Well, I've no tea or coffee,' she said. 'If you want a drink it'll have to be either tap water or cordial.'

Mark wanted to say that he didn't need anything, but in truth he was parched, so he told her a glass of water would be perfect.

'Aren't you going to come in and sit down?' she asked, filling his glass. 'You're making me nervous standing there in the doorway.'

'Sure,' Mark said. 'I, um, wasn't sure whether you'd want me to or not. You didn't seem too pleased to see me outside a minute ago.'

'Sorry.' She placed the glass on the kitchen table, gestured for Mark to grab the wooden chair in front of it and then sat down opposite. 'I was just a bit, er, taken aback to see you. You could have called ahead to let me know you were coming.'

Mark cleared his throat. 'Really? Like you did when you turned up in Manchester, you mean? Plus you've not exactly been answering your phone recently.'

Diane sighed again. 'Fair point. So what's going on? How come you're here? I'm guessing you didn't travel all this way just to see me, especially not dressed like that.'

'I've been visiting the office of a company we recently took over in Southampton.'

Diane raised an eyebrow. 'Right. Not that close then. You must have been keen to check up on me.'

'It didn't take long by train, actually. But yes, of course I'm keen to catch up with you, Diane. What do you expect?'

'Does Hannah know you're here?'

'Of course.'

Diane nodded, scratching the side of her neck with one finger. 'And Mia?'

'Yes, Mia too. She's the one who gave me your address. I, um, think she'd appreciate it if you stayed in more frequent contact with her while you're apart. She obviously misses you.'

Diane scowled at Mark in a way that instantly reminded him of Hannah. The look she used was the exact same one his wife did when she was annoyed with him. It literally could have been her at that moment. The shocking similarity of it felt eerie and disconcerting; it brought up unpleasant memories, which he instantly wanted to eject from his mind.

It appeared that Diane was about to say something – no doubt to rebuke him for daring to question her actions as a mother – but, for whatever reason, the words never came. Instead she closed her eyes and took a couple of long, deep breaths. Puzzled by this apparent attempt by his sister-in-law to calm herself down, which was very untypical of the hot-headed Diane he remembered, Mark resisted the temptation to speak further. He watched and waited.

Eventually, speaking in a steady, almost robotic voice,

she asked: 'How is Mia? Has she settled in with you and Hannah okay?'

'Yes, she's doing fine,' Mark replied. 'Hannah's even found her a friend of her own age. Well, in the year below her at school, I think, but near enough. It's this lad called Todd, who's the grandson of one of our neighbours. They seem to get on pretty well.'

Diane looked pleasantly surprised by this. 'Really? That's nice.'

As Mark took a big swig from his glass of water, it struck him as weird their chatting about Mia like this, as if she was simply his niece. There was one heck of an elephant in the room and he had a strong feeling Diane wasn't going to be the one to mention it.

He coughed nervously before leaning forward on the table, balling his hands together and resting them under his chin. 'What about you?' he asked. 'How are you getting on with, um, sorting things out?'

'So you're here to check up on me, are you?' she snapped. 'Makes sense. Hannah's idea, was it?'

'Mine actually. There's no need to have a go at Hannah. She's the one currently looking after your daughter, remember.' He left a long pause before adding the next bit, which took some courage. 'Or should I say *our* daughter?'

So there it was. He'd said it. Now he stared across the kitchen table at Diane and waited.

Her eyes darted all around the room, looking everywhere apart from at him, like cornered prey desperately seeking an escape route.

He waited.

Diane continued to squirm.

Then finally she spoke. 'I don't know what to say to you, Mark.' Still refusing to meet his eye, she stared down at the table, rolling around a stray peppercorn with one finger. 'That's why I wrote you the letter rather than speaking directly to you in Manchester. It's . . . I don't know. Where the hell do I even begin?'

Mark fought to keep his voice steady, his temper under control. 'What about explaining why you chose to lie to me for all these years? Why would anyone deliberately keep a father and his child apart, unaware of each other? It's beyond me, Diane. I get furious just thinking about it.

'I keep casting my mind back to that time after your mum died, in 2008, when I specifically asked you if I was Mia's father and you lied to my face. Well, I assume you did. Unless you're actually lying now? How the hell am I supposed to know if what you're telling me today is the truth? Do you have any proof? You told me previously that another man was definitely the father.'

Mark was surprised to see tears rolling down either side of his sister-in-law's face. He'd seen her cry before: at her mum's funeral and even the other day in Manchester, when she'd begged for his and Hannah's help. But it certainly wasn't something he'd seen her do often. The Diane he knew of old was too hard, too cold to cry.

Seeing her so emotional in their apartment had shocked him; he'd wondered how sincere it was and how much to elicit their sympathy. But witnessing it again now, when it was just the two of them and he was staring right at her, centimetres away, it didn't feel fake. Either she was a damn good actress – something he couldn't entirely rule out, based on past experience – or she felt genuine remorse, as she'd suggested in that bloody letter.

Much to his frustration, Mark felt his resolve to take her to task weaken. It was too much like watching Hannah get upset. But was that exactly what Diane intended? Was she manipulating him as she'd done so successfully years earlier? God, how on earth was he supposed to know the answer to that?

He reached into the inside pocket of his suit jacket, which was hanging over the back of the empty chair next to him, and pulled out a pack of travel tissues. 'Here,' he said, handing it to her. He wanted to leave it at that; not to appear to weaken. But before he knew it, he found himself asking if she was all right. He did at least manage to stop himself apologising for anything, which would have been ridiculous.

How the hell could he be feeling sympathy towards someone who'd caused him so much pain and misery? There had been a time when he'd violently hated Diane for what she'd done; what she'd made him do. Even after years had passed and he'd learned to live with it, Mark had always viewed her as an adversary not to be trusted.

'Look me in the eye and tell me one thing,' he said, once Diane's tears began to abate. 'Do you promise me, hand on heart, that Mia is my daughter?'

She nodded and, meeting his gaze, replied: 'Mia *is* your daughter, Mark. I've lied to you in the past. I've made such a mess of things. I hold my hands up to that. I apologise for it – and I totally understand why you'd doubt what I'm saying now because of it. But she's yours, one hundred per cent.'

'Can you be absolutely sure?' Mark asked. 'I mean . . . what about that old boss of yours? You told me he'd taken a paternity test.'

'That wasn't true,' she replied in little more than a whisper.

'What do you mean?'

'It was a fib. I panicked and made the whole thing up.' She looked down at the floor, abashed; avoiding his gaze. 'It was a kneejerk response to you guessing the truth. There was no one else at that time. It could only ever have been you after our night together.'

Mark felt a stab of fury in his stomach at Diane's use of the word *fib*, which she made sound so casual and unimportant. Then there was the way she referred to that night: like it was something normal that had happened between the two of them. Like it was just one of those things. The truth was much darker – far more messed up and warped. But he couldn't afford to go there, so he suppressed his anger, crushing it down before it exploded up into his chest and out via a string of expletives. And yet, from the shadow that fell across Diane's face, Mark suspected he hadn't totally managed to conceal the fire burning within.

'Would you like another drink?' she asked, gnawing on one of her stubby fingernails.

Mark looked over at his glass and was surprised to see it empty. 'Um, okay, yes. Another glass of water, please.'

As Diane fetched this, Mark felt a wave of tiredness crash over him. It had been a long day, what with all the travelling and the work, and now his head was starting to hurt. The heat didn't help. Nor did the fact that he'd not had anything to eat since a late lunch around 2.30 p.m. and his stomach was starting to grumble. Plus this hard chair he was perched on was crying out for a cushion.

He thought back to how Diane moving a young Mia down here and cutting off communications with Hannah had secretly been a relief to him, even though he'd hated what the split had done to his wife. Prior to that, every time he'd seen his sister-in-law, he'd had to fend off memories of that damn night: the booze-fuelled, steamy passion and then the shocking reality of what had just happened, like an ice spike hammered into his skull.

While Diane had been out of their lives, he had at least been freed from the constant fear that she might tell her sister what had happened at any moment. The fact she hadn't said anything so far was her one saving grace in his eyes, although he realised Hannah would view this differently.

Now that fear of discovery – and the destruction it could cause to his marriage – was back with a vengeance.

'I can't stay much longer,' Mark said. 'Otherwise I'll miss the train and won't be able to get back to Southampton tonight.'

'But there's so much still to talk about. Why don't you stay the night and get the train back in the morning? That would give us more time. Have you eaten? We could order a takeaway if you like.'

'Stay the night?' Mark repeated.

'There's a spare room. The bed's already made up. I could drive you to the train station in the morning.'

'Um, I'm not sure that's—'

'Listen, now you're here, Mark, there's a lot more I need to speak to you about.' She lurched forward so she was half leaning over the table, staring him straight in the eye and wearing a look of intensity and desperation. 'This could be the last chance I get.'

'What the hell does that mean?' Mark asked, sliding a few centimetres back into his chair in an attempt to regain some personal space.

She was crowding him. He could feel the heat of her breath on his face and it wasn't pleasant, like she could really do with brushing her teeth.

But all of that faded to insignificance when Diane uttered her next sentence.

'It means I'm dying, Mark.'

CHAPTER 13

'Hello! You're back. How was the trip?'

'Mia, how are you? I didn't expect a welcoming committee, but it's nice to have one.'

She flashed her uncle a sheepish grin. 'Oh, I wasn't waiting here for you. I was just, er, nipping to the bathroom.'

She stood there in the hallway while Mark, who looked worn out and dishevelled, dropped his overnight bag on the floor before removing his jacket and placing it on a hanger on the coat rack.

There was an awkward moment when he looked up and, seeing his niece there, watching him, interpreted this as her waiting for a proper greeting. So he leaned forward and planted an unexpected kiss on her cheek.

'Hello,' she found herself repeating. 'Um, Hannah said you did manage to catch up with Mum yesterday evening.'

'That's right.'

'How was she? Did she, er, say when she'd be coming back for me?'

Her uncle smiled, although his eyes didn't join in with his mouth. 'Is it okay if I freshen up first, Mia? Then we can all sit down together and I'll bring you and Hannah up to speed. I've been dreaming of a shower all the way home. I feel so hot and sticky, although it's definitely not as warm now as it was in Bournemouth yesterday. It was roasting.'

'Sure,' Mia replied. 'Hannah's in the kitchen, by the way. I'll, um . . .' She pointed in the direction of the bathroom.

'Please. You carry on, love.'

She hadn't actually been on the way to the bathroom when Mark had walked through the front door. She'd been listening out for him for the past hour or so, splitting her time between the lounge and her bedroom, trying to read but struggling to concentrate. Hannah must have noticed she was on tenterhooks, but she'd been good enough not to say anything.

As soon as Mia had heard the key, she'd darted towards the entrance of the apartment, desperate to know what her uncle had discovered. She hoped for some explanation about what her mum was up to and a date when she could return home: preferably soon, while there was some of the school holidays left to enjoy with her friends. Hearing Mark say how warm it had been down there was enough to make her feel homesick. She longed to sunbathe or play ball games on the beach; to enjoy a refreshing dip in the sea.

It was for this reason that she'd not been messaging as much with her friends back home in recent days. It only made her envious and sad she wasn't with them.

Meanwhile, not wanting to look like a total loser, she'd told them a few porky-pies about what she'd been up to in Manchester.

For a start, Mia had claimed to have befriended a group of local kids, who she was supposedly hanging out with most days. She'd taken some surreptitious pictures on her phone of teenagers skating and hanging out in Cathedral Gardens, an open space near Victoria railway station, then used these to bring her fictional friends to life.

Unbeknown to Todd, she'd also woven him into this fantasy as a guy she had a crush on – older not younger – who she was gradually getting close to in the hope that something might happen between them. She'd not used a photo of the real Todd, as it would be obvious he was younger than her, but rather one of a particularly hot skater she'd managed to snap from a distance and zoom in on.

She and Todd had spent most of today out and about together. Todd had called round for her after breakfast and she hadn't returned to the apartment until gone 5 p.m. They'd both agreed to try to swipe some alcohol from their relatives. It had been Mia's idea, mooted while they were messaging each other the previous night. It was out of character for her to do such a thing, never mind suggest it, but she'd been emboldened by hearing her friends going on about various parties and nights out she was missing. She'd felt a yearning for some real excitement and adventure of her own, hoping this might shake things up a little and help the day pass more quickly as she anxiously awaited her uncle's return.

Initially Todd hadn't been too enthusiastic. But in the event, he'd been the one to come up with the goods.

'So, what have you got?' Mia asked him once they were alone in the lift that morning, heading down.

'Sorry, nothing,' Todd said, looking at the floor.

'So what's with the backpack?' she asked, nudging him in the side, having noticed a flash of a grin escape from the corner of his mouth.

'Okay, okay.' He turned to face her with his hands aloft. 'Busted. I'm winding you up. I got two bottles of wine.'

Mia was impressed. 'Serious? Isn't that too much? Won't she notice?'

He shook his head as the lift arrived with a thud at the ground floor and spat them out. 'No way.' Once they were safely outside in the warm, breezy air, he added: 'You should see how many bottles she has in the pantry. I think she's in a wine club or something. I picked two at random.'

'Red or white?'

'White. Have you ever tried red? It's disgusting. My dad's always drinking it. Plus it stains your teeth, which would be a dead giveaway.'

'Isn't white supposed to be served cold?'

Todd shrugged. 'Don't ask me. I just got some alcohol, like you asked. How did you get on?'

'Yeah, about that—'

Todd started to laugh. 'Oh, come on. You didn't get anything, did you? There can't be much in that little handbag.'

Looking around first to ensure no one was watching,

Mia unzipped her bag and pulled out a small glass bottle of clear liquid, which she flashed at Todd before tucking it away again.

'What's that?' he asked. 'Vodka? Gin?'

'It's kirsch.'

'You what? I've never even heard of that? Where did you find it?'

'It was tucked away at the back of the cupboard under the kitchen sink, like it had been forgotten.'

'What is it, though?'

'Well, I looked it up online and, apparently, it's a kind of fruit brandy made from cherries. It's strong too – forty per cent alcohol – although it does smell a bit odd.'

Mia had wanted to bring something better than this, but she'd bottled out, fearing anything bigger would get noticed.

When she'd suggested the idea of getting their hands on some alcohol yesterday, she'd made out to Todd like it was something she did all the time. This was far from the truth. Other than sneaking the odd sip from her mum's glass at home, she'd only tried it a couple of times: once at a house party thrown by an older girl from school and another time at a beach party about a week before she'd come to Manchester. It had been alcopops she'd drunk the first time and cider the second; on both occasions, she'd stopped before getting too wasted, unlike some of her friends, who'd embarrassed themselves and/or been violently sick.

So why now?

Everyone had to rebel from time to time. And wouldn't

it be great to have something juicy – not made up for once – that she could tell her friends she'd done in Manchester?

After wandering in the direction of the city centre for a few minutes, Mia grabbed Todd's arm and jerked him to a halt. 'Hang on,' she said. 'Wouldn't a park be better: somewhere quiet where no one will notice what we're up to? We don't want to get arrested.'

'Good point,' Todd replied. 'Um, have you been to any parks here before?'

'What about the Whitworth?'

Todd had no idea where she was talking about, so she explained it was an art gallery she'd visited with her aunt.

'An art gallery? How's that a good place to get drunk?'

She explained it was located in a big park and, ten minutes later, they were on a bus heading down Oxford Road towards Manchester University. At this point, Mia started to feel anxious. Todd was chatting away about how he'd got further than ever before on one of his PlayStation games; she nodded occasionally, pretending to listen.

'Are you okay?' he asked her when they left the bus.

'Yeah, why?'

'I don't know. You seem quiet.'

Mia had been thinking about her mum. Hannah had told her over breakfast that Mark had met up with her at the house last night, but he hadn't told her anything so far. Mia had a bad feeling about the situation, which she couldn't shake. She'd nearly messaged her mum loads of times this morning, but something had stopped her. She didn't want to tell any of this to Todd, though. She preferred him to think of her as this chilled, older, worldly-wise girl who took everything in her stride. Admitting she was homesick and worried about what the hell was going on with her mum didn't exactly fit in with that.

But as they crossed the road, which was really busy despite none of the uni students being around due to the holidays, the whole getting drunk thing seemed like less and less of a good idea. Nonetheless, she continued in the direction of the park with Todd at her side.

'So what shall we start on first?' he asked after they'd found a quiet spot, tucked away behind a bush.

'I'm not sure. You pick.'

'Can I have a smell of your weird stuff?'

'Sure.' She opened her handbag and pulled the small bottle out, handing it to Todd, who was sitting cross-legged on the grass next to her.

As Mia shuffled around, trying to get comfortable without giving anyone – especially Todd – a view up her skirt, she wished she'd thought to wear trousers or leggings. Even shorts would have been better.

A young family playing catch with a bouncing Yorkshire terrier in the distance grabbed her attention. Then Todd let out a high-pitched scream and she nearly jumped out of her skin. She turned to see he'd leapt to his feet and, in the process, dropped the bottle of kirsch on the floor.

'What the hell?' she cried out, stretching over to grab the bottle, only to find it was already drained.

Todd had darted a few feet away from her and was staring anxiously at the bush, gesticulating that Mia should follow him.

'What's the matter?' she asked.

'There's something in there,' he said, eyes wide, pointing at the bush. 'I think it's a rat.'

'What?' Mia yelped, finally listening to her friend and springing to her feet.

She moved over to where he was standing, leaving her handbag behind, next to Todd's backpack. The pair of them stared at the bush, scouring it for movement.

'Are you sure you didn't imagine it?' Mia asked after a few minutes had passed and there was no sign of any rat.

'I saw its eyes glaring at me,' he whispered. 'It was terrifying.'

'I noticed.' Mia started to giggle. 'That was quite a scream.'

'Don't,' Todd replied, cracking a smile. It was soon wiped away, though, by a rustle in the bush as some of the leaves and branches moved.

'Oh my God!' Mia cried, grabbing hold of Todd's hand. 'Did you see that? Are you sure it's a rat? I hate rats. Yuck. They're disgusting.'

'I know – me too. I was on a school camping trip once and someone brought along a copy of this ancient horror book called *The Rats*. He read a bit of it one night and I was terrified. I pretended not to be, because – you know – I didn't want to look like a wuss, but I hardly slept that night. I've had a thing about rats ever since.'

'I'd never have guessed,' Mia said, realising she was holding Todd's hand and gently letting go.

'You'd have screamed too, if you'd been the one to see it,' he said.

'Too right I would, but I'm a girl. Aren't you guys supposed to be the ones who come to our rescue in these situations?'

'Um, heard of feminism ever?'

Mia rolled her eyes. 'That doesn't apply when rodents are involved. Obviously. You could redeem yourself by going to get our bags. You needn't bother with the kirsch. It's empty.'

'Sorry about the bottle,' Todd said, 'but I'm afraid there's absolutely zero chance of me going anywhere near that bush. Ladies first. I insist.'

They both started giggling at the ridiculousness of the situation, at which point Mia spotted a scruffy-looking chap veer off the nearby path on to the grass, heading in their direction.

The man, who looked to be in his late thirties or early forties, had long, curly ginger hair and a matching beard. As he approached – dressed in combat boots, tatty jeans and a woollen jumper that belied the summer weather – his smell announced itself before he did. It was the unmistakeable reek of someone who'd been living and sleeping rough in the same clothes, without washing, for too long. It wasn't uncommon to see such folk back home, especially during the summer months, so Mia wasn't fazed. Her mum had taught her to be charitable towards them rather than afraid, pointing out that they were 'just normal people down on their luck'.

'What are you two looking so stressed about?' he asked

them in a softer than expected voice that, to Mia's ears, sounded northern but not Mancunian.

'Um, I er . . .' Todd had a tremor in his voice as he looked at Mia rather than their new companion. The pupils in his eyes looked stretched to capacity and he appeared almost out of breath. She wanted to tell her friend to calm down, but instead she replied to the man, trying not to wrinkle up her nose at the smell. 'My friend here saw a rat in the bush.'

'A rat?' he said, his breath stinking of alcohol, even though he seemed articulate enough. Turning to look at Todd, he asked: 'Are you sure?'

He got a vigorous nod in reply.

'I haven't seen it myself, but there's definitely something in there,' Mia said. 'The bush was moving around before you got here and there was a rustling noise.'

'Hmm,' the man said. 'I can't say I've seen any rats around here. Are you sure it wasn't just a—'

Before he had a chance to finish the sentence, there was more rustling and moving branches, followed by the sudden appearance of a grey squirrel.

Mia stifled a scream, having initially mistaken it for the rat – and then, as the truth dawned on her, she started to laugh.

The fluffy-tailed animal beamed its dark eyes at them for a long moment before darting up a nearby tree.

'Exactly,' the man said. 'A squirrel. That's what I was about to say. There are loads of them in this park and they're not afraid of us at all. They'll come right up to you if you have some food.' He turned to Todd again and threw him a good-natured grin. 'Do you reckon that might be what you saw, lad?'

The teenager looked down at the ground before muttering: 'Um, maybe, yeah. I only really saw its face.'

'Don't worry,' the man said. 'It's an easy mistake to make.' He looked back at Mia and gave her a private wink, adding: 'They don't look that different, do they? It's only the cute bushy tail that stands them apart really. But they are much easier to love than rats; that's a fact. I reckon you can return to your bags in safety now, kids.'

Mia expected the man to tap them up for some change before leaving. But he didn't – and, as a result, she felt bad for thinking so.

She and Todd returned to where they'd been sitting. Once the man was safely out of earshot, Todd whispered: 'He was a bit of a weirdo, wasn't he? He totally stank. Do you reckon he was a tramp?'

'I think he was probably homeless, yes. Tramp isn't a very nice word. He was only trying to be helpful.'

Todd frowned. 'If you say so. Are you sure he didn't nick anything while he was talking to us? He could be a skilled pickpocket, for all you know, like Fagin's gang in *Oliver!*'

'What are you on about?'

'It's the musical version of *Oliver Twist*. We, um, put it on at school a few months ago. I was one of them.'

'Sorry?'

'One of the thieves. You know, the Artful Dodger and all that. I didn't play him, though. I was just in the chorus.'

Mia vaguely knew what he was talking about now. She

seemed to remember seeing the film on TV once. 'It's not very nice to assume he's a thief, Todd,' she replied, cutting to the chase. 'You shouldn't be so quick to judge. He didn't go anywhere near my handbag.'

'If you say so. I kept my hands in my pockets the whole time he was here. My dad reckons no one needs to be homeless. He says they're usually people who don't want to contribute to society, because they'd rather be off their heads on drugs or drink.'

Mia decided at this point that she definitely had no further interest in getting drunk with Todd.

'I'm not really feeling like this any more,' she said after he suggested opening the wine.

'What? How come? Is it because I dropped your bottle? I am sorry about that. I didn't mean to. It was an accident. It smelled pretty awful anyway.'

Mia got to her feet, smoothing down her skirt with her hands. 'I know. Don't worry, that's not the reason. Come on, let's go.'

Todd also stood up. 'Is it something I did? Is it about the rat – or what I just said about that, um . . . bloke?'

'You could have been nicer about him, sure. No offence to your dad, but I think what he told you about the homeless isn't very fair. No one wants to be living on the streets.'

Todd winced. 'Sorry. I didn't mean—'

'Never mind. The drinking seemed like a good idea earlier, but now it feels, um, juvenile.'

'Right.' Todd picked up his bag and zipped it shut. He looked so dejected that Mia wondered if she'd gone too far in what she'd said. She had been disappointed by his reaction, though, because it was so far removed from her own. Mind you, it wasn't his fault what his parents had taught him. And he was only thirteen.

'I'd better find a bin for this,' she said, bending down to pick up the discarded kirsch bottle and emptying out the drop of clear liquid remaining before screwing the lid back on.

When she looked up again, to her surprise, Todd was running in the direction of the homeless guy, who was now sitting on a park bench in the distance.

What the hell?

She thought about going after her friend, but before she had a chance to make her mind up, he'd already reached the man. She watched the pair interact, although they were too far away for her to hear what they were saying.

Todd had his back to her and was blocking her view of the seated man, so she couldn't even see their facial expressions. There was some gesturing and then Todd unzipped his backpack, pulled out the two bottles of wine and handed them over. Next thing, Todd was waving goodbye and running back in her direction; she could now see that the man was grinning. He raised one of the bottles into the air and mouthed what looked like 'cheers'.

'Cheers!' she shouted back with a wave.

'You gave him the wine,' Mia said when Todd returned to her side.

'Yep. I asked him first if he liked wine, which he does, and then I offered him the bottles. He seemed pleased.'

Mia couldn't help thinking they would have been better

giving him some food or even cash. But what the hell? If it made him happy in the short term, why not? He'd no doubt be buying alcohol at some point anyway, judging by how much he smelled of the stuff. It was a nice, well-meaning gesture on Todd's part; enough to make up for what he'd said before.

'I thought I might as well pass the bottles on to someone who wanted them. I'm sure Gran won't miss them and, if I tried to put them back, I'd run the risk of getting caught in the process.' He winked before adding: 'It'll be nice not having to lug them around any more.'

'Fair enough.'

'So are we heading back into town?'

'Um, we could have a look around the art gallery first, if you like, or there's a museum a bit further up Oxford Road where there's a dinosaur skeleton.'

Todd pulled a face. 'I'm not really into museums and art galleries. Sorry. And I think I've seen the dinosaur before. It must be the place Gran took me last summer. I'm actually a bit hungry. Do you fancy popping to that McDonald's we passed on the bus earlier? It's only a short walk, I think.'

'Go on, then,' Mia said, laughing inside at the fact they were surrounded by culture but chose instead to go for a Maccy D's. 'I reckon I could handle a chocolate milkshake.'

'It's the cheeseburgers I love. Yum.' Todd rubbed his stomach with one hand to emphasise his point as they headed back to the park entrance, Mia dropping the empty kirsch bottle into the first bin they passed.

As they walked, they joked about how angry their

respective parents would be if they found out about them stealing the alcohol from their relatives.

'How come it's just you and your mum, actually?' Todd asked next. 'Unless you don't want to talk about it.'

'No, it's okay,' Mia replied. 'It's always been this way. My dad's never been on the scene. Mum doesn't like to talk about him. Any time I've brought him up, she's just said he's a waste of space who's not interested in being a father – and we're better off without him in our lives.'

'So you don't even know who he is?' Todd asked, his mouth agape. 'That's mental. Don't you even want to find out?'

'I don't know really. It's hard to miss someone you've never known. But then occasionally – when I spend time at friends' houses, for instance, and see what a regular family looks like – I do think about it. I wonder where he is and what he's doing; if I look like him and whether he ever thinks about me.'

'Don't you reckon she'd tell you if you went on about it enough and wore her down?'

'She'd probably just get mad, to be honest. Mum really doesn't like to talk about it. She's doing what she believes is best for me. And if he isn't a very nice person, who's not interested in the fact he has a daughter, then I am probably better off without him. It's not like he's ever made any effort to contact us.'

'It must be weird, though. I can't imagine. What about your aunt and uncle? Do they know who he is?'

Mia shook her head. 'Mum's always said she's never told anyone. I did ask my grandad once, a couple of years ago, and he said he didn't know. I don't think he was lying. Whoever my dad is, it's likely he's from around here, because Mum lived in Manchester when she had me.'

'It could be that dude I gave the wine to,' Todd said with a smirk.

'Very funny.'

As they arrived outside McDonald's, Mia decided to change the subject to something lighter. 'Anyway, Todd, since you're being a comedian, tell me more about your time on stage in that musical.' Mia fought to keep a straight face. 'I guess there must have been lots of singing and dancing involved. You'll have to give me a rendition.'

Todd groaned as he held open the door for her. 'Why did I tell you about that? I was awful, honestly. My English teacher roped me into it because they were short on numbers. My singing voice is so bad they actually told me to mime.'

This made Mia giggle. 'Maybe don't sing after all, then.'

Back in the present, Mia was lying on her bed, staring at the plain white ceiling above and trying to stay calm when there was a knock at her door.

'Come in,' she said.

The door swung open and Hannah's head appeared. 'Have you got a minute, love? Your uncle wants a word with us both about what happened yesterday with your mum. We're in the lounge.'

'Okay. I'll be there in a sec.'

Mia took a deep breath, closed her eyes for a moment and wished for good news.

CHAPTER 14

Mark had been dreading his arrival back home. He'd spent most of the train journey from Bournemouth to Southampton that morning thinking about what to say. Then he'd barely been able to concentrate on work during the day.

It hadn't gone unnoticed. Adam had quizzed him about it over lunch, when the pair of them had slipped out to a nearby boozer, taking advantage of the fact that Wilder was tied up with a previous appointment.

He'd been sipping on a gin-and-tonic in a quiet corner, waiting for his chicken salad to arrive; hoping it wasn't as bland as everything else in the cavernous chain pub, from the sleepwalking staff to the dreary background music. Having finished replying to an email, Adam – sitting directly across from him – had jammed his mobile back into his jacket pocket and muttered something about never getting a moment's peace. Then he'd thrown Mark a quizzical glance, asking: 'So how come you didn't make it back last night? Is everything all right?'

'It took a bit longer than expected, that's all. I missed the last train, so I had to take the spare room and catch an early one back this morning.'

'At least you managed to get changed before hitting the office,' Adam had said, smirking, after taking a sip from his pint. 'Otherwise people might have thought you'd been a dirty stop-out.'

'Hardly.'

'Seriously, though. Did you manage to sort things out with your sister-in-law? What's her name again: Deborah, is it?'

'Diane. Yeah, it's . . . complicated.'

'I thought as much. You've been away with the fairies all morning.'

'Is it that obvious? Sorry, mate.'

'Don't worry about it. I only caught on because I work with you all the time. It's fine, honestly. Wilder's too wrapped up in his own crap to notice. Besides, I think he's terrified of you after all the financial stuff you reeled off yesterday.'

Mark, who'd been occupying his hands by tearing up beer mats under the table, had laughed at this. 'Well, that's what you asked me along for, right?'

'Exactly. Are you okay, though? If there's anything I can do to help . . .'

Mark had lied, claiming to be fine, despite this being far from the truth. He'd then done his best to put his – and Diane's – troubles out of his mind for the rest of the afternoon, although he hadn't been particularly successful.

It had been the same story at the airport, during the

short flight back to Manchester, and then the cab ride home. One thought had barely left his mind the whole time, bouncing around inside his skull like a rubber ball: what the hell was he going to tell Hannah and Mia when he got back?

Finding Mia waiting by the front door of the apartment had thrown him, but luckily he'd had the excuse of needing a shower first, which had bought him some extra time. Not that it had helped much.

Now he was facing the pair of them in the lounge, hair still damp from being washed, and no clue what to say.

His mind flashed back to twenty-four hours earlier when it had been Diane's face staring expectantly at him, rather than those of her sister and daughter. But unlike them, it hadn't been explanations she'd wanted. It had been Mark's reaction to the bombshell she'd just dropped at her kitchen table.

'Aren't you going to say anything?' she asked him, her face eerily calm.

Like what? How was he supposed to respond? She'd just told him she was dying! And this was Diane, of course, which made things even more complicated. Was it true – or merely the latest move in some elaborate game she was playing?

'Um,' he replied eventually, shaking his head as the words shuffled out. 'I don't know what to say, Diane. What . . . how?'

She sat back in her chair at this point, rather than

continuing to lean over the table, but it did little to ease the tension.

'It's cancer,' she said, her voice little more than a whisper. 'Pancreatic. Terminal.'

As she uttered these words, the look in her eyes – or rather the absence of anything there, like a vacuum, bereft of hope – shattered Mark's remaining defences. He reached forward and placed his right hand over hers as it gripped the kitchen table: one human to another, the past temporarily forgotten.

'Diane, I'm so sorry. Does Mia—'

He felt her hand stiffen at the mention of her daughter's name. 'No – and she mustn't! She can't go through what Hannah and I did with Mum. You remember that, right? It was horrendous watching her slowly waste away. I don't want that for my daughter, especially at her age. That's why I brought her to you.'

Diane went on to explain how her cancer diagnosis had been a bolt from the blue just a few weeks earlier. She'd been feeling under the weather for a while – tiredness, weight loss and some niggling stomach pains – but hadn't thought much of it. The possibility of such slight symptoms being anything serious hadn't even entered her mind, until she'd finally got around to having them checked out. Her GP had quickly escalated things and, next thing she knew, an oncologist was delivering the devastating news.

'But how could you hide that from Mia?' he asked.

'It's all happened so quickly, you wouldn't believe it. I've barely got my head around it myself. Mia was at school when I had the hospital appointments. I made the decision not to tell her.'

'But . . . who have you told? You can't do this alone, Diane. How long have you even—'

'A few months, best-case scenario.'

'What? Jesus, Diane. And there's nothing—'

'It's incurable.'

'You have to tell Mia. And what about your dad and Hannah? They're your family, Diane. They have a right to know. You've told your dad at least, right?'

'No, I don't want my family watching me die before their eyes. We've been through that already with Mum and look where it left us. The trauma ripped us apart.'

'So what are you going to do?'

'I want to die on my own terms, before things get too bad. Quick and painless, while I'm still me.'

'What does that even mean?' He threw his hands in the air, incredulous. 'What exactly have you been doing since you left Mia with us, Diane?'

'Mark? Hello, Earth to Mark!' The insistent sound of his wife's voice brought him back to the present: the last place he wanted to be, considering the dilemma he faced.

He blinked and dragged one palm up over his forehead into his freshly washed hair, beads of moisture running into the gaps between his fingers. 'Sorry, I guess I'm tired,' he fudged. 'I've had a long couple of days.'

Knowing what he now did about his sister-in-law and the shocking reason for her recent actions, Mark's gut instinct was – of course – to tell Hannah and Mia the truth. It would be a disastrous conversation, naturally; goodness only knew how Mia would react. She'd probably want to head back down to Bournemouth immediately.

But it wasn't that simple.

Diane had made it crystal-clear she didn't want her daughter or sister to know about her condition. She'd also said in no uncertain terms that should he decide to tell them anyway, she would be forced to reveal the truth about him being Mia's father. Despite Mark pointing out how unfair that was, considering how it had come to pass and the fact he'd only just learned the truth himself, Diane had been insistent.

'Fair or unfair, that's how it is,' she'd said. 'I absolutely don't want them to know – and the same goes for my father.'

'So why have you told me?' he'd asked. 'Is this just another way for you to torture me, Diane? You seem to take great pleasure in putting me in impossible situations.'

'Honestly, this isn't about you,' she'd insisted. 'You came here tonight and, well, telling you suddenly seemed to make a strange kind of sense. But I can't let that get in the way of how I need things to happen.'

And still Mark wrestled with what to do; what to say. Was protecting his secret, and thus saving his marriage, more important than telling a girl – his own daughter, as it now seemed – her mother was dying? Didn't he at least owe Hannah the chance to try to make peace with her sister, rather than be haunted by regret for the rest of her life? But how could that ever happen if she found out about his and Diane's night together? And what would the uncovering of this sordid secret do to Mia?

Dammit, he was in an impossible situation. Lying to Hannah and Mia about what had happened yesterday seemed like the only option for now. However, if either of them later discovered he'd actually known more, that too could prove disastrous. Talk about being stuck between a rock and a hard place.

'So, er, yes,' he found himself saying, although it was like he was outside his body, watching as an observer rather than a participant in the conversation. 'I did manage to track Diane down yesterday.'

'You went to our house?' Mia asked. 'Is that where you found her?'

'That's right. I took a taxi from Bournemouth railway station. Diane wasn't home when I first arrived, so I got the third degree from your next-door neighbour.'

Mia, who was sitting opposite him, next to Hannah on the sofa, lit up at this. 'Rod, you mean?'

'That's right. Big chap.' Mark hunched his shoulders forward and clenched his fists in front of his chest. 'I wouldn't want to mess with him.'

'He's lovely really. He's just a bit protective of me and Mum.'

'I noticed.' Winking in a bid to keep the mood as light as possible, he added: 'Anyway, luckily Diane got back before he moved on to roughing me up.'

'How's she doing?' Mia asked. She leaned forward, her green eyes all the more piercing for not being circled by her dark make-up.

'Well . . .' he replied, realising the crucial nature of the next few words he would utter. He looked at the concern etched into the teenager's face and wondered, not for the first time, whether she already had some idea her mother was ill. Diane may not have told her anything, but she was a bright kid. She must have been wondering what had led her mum – the person who'd single-handedly brought her up – to suddenly take the drastic measure of driving all the way to Manchester and leaving her here, with him and Hannah.

'We had a good long chat,' he continued. 'So much so that I missed the last train back to Southampton and had to stay the night in your spare room. Luckily your mum was good enough to give me a lift to the station early this morning.'

He looked at Hannah as he said this, knowing she was hearing it for the first time; she looked confused and surprised rather than angry, which was probably as good as he could hope for in the circumstances. He realised he probably ought to have mentioned it when they'd spoken on the phone earlier. But he'd bottled out, keeping the conversation deliberately short and blaming it on being busy with work.

'Did she say when I can go home?' Mia asked. 'Has she got herself sorted out?'

Mark took a deep breath, but before he could continue, he was interrupted by the sound of Hannah's mobile phone ringing.

He looked at his wife, expecting her to answer it or at least check who was calling, but she waved her hand dismissively and told him to ignore it. 'If it's important, they'll leave a voicemail,' she said.

But no sooner had the ringing stopped than it started up again. And when this happened another time, Hannah frowned and walked across the room to her desk, where she pulled the mobile out of her handbag and announced: 'That's odd. It's Dad.'

'I thought he was on a cruise in the Med,' Mark replied, but by that point Hannah had already answered the call.

As she strode out into the hallway with the phone to her ear, he heard her ask her father if everything was all right, before requesting him to slow down because she couldn't understand what he was saying. Then there was the sound of a door opening and shutting, which Mark took to mean she'd gone into the bedroom. While this wasn't particularly unusual behaviour – Hannah often lay on the bed to take phone calls she knew might last a while – Mark had a bad feeling. Frank didn't call very often, especially not when he was away on holiday. There had to be something wrong.

'Do you think everything's okay?' Mia asked him, her furrowed brow giving away her own concerns.

Mark forced his mouth into a smile, which he hoped looked more convincing than it felt. 'Oh, I wouldn't worry. I'm sure it'll be nothing. I hear you and Hannah went out for dinner yesterday. Somewhere in the Northern Quarter, wasn't it? Did you enjoy it?'

'Yes, thanks,' Mia said.

'Good, good. And what have you been up to today? Anything exciting?'

'Todd and I hung out together for a bit.'

'That's nice. It's great you two get along. Did you—'

Before Mark could ask his question, Mia posed two of her own. 'Do you think Grandad's call might be to do with my mum? How was she when you said goodbye to her this morning?'

Mark gulped. 'What makes you think it's about Diane, love? It could be anything. Your grandad's not even in the UK at the moment. It's probably to do with his holiday. Maybe Joan's fallen ill or something.'

Mia didn't appear convinced. The look on her face was locked somewhere between pensive and terrified.

Then they both heard the muffled but unmistakeable sound of Hannah letting out a sudden hair-raising shriek from the other room. They looked at the open doorway of the lounge and then back at each other in perfect sync.

'That doesn't sound good,' Mia whispered. 'Had you better check on her?'

Mark's heart was racing so hard he feared she might see it thumping through his fresh grey polo shirt. 'Yes,' he said, jumping to his feet.

'Do you want me to come too?'

'No, Mia,' he replied, more abruptly than intended. Adopting a softer tone, he added: 'I've got this. Don't worry. I'm sure it's nothing: probably a storm in a teacup.'

She nodded once, remaining where she was on the couch, yet looking unconvinced.

'Back in a minute,' he added, before walking to the bedroom with feigned calmness. He paused in front of the closed door, fingertips resting on the cool metal handle,

210

as he listened for a moment but heard nothing. Taking a deep breath, he pressed down and felt the door swing open, revealing a silent Hannah perched on the edge of the bed, her head resting in one hand; the other trembling slightly, but still holding her mobile to her ear. 'And then?' she puffed breathlessly into the phone before looking up at Mark with a blank stare: the redness of her tear-soaked eyes like gaping wounds in the sheet-white skin of her face.

'Is everything okay?' he mouthed.

She shook her head in slow motion and absent-mindedly waved him away.

Mark nodded, whispering: 'You know where I am.' He backed out of the bedroom, gently closing the door behind him, and stood in the hallway wondering what on earth was happening and what to do next. He knew Mia would be crying out for answers when he returned to the lounge, yet he had none to give. Despite what he'd told her, he too had a horrible, deep-seated feeling that this was something to do with Diane.

He darted into the main bathroom, locking the door behind him before sitting down on the closed lid of the toilet seat and holding his head in his hands.

What was he doing? Why was he hiding here rather than speaking to Mia? She was his daughter, for goodness' sake. Wasn't she? In truth he still hadn't fully accepted this, despite everything Diane had told him. Even though she'd seemed so sincere, he couldn't forget the way she'd manipulated him before. Was this genuinely the reason, though, or was he burying his head in the sand and using that as an excuse? Maybe it was a bit of both. God, what a mess everything was in . . .

Mark had never wanted to have children. He'd decided that years ago – and he had good reason for it, based on the tragedy he'd lived through when only a child himself, which had torn his family to shreds.

He'd always been upfront about this with Hannah. He'd made sure she was okay with it before asking her to marry him. He'd genuinely been prepared to walk away, painful as it would have been, if she hadn't been able to accept this. Not having children was definitely a compromise on her part. Mark had never kidded himself about this fact. But it had been her choice, rather than something he'd imposed on her. That was important. And they'd had a good life together as a result, full of the kinds of freedoms parents of young children didn't have: the regular luxury holidays and nights out, for instance. You could even argue that it had granted Hannah the opportunity to pursue her dream of becoming a professional author.

But all of that was, of course, built on a lie when you brought Diane into the picture. Specifically that one illicit night they'd spent together and, as he was now finally starting to accept, the child it had produced.

There was one key moment in his and Hannah's relationship when Mark had questioned whether she regretted her decision to forego parenthood. And that was after seeing the look in her eyes when she'd taken him to visit Diane and Mia for the first time in hospital. He hadn't said anything to her at the time. He hadn't dared to, fearing the answer and where it might lead.

Hannah had soon settled into the role of loving aunt. And how she'd loved that little girl! She'd doted on her, showering her with affection and gifts galore at every opportunity. It had been losing contact with her niece that had smashed one of the biggest cracks in his wife's psyche following her and Diane's spat. Young Mia had been a beacon of hope in the devastating wreckage left by her mother's death. So when that too had been taken away from her, only darkness had remained.

How would Hannah feel about Mia, with whom she was now finally reunited and starting to bond, if she discovered the terrible truth of her origin?

Mark levered his resistant body into a standing position. He walked over to the sink, ran the cold tap and splashed water on his face before staring at himself in the mirror. He searched his tired, unshaven doppelgänger for some hint of Mia and, as he did so, felt a gear shift in his conscience.

He remembered how he'd felt all those years ago, while looking after Mia for a couple of days at Diane's house. That gut feeling he'd had about her being his daughter – it had been right. And when he'd felt it back then – when it had punched him so hard in the belly he'd been unable to think of anything else – he'd known he had to do right by her, despite all that it might cost him. He'd recognised that he couldn't run away from his responsibilities like his own dad had. He'd understood that what he wanted wasn't the most important thing any more.

The same was true now. He was a father. Mia's father. That mattered more than anything else. It was time for him to stand up and accept his duty.

At that moment his phone, which was on silent in his trouser pocket, announced the arrival of a message with a short vibration. He pulled it out and saw, to his surprise, that it was from Hannah.

Can you come to the bedroom NOW? Need to speak to you alone urgently. Don't let on to Mia.

CHAPTER 15

Hannah sent the text message and waited. It had been the only way she could think of to get Mark's attention without also alerting poor, poor Mia. She desperately needed to speak to him alone first, because . . .

Oh my God. How could this be happening? None of it felt real. Could it be a dream? She wanted to pinch herself, but suddenly all of her limbs felt like lead and the idea of moving even a muscle seemed impossible. What was happening? Was this what extreme shock felt like?

How could Diane have done that? How could she really be . . . ?

Hannah couldn't bring herself to finish the thought. It was too much. It was incomprehensible. And how could she, of all people, not have sensed that something so horrendous had happened to her own flesh and blood just hours earlier?

Still sitting there on the edge of the bed, where only

moments ago she'd been speaking to her dad, she started to feel light-headed. Oh no. Was she going to be sick?

The bedroom door swung open in slow motion and Mark was standing there again, like when she'd sent him away. How long ago was that? It felt like hours.

She opened her mouth to say something. Tried to stand up, but . . .

Next thing she knew, Hannah was lying on the opposite side of the bed – her own side – feeling groggy. Mark was crouched on the floor at her side.

'What happened?' she asked, instinctively trying to sit up, only to feel Mark's hand on her chest, encouraging her to stay put. 'I—'

'Easy,' he whispered. 'You fainted. Luckily it happened just as I walked in and I managed to catch you.'

'How long was I—'

'Only a moment. I carried you over here and laid you down. How do you feel?'

'Woozy.'

Mark pursed his lips and gave a gentle nod of his head. 'Exactly. So best not rush to get up again straight away. Close your eyes for a moment, if it helps. I'm right here if you need anything.'

'Thanks, love. I might just do that.'

She enjoyed a few seconds of peace before the blaring klaxon of reality started up again in her skull and her eyes teared up in response. 'Oh, Mark!' she said, wishing she didn't have to repeat her father's words out loud; knowing it would only made them more real. 'Something awful has happened.'

She felt his hand, which was wrapped around hers, stiffen.

'I . . . whatever it is, Hannah, I'm here for you. Okay? Take your time. I can see you're very upset.'

'Where's Mia?' she asked, lowering her voice to the faintest of whispers. 'I don't want her to hear this. Not yet. Not before I know what to say.'

'In the kitchen, I think. Maybe the lounge.' His reply was also a whisper, but still she warned him to keep it down.

Hannah took a long, slow breath before she spoke again. And when she did, it was even quieter still, delivered straight into her husband's waiting ear.

He smelled clean from his recent shower – his hair freshly shampooed – and she couldn't help but think what an awful match that pleasant scent was for the horrendous news she had to impart.

'It's Diane. She's gone.'

Mark's head jerked back at this. 'What do you mean? I saw her this morn—'

'Shh! Keep it down. I'm serious.'

'Sorry, but what are you talking about? What do mean gone? Gone where?'

An eerie calmness descended on Hannah as the words finally came out. Bizarrely, she imagined herself as a TV news anchor reading from a teleprompter. 'She's dead, Mark. She walked out in front of a train this morning. Dad just got a phone call from the police. Her mobile was, um, destroyed in the, er . . . accident. But somehow they managed to work out who she was and, after breaking into the house, found Dad's number. Thankfully he had his phone turned on and there was a signal. He's already busy trying to find a flight home.'

She paused and looked at Mark's face. It was twitching and blinking and shaking in a way that reminded Hannah of one of those pre-CGI horror movies when someone transformed into a werewolf. It was a more extreme reaction than she'd expected – particularly as she knew Mark had never much liked her sister, even before the big falling-out. But she supposed it was something to do with the fact that he'd only just seen her. Come to think of it, he may have even been the last person who spoke to her. Hadn't he said she'd given him a lift to the station that morning? How could he not have picked up on what she was about to do?

She must have gasped as this last thought occurred to her, judging by the abrupt change of expression on Mark's face. It had at least returned to a more human look, albeit one of horror and bewilderment.

'Hang on,' he said, lowering his voice as she threw him another warning glance. 'You're saying she killed herself? That she jumped in front of a train – this morning? I don't. I can't. What time was it?'

'I don't know, Mark. Why? Because she dropped you off at the train station. That's what you said, right?'

'Yes. Exactly. Oh my God!' His mouth hung open, like it had run out of words to say. Hannah considered asking him further about this. But a sudden, jarring knock at the bedroom door focused her mind on more pressing matters – namely, how to break the devastating news to her niece.

'Hello?' Mia's voice called from the other side. 'Is everything okay in there?'

Hannah and Mark threw each other a rabbit-in-the-headlights look and then both turned back to the door. Hannah was terrified it would open and she'd be face to face with her niece yet utterly unprepared what to say. Thankfully, Mark responded in time to stop this.

'Could you give us a minute, please, Mia?' he said, somehow managing to sound composed. 'We'll be out soon. I promise.'

'Is Hannah all right?' the teenager's little voice asked, breaking her heart. Too choked up to reply, Hannah begged Mark with her eyes to say something.

'She's, um, in our bathroom,' he lied, wincing and shrugging by way of apology for not coming up with anything better. 'We'll explain everything very soon, I promise.'

'Okay, if you're sure.'

Neither of them said a word as they listened to Mia's footsteps walking away from the door.

Eventually, Hannah turned back to her husband. 'Do you think she heard anything?'

He shook his head.

'I hope not. That would be the worst thing of all.'

'Don't worry. But we are going to have to tell her. Do you want to do it or—'

'I was thinking maybe we could do it together.' Hannah's heart was thumping its way out of her chest. She felt breathless. 'What do you reckon?'

Mark gave a solemn nod. 'Okay, but you know more details about it than I do. So . . .' He stopped speaking for a few beats; his eyes looked ready to burst as he circled his lips into a small O shape and slowly exhaled. 'Sorry. I'm struggling to get my head around this. I was with her only hours ago. I can't comprehend the fact she's gone. And to do it in such a way. Bloody hell!'

'Did she give any indication—'

'Let's not do this now, Hannah. It's not the time. We need to break the news to Mia fast before she finds out some other way. Imagine if she comes across a news article online or someone calls her about it on her mobile.'

Hannah's jaw dropped. She hadn't even considered this possibility. 'You're right. Let's do it immediately.'

CHAPTER 16

Mia knew for sure that something was terribly wrong when her aunt and uncle walked together into the lounge – Mark with his arm held supportively around Hannah's waist. Both of them were deathly pale, their eyes wide open and bodies moving in a jerky, awkward fashion. They looked every bit as nervous as she felt.

Mia stopped chewing her fingernails and sat bolt upright on the couch. 'Hi,' she said in a tiny voice. 'What's going on?'

Hannah sat down next to her and took her hand as Mark knelt before her.

'What's happening?' Mia said, shaking her head, fear and confusion oozing out of every pore. 'You're scaring me.'

Hannah appeared to be about to say something, but instead she hesitated, turning from Mia to her husband, her already red eyes filling up with fresh tears. She shrugged helplessly.

Nodding, Mark took a deep breath and looked Mia in the eye. 'We have some very bad news, I'm afraid,' he said. 'There's no easy way to tell you this. Your grandad received a call earlier from the police who, um, told him that your mum had been found dead this morning. I'm so terribly sorry.'

Mia scowled at her uncle. She'd heard the words that had just left his mouth, but they made no sense. They couldn't be true, so she rejected them. 'What are you talking about? You were with her this morning. Why would you say such a thing?' She turned to Hannah. 'Why's he lying to me? That's not what Grandad told you, is it? What's going on? Please tell me the truth.'

Hannah's eyelids flickered shut. It must only have been for a few seconds, but to a panicked, befuddled Mia it felt like forever until they opened again and, with a pained sigh, her aunt finally spoke. 'I'm afraid that is the truth, my love. Diane's gone.'

As soon as those devastating – impossible – final words had left her mouth, Hannah fell forward on the seat and started sobbing into her hands.

Mia watched her for a moment in silence. She felt nothing, like a cold cloud had descended on her brain and numbed it, temporarily blocking her thought process.

And then suddenly Hannah was trying to wrap her arms around her – to pull her in to a hug – and it was all too much. She shoved her away and leapt to her feet, bawling: 'Why are you both lying to me? I want to go home right now! I want to see my mum.'

As her aunt flopped away from her, lost in another wave

of tears, Mia refocused her fury on Mark. He remained kneeling before her, his hands held up in front of his face as if to defend himself.

'You said you saw her!' she yelled. 'You said you stayed at our house and she took you to the train station this morning. So how can any of this be true? Unless . . . you did something to her. Oh my God, is that it? Tell me the truth now or I swear I'm going to call the police and report you. Tell me the truth!'

The teenager's demand, delivered with a deafening scream, had an instant effect on Hannah. Reacting like an ice bucket had just been emptied over her head, she jerked upright on the sofa and her voice took on the tone of a stern school teacher. 'You need to calm down and listen to what we have to tell you, Mia,' she snapped. 'I know what you're hearing must be a dreadful shock. It was to me too – and I can totally understand why you want to lash out, believe me. But we're not the enemy here, Mia. We're your family and we all need to stick together. Think about it for a minute. Why would we make up something this horrendous? Have we done anything during your stay with us to suggest we'd do something so despicable?'

Stunned back into silence, Mia stared at her aunt for a long moment. Her haywire brain continued to spark and fizz inside her head until it finally started to regulate itself and slow down.

'But she's not your mum,' she said, her slight, shaky voice cutting into the stillness that had descended on the room. 'You don't even like her. Why else have you ignored each other for so long?'

'She's my sister,' Hannah replied, her voice brimming with emotion. 'And despite everything that's gone on between us, I love her. Just as I love you.'

Upon hearing this, something inside Mia broke; she collapsed back next to her aunt on the settee and was consumed by a torrent of tears.

'It can't be true,' Mia said eventually, sniffling and dabbing her cheeks with tissues Hannah had passed to her. 'It can't! How can my mum be gone?'

And then, after looking from her uncle to her aunt, Mia asked the question she'd been avoiding until now, because she knew saying the words would make it real. 'How did it happen? How did Mum die?'

Hannah's face twitched as she seemed to try to form the words to give Mia her answer, but they never came. She shook her head and let out an exasperated sigh.

'There was a terrible accident, love,' Mark said in a slow, steady voice. 'She was hit by a train sometime after she dropped me off at the station. We're, er, not exactly sure what happened yet.' His eyes trailed from Mia to Hannah and then back again. 'I had no clue about this until Hannah told me a few minutes ago, Mia, I swear to you. Your mum was very much alive when I said goodbye to her. I've no idea what happened, but I'm as shocked as you are.'

'She was . . . hit by a train?' Mia asked with a gulp. 'Like someone pushed her off the platform?'

Now Mark looked to Hannah for assistance.

'It didn't happen at the station,' she said. 'It was somewhere along the line.'

'Oh.' Mia frowned. Her eyes darted all around the room, jumping from one spot to the next, as she tried – and failed – to make sense of what she'd just heard. 'What was she doing there?'

'I only know what your grandad told me,' Hannah said. 'He was going by what the police had told him. But early indications are that she was alone at the time and, um . . . damn, this is hard to say. I'm, er, afraid it appears this was something she did deliberately to herself.'

'You're saying she killed herself?' Mia whispered, at which point her eyes squeezed shut, thrusting her into darkness as a fresh storm of tears swept in, rolling down her face in a never-ending cascade.

'I'm so sorry,' she heard Hannah say somewhere in the distance. But her aunt's words were of little comfort as Mia's mind whirred, considering the unthinkable situation in which she found herself. How could her mum really be gone . . . forever? And how could she have done such an awful thing deliberately, without even saying goodbye? It couldn't be true. Surely it couldn't be true. Her mum would never do that to her, would she? She loved her, didn't she?

But if she really was gone, where did that leave Mia?

Alone.

An orphan.

Who would look after her? Where would she live?

Here she was with an aunt and uncle she was only just getting to know. They had their own lives to lead. Surely they wouldn't want to be burdened with her. So what would she do? Was there any way she could return to Bournemouth? Unlikely. So where would she go? Her grandad's place? What about Joan, who'd never shown a lot of interest in her? Would she really want a teenager messing up her immaculate house?

God, this was awful. All she wanted now, more than anything else in the world, was to be back with her mum in their own house. How had that become an impossible dream in the space of one conversation?

The tears wouldn't stop falling . . . and when she felt her aunt reach out to her again, this time she accepted. In her fragile state, she realised human contact was exactly what she needed; once she and Hannah had found each other, both shaking with emotion, she clung on tight.

'Your aunt and I are both here for you, whatever you need,' Mark said after a little while, his kind words like ointment on her raw wounds. 'You don't have to do this alone.'

Next thing Mia knew, her uncle had made them all a cup of tea.

'Thanks, darling,' Hannah said to him, easing herself away from a shuddering Mia while continuing to stroke her hair. 'Here, look. Mark's brought us all a nice cuppa and some biscuits.'

Mia nodded, sniffling and wiping away her tears with both hands, while staring down at her feet. Now her eyes were open again, she felt uncomfortable and embarrassed about letting herself get so emotional in front of her relatives. She couldn't bear the idea of eating or drinking anything at that moment. It would probably have made her throw up.

As if able to sense this, Hannah reached over and

squeezed Mia's shoulder, telling her: 'It's important to let our emotions out, love, at a time like this. We might have only just found each other again, but we're family. That's what's important. Everything must feel so bleak and hopeless right now. I can't even imagine what you must be going through. But like your uncle said: we're here for you, whatever you need. Your grandad will be flying back as soon as possible too. We'll find a way forward together, okay?'

Mia nodded but continued to stare at her feet, lost for words. After its recent stint on overdrive, her brain now appeared to be shutting down. She felt shattered. As her aunt and uncle muttered something between themselves, all Mia could think of was going to bed and escaping this harsh reality for a while.

'Is it okay if I go to my room for a bit?' she asked. 'I think I need to lie down.'

'Oh, right,' Hannah replied. 'Yes, of course. Would you like to take your tea with you?'

'Sorry, I don't think I can manage it.' She stood up to leave, steadying herself on the arm of the sofa, before adding: 'Would you let me know if there's any other news?'

'We will, I promise. If you need anything, please shout.'

'Thanks.'

And then she headed straight for her bedroom, flopping on top of her quilt, curling up into a foetal position and sobbing herself to sleep.

CHAPTER 17

Diane was gone, taking a piece of Hannah with her. This ought to have been easier to accept, bearing in mind their lengthy feud and the fact they'd been apart from each other for so long. But if anything, that made it worse.

Now Hannah would never get the chance to properly make things right with her sister. In her heart of hearts, this was something she had hoped would happen one day. Knowing she could have done more to achieve this during Diane's recent visit – maybe even averting her death in the process – was hard to stomach. It was a regret she'd have to find a way to live with somehow.

Meanwhile Mia, who'd just left the lounge and gone into her bedroom, closing the door behind her, would have to find a way to live without her mother. Hannah knew the heartbreak of losing a parent only too well. But in her case, she'd had a father, a sister and a husband to support her in the immediate aftermath of the death; she'd been a fully grown adult with her own life. Plus her mum had

228

been sick for a long time beforehand, so Hannah had had time to prepare herself, as much as one could for such awful grief. Mia, on the other hand, was an only child, still at school, with a dysfunctional family ripped apart by a long-standing feud. She'd had no preparation whatsoever for the agonising ordeal of her mother's death.

What that poor girl was facing was so much worse than anything Hannah had experienced. It was unimaginable. And then there was the way Diane had died: taking her own life in such a dramatic, brutal fashion. Hannah knew Diane could be selfish, but how could she do that to her own daughter? How could she abandon her like that? It wasn't just leaving her to fend for herself, which alone would have been bad enough. It was doing so in a way that would scar Mia for the rest of her life, probably blaming herself and forever questioning if there was something she might have done to stop it.

That girl desperately needed care and protection, and Hannah swore to herself there and then that she would make sure she got it.

'Poor, poor kid,' Hannah whispered as she emerged from her thoughts and saw Mark watching her, concern etched into every line on his face. 'How the hell is she supposed to cope? How could Diane do this to her – leave her alone like this?'

'Well, she didn't, did she?' Mark replied, much to her surprise.

'Sorry, what?'

He scratched his forehead. 'I didn't mean . . . There's no excuse for what she did, obviously. It beggars belief.

What I'm trying to say is that she didn't leave her alone. She left her with us.'

'Yes, temporarily. Unless . . .' She'd not understood what Mark had been getting at initially, but then the penny dropped. Her mind leapt back to that conversation between her and Diane all those years ago, at a time when Mia was just a baby and they'd still had a normal sisterly relationship. They'd been taking a walk together in the park on a frosty winter's day, both dressed in thick coats, scarves and gloves. Mia had been wrapped up tight and warm in her pram, which Hannah had been enjoying pushing while Diane walked alongside. They'd been chatting about how Diane had been coping so far as a single mother, their words puffing out before their mouths in cold, moist clouds of breath.

'So, how are you managing, Di? It's not too much, is it? I often think how it can't be easy raising a child alone.'

'I'm not alone, am I? I've got you for a start.'

'I'm always happy to help – you know that. But I think you also know what I mean. Being a single mum isn't a walk in the park.'

Diane smiled at her sister's joke. 'Very good, Han. You ought to try stand-up. Having Mia was my choice and I'm happy with the way things are right now. I wouldn't change it for the world.'

'No, of course not. Mia's amazing. You know I love her to bits and you're doing a wonderful job with her. It's just . . . you pretend like she doesn't have or need a dad, but—'

'But what?' Diane started to walk faster along the tarmac

230

path, forcing Hannah to increase her own speed pushing the pram to keep up.

'Wait. Don't get the hump. Whether or not Mia's father is in her life is up to you. I totally get that. But whoever he is – and I can't believe you still haven't told anyone, least of all me – he ought to be making some kind of financial contribution, don't you think? He was there too when it happened. He should bear some responsibility.'

Diane came to an abrupt halt and turned to look at her sister. 'I don't need anything from any man. I'm coping just fine, thank you very much.'

Hannah considered mentioning that she knew their parents were propping her up with handouts. It was something her mum had let slip after Hannah had queried how Diane could manage on her maternity pay alone. However, she thought better of saying so, realising it would only lead to a needless argument. And how could she begrudge her sister that parental help at such a crucial time in her life?

She decided to drop the matter. Diane didn't exactly have a good track record when it came to her boyfriends. They had a tendency to be good-for-nothing losers and users, so it was probably best for all concerned if the mystery father remained out of the picture. It was a bit odd she'd never let on who he was, mind. But hey-ho, that was her sister for you. She always liked to do things her own way.

'What are you staring at?' Diane snapped at a middle-aged man walking in the opposite direction, who'd been looking from one sister to the other. It was a common enough occurrence when they were out together and something that had never particularly bothered Hannah. If anything it amused her; Diane, on the other hand, often tended to lash out in such a way.

'Do you have to be so aggressive, Di?' Hannah said quietly.

'What? It's annoying! So we look alike. That doesn't give people the right to gawk at us. Anyway, since we're talking about me being a single mum and all, I have something I've been meaning to ask you. Something important.'

'That sounds serious.'

Diane chewed on one of her fingernails. 'It is actually. It's about what will happen to Mia if, God forbid, anything should happen to me while she's still a child.'

'Oh, right. That's a bit of a morbid thought.'

'Well, it's something I need to think about now I'm a parent; all the more so because I'm doing it alone. Anyway, I'm getting a will sorted and I was hoping you and Mark might be okay with being named as Mia's guardians, on the off-chance I cark it.'

Hannah had guessed this might be where the conversation was headed. Although it wasn't something she'd considered previously, her initial reaction was that she'd be only too happy to take on this responsibility for her sister and, of course, her beautiful niece, who she doted on. Her only concern was Mark. He too was very fond of Mia, but he'd always said he didn't want children, so she wasn't sure how he'd respond to this.

'Wow. I'm honoured to be asked,' she said, grabbing

Diane and pulling her into a hug. This was the truth. She was also a little surprised, since she and her sister hadn't always seen eye to eye over the years. Diane's pregnancy and, even more so, Mia's birth had seemed to bring them closer together, though. She'd accompanied her sister to several of her prenatal appointments and classes; she'd been the one there with her in the birthing room at the hospital; and now she felt like her niece was the closest thing she'd ever have to a child of her own. Privately, there had been a little jealousy at first, but rather than give in to the green-eyed monster, Hannah had opted to embrace the situation and make the best of being an aunt.

She really wanted to say yes straight away. But she knew it wasn't fair to do so without first speaking to her husband.

'Don't worry, Han,' Diane said. 'I'm not expecting an answer immediately. I realise it's something you and Mark will need to discuss first. Just let me know as soon as you can. Mum and Dad are the other option, but they're not getting any younger and with Mum's health as it is—'

'No, of course. I totally understand. I'll speak to Mark as soon as possible.'

'Are you okay, darling?'

The sound of Mark's voice, laden with concern, brought Hannah's mind crashing back to the harsh reality of the present.

He'd moved next to her on the couch and slipped his arm around her waist.

'Sorry, what was that?' she asked, shaking her head to clear it.

'Your eyes glazed over for a moment there. You looked like you were miles away.'

Hannah sighed. 'Sorry. I guess I just, er, got lost in my thoughts. What you said before. It triggered something: a memory. When Diane first asked me about us being Mia's guardians if—'

'Ah, right.'

'I thought at the time you might not want to take on the responsibility, because of not wanting kids. But you were great. You agreed without hesitation.'

'Yes.'

'And you think Diane brought Mia here because that's what she still wanted?'

Mark rubbed his nose and looked over at the open lounge door, his wary eyes acting as a reminder of the need to keep it down, so Mia couldn't overhear them. 'With hindsight, I think that's a definite possibility. I suppose we'll have to wait and see what it says in her will, assuming there is one.'

'Well, there definitely was back then. I guess it depends if she's changed it since.' Hannah hung her head and let out a whimper. 'I can't believe she's really gone, Mark. Every time I think about what happened – what she did to herself – I feel like I'm going to vomit.'

CHAPTER 18

'Everything okay today, mate? You look like death warmed up.'

Mark looked up from the printout he'd been staring at for the past fifteen minutes. He saw Adam's cheery face beaming at him from the side of his desk, like everything was still okay with the world, which couldn't have been further from the truth. Mark squeezed a pursed smile out for his colleague nonetheless. 'Charming.'

'Seriously, though. You look shattered. What happened?'

'I didn't get a lot of sleep last night.'

Adam frowned. Lowering his voice after looking around to ensure no one nearby was eavesdropping, he said: 'Is this to do with whatever was bothering you yesterday? I know it's not what us blokes usually do, but if you need to talk about it . . . we're both modern men, right?'

This last comment was delivered with a wry grin, but Mark could tell Adam was being sincere. 'Shall we pop to the kitchen for a minute?' he said after glancing over that way to confirm it was empty. 'It's probably best if I do tell you what's happened.'

Once he'd brought Adam up to speed under cover of the boiling kettle, his friend shook his head, looking dazed. 'Bloody hell,' he repeated several times. 'How was she when she dropped you off at the station, your sister-in-law? Did she give you any impression that she might be on the edge?'

Mark shook his head. Diane had seemed calm and collected that morning. Despite everything she'd told him the night before, there was no way he'd seen this coming when he left her.

'Why are you in work?' Adam asked. 'No one would have blamed you for taking some time off.'

'Well, she's only a relative by marriage, at the end of the day. I did think about it, but I decided it would have been worse, sitting at home with Hannah and Mia, twiddling my thumbs, rather than coming in. At least here there's plenty to keep me busy and take my mind off it.'

'Isn't there loads to organise for the funeral and so on?'

'There will be, but it's too early yet. The body won't even be released for a bit . . . whatever state it's in.'

Adam winced. 'God, I hadn't even thought about that. What an awful way to go.'

Seeing another member of the team on their way to the kitchen with a handful of mugs, Mark asked Adam to keep the information to himself then suggested they ought to get back to work.

'I want to die on my own terms, before things get too bad. Quick and painless, while I'm still me.'

236

Those words of Diane had been bouncing around inside Mark's head ever since Hannah had informed him of her death. They troubled him again now as he returned to his desk and pretended to be busy while lost in his thoughts. She'd made it quite clear she was suicidal – and what had he done? Nothing. He should never have left her alone having heard that. The problem was that she'd backtracked after saying it: with hindsight, probably to throw him off the scent after realising he might tell someone and try to stop her. But she'd been convincing, claiming she hadn't meant it.

'Don't worry, Mark, honestly,' she'd told him as they'd continued to chat in her kitchen. 'I'm not actually going to do anything stupid. I read in some pamphlets they gave me that it's normal for terminally ill patients to say such things without really meaning them. It's a way of taking back control, apparently; to counter the feeling of our lives no longer being in our own hands. Although you could argue they never were in the first place. Is it better to know you're going to die soon or for it to happen unexpectedly? Yep, these are the kinds of happy thoughts occupying my head at the moment.'

He cast his mind back to their car journey to the train station. Diane had seemed quite bright, considering. Definitely better than the night before. But now he wondered if that was because she'd already made the decision to take her own life. Had knowing this given her a sense of liberation, of serenity?

He hadn't told a soul about any of this or her terminal cancer diagnosis. Unsurprisingly, Hannah in particular had probed him for information about his visit to her house and whether he'd seen or heard anything to indicate what she was about to do. He had considered mentioning the cancer at least, but he couldn't see what good it would do to tell her now. The diagnosis would come to light eventually as part of the inevitable inquest into Diane's death. And since no one other than Diane knew she'd told him, why complicate matters?

Mark thought back to what he'd decided about Mia and his parental duties towards her just moments before hearing the news of Diane's death. He'd resolved to stand up and accept his responsibilities. This was something even more important now than before. And yet what did it mean exactly? If his suspicions about Diane's intentions for Mia's future were correct and Frank didn't throw up any opposition, there was a good chance she'd be coming to live with them. This would take some adjusting to for everyone, but he wouldn't be opposing it. How could he in the circumstances?

The person most likely to be against it was Mia herself, who'd have to leave her home, school and friends behind. What with all the grief she'd be experiencing, and no doubt the anger she'd feel in light of her mum's extreme actions, it was going to be tough enough for the kid already. Did she really need to discover that her uncle was in fact her father, on top of everything else?

Mark's current thinking was that telling Mia now would be a mistake. If he did so, he'd have to tell Hannah too, thus putting their marriage on the line. And that would benefit no one. Mia would face an unsettled future when

238

she most needed stability, while Hannah would be left incredibly vulnerable ahead of her novel being released.

What a shambles. Even with the wildcard that was Diane no longer on the scene, Mark still feared she might have left a message somewhere for her daughter or sister. He thought back to the letter she'd handed him in the car park. It seemed so long ago now, although it was actually less than a fortnight. What was it she'd said about the truth?

He slid open his desk drawer and rummaged around with his hand near the back until he found the envelope he'd stashed there and the single sheet of folded paper it contained.

He opened it on top of his keyboard and scanned through it until he found the words he was looking for. She'd written first that it was *time for the truth* and then later: *Secrets and lies are no good. They eat you up inside.*

Mark felt his heart pounding in his chest as he read these few words over and over again, wondering what implication to draw from them. How much of the truth had Diane wanted to reveal? She had also threatened to tell Hannah and Mia his big secret if he'd told either of them about her cancer. What if she'd written something down – a letter or a draft email perhaps – in anticipation of this? If so, anyone could find it while going through her things.

Mark was so absorbed by these terrifying possibilities that he didn't notice Sharon from reception walking up to his desk until the very last minute. Panicking she might see the compromising contents of Diane's letter, he shoved it into the inside pocket of his jacket and tried not to look flustered.

'Hi, Sharon,' he said. 'Is everything all right?'

The pained expression on her face immediately told him otherwise. 'I'm so sorry to bother you,' she replied in little more than a whisper. 'I know you asked me to hold all your calls, but . . . there's a policeman on the line.' As she delivered this last part of her news, Sharon's eyes were screwed up so tightly they were almost closed.

'I see,' Mark replied in a voice that was calmer than he felt.

'He was insistent that he needed to speak to you.'

'That's fine. I know what it will be about.' Mark paused, weighing up whether it was better to tell her nothing and risk the office gossip machine going wild at his expense, or to give her a titbit. Opting for the latter, he added: 'Someone I know was involved in a nasty accident yesterday.'

'Oh dear. I am sorry.'

'Thanks. So is this policeman still on hold?'

'Yes.'

Mark looked to the nearest meeting room, which was empty, and asked her to transfer the call to the phone in there.

As Sharon raced back to her desk, Mark walked to the meeting room, avoiding the eyes of his colleagues. He shut the door and waited for the phone to ring.

CLIENT SESSION TRANSCRIPT:
HCOOK080819

H: Thanks for squeezing me in for another session, Sally.

S: Of course. I'm sorry it can't be for as long as usual, but I juggled things about as best I could. I thought a short session today and again tomorrow would hopefully be okay for you.

H: Yes, perfect. Much appreciated.

S: Please accept my condolences, Hannah. Such awful news about your sister.

H: Thank you. Yes, I'm still struggling to wrap my mind around it all, to be honest. God knows what must be going on inside Mia's head.

S: If you think she could do with seeing a counsellor at any point, I have a colleague I can thoroughly recommend, who specialises in helping children to manage grief. It's probably too soon right now, but you know, eventually.

H: Thanks, Sally. I'll definitely bear that in mind. She got very frustrated this morning about mislaying her mobile phone, which I took as a symptom of her anguish. But otherwise she's not been very forthcoming so far. I'm just trying to be as supportive and sympathetic as I can without crowding her.

S: That sounds sensible. For the moment it's probably best to let her deal with things however she's most comfortable and at her own pace.

H: Good to know.

S: So have you found out exactly what happened to your sister yet?

H: There's a police investigation going on, but I think that's a formality. It seems that . . . Diane walked out in front of a speeding train.

S: Goodness. That is tough. Please take your time. Help yourself to tissues.

H: . . . Sorry about that. It's all still so fresh. So raw. One minute I think I'm okay and the next I'm in a state.

S: It's totally understandable.

H: Is it though? Do I actually have any right to mourn my sister, considering the state of our relationship?

S: You have every right to feel whatever you feel.

H: What about guilt? I can't stop thinking this is partly my fault. If I'd been more welcoming to her when she reached out to me, maybe she'd never have been driven to do such a dreadful thing. Perhaps I could have stopped this.

S: You can't think like that. The past is the past. There's no way of altering it now and you'll never know if there was anything you could have done to change

242

it. You don't know what was going through Diane's head when this happened. If things are as they seem, then she did this to herself. And it's not like you turned her away, is it? She asked for your help and you gave it to her. That's more than a lot of people would have done in the same situation.

H: I feel very angry too. How could Diane kill herself knowing she'd be leaving behind a fourteen-year-old child? She ought to have put her daughter above every other consideration. Whatever drove her to this brutal act, I can't comprehend how she could be so selfish, especially having experienced the agony of losing a mother herself. That poor girl: abandoned by the only parent she's ever known. It's beyond me how she's turned out as well as she has. I was just starting to accept that Diane must have been a half-decent parent. But how can I possibly believe that now? And to think my sister once had the audacity to tell me I'd make a terrible mum!

S: When was that?

H: It was on the day we had our big falling-out, in October 2008, when we both said a lot of nasty things to each other. But that particular comment really stood out for me.

S: Why's that, do you think?

H: It was so deliberately hurtful: like a knife in my heart after all the love I'd showered on her daughter. How could she think that, never mind say it out loud? I suppose not being a mum was still a sore spot for me, particularly in the aftermath of our own mother's death. I'm not sure why, but after she passed away, I found it really hard. It was part and parcel of my grief, I suppose. Somehow losing one close family member gave me this massive urge to want to create another. I think it was also because of the way Mum had been surrounded by her family at the end, which I know gave her great comfort. I couldn't help but imagine myself not having that in the same situation. If Mark was to die first, I kept thinking, who would there be for me? Would I die alone? It sounds selfish to worry about that, but I couldn't help it.

S: Did you discuss this with Mark?

H: Almost. I thought about it a lot. At one point it felt like I kept seeing mums and daughters together wherever I went. But in the end I decided it wouldn't be fair to put that on Mark, knowing he didn't ever want children. He'd been upfront and honest, giving me a choice before we got engaged, and I'd picked him instead of having kids. I also had the feeling that, if I pushed it, he might give in, feeling sorry for me about my mum's death and wanting to ease my pain. That's the type of kind, considerate husband he is – and I couldn't bring myself to push him into something so important, knowing his heart wouldn't be in it.

S: It sounds to me like you're every bit as kind and considerate in your relationship as you say he is, Hannah. A lot of people wouldn't have been able to show that kind of restraint.

H: That's nice of you, Sally. I had similar feelings after Diane and Mia moved away, but by that stage I knew

I wasn't in any suitable mental state to have a child anyway. And as you know from our earlier sessions, Mark was an absolute rock during my breakdown. I couldn't have asked for someone more understanding and patient. I'd never have got through it without him. I had suicidal thoughts then, when I considered my life was worthless, but I could never have acted on them, knowing what it would do to Mark and even to my dad. That's why I'm really struggling with Diane's actions. I keep wondering if, by taking Mia in, I enabled my sister to do this. Mind you, otherwise she might have done it with Mia still around, which would have been so much worse. Imagine if she'd killed herself at home and Mia had found her. It doesn't bear thinking about.

CHAPTER 19

'Good. You're home,' Hannah said when Mark walked into the kitchen. She turned off the electric hand blender. 'I didn't hear you come in.'

'Well, no. You wouldn't hear much over that racket.' He gave her a kiss and a little hug, peering over the large pan she was busy with on the hob before adding: 'Smells nice. What is it?'

'Carrot and tomato soup. I found a recipe online.'

'Lovely.' Mark smiled before his face turned serious. 'How's, um, everything going? How are you doing?'

'Well, I'm making soup now and before that I made a fridge cake. There was no chance of me getting any writing done today. I don't have the concentration to read a book, never mind create one of my own. I'm doing what I can to keep busy in a way that doesn't involve too much thinking.'

'That sounds fair enough to me, love. You have to deal with the news in whatever way works best for you. Is it chocolate?'

'Sorry?'

'The fridge cake.'

'Oh, right. Yes.'

'Great,' Mark replied, already heading towards the fridge. 'I'll have a piece of that.'

'Not until after tea, you won't.'

'So I take it you haven't heard much more about Diane today, then?'

Hannah shook her head. She felt tears coming again but fought them off by taking a couple of steady breaths and diverting her mind from trigger thoughts. These were skills adapted from those she'd learned to overcome anxiety in the aftermath of her breakdown, which had served her well for some time now. Mark knew to be patient and say nothing at this point, rather than draw attention to her emotional state, which would only make it worse.

Once she'd gathered herself, she replied: 'No. Dad's back in the UK now and heading to Bournemouth tomorrow. He's the one dealing with the police and so on. I've spoken to him a couple of times, but it doesn't sound like anything's going to happen very quickly.'

Mark nodded. 'Yes, about the police. They rang me at work earlier. I'm not sure where they got the details from, but—'

'Oh, I'm so sorry!' Hannah said, raising a hand to her mouth. 'Dad mentioned that this morning and I was supposed to warn you, but I totally forgot. The neighbour had mentioned you to the police, because of your visit, and Dad didn't have your mobile number to hand. He told them the name of your company instead and said they'd be able to get hold of you there. Sorry, I can't believe I forgot to tell you. Dad specifically asked me to as well.'

'It's fine. I had a feeling they might need to speak to me.'

'What did they want? What did they ask you?'

'Just what we'd been talking about: her state of mind and that kind of thing. They're obviously trying to get to the bottom of why she did what she did. There wasn't much I could tell them. Anyway, what about Mia? How's she doing? Is she in her room?'

Hannah shook her head. 'She's still in shock, I think. There's so much for her to process. She moped around the apartment until just after lunch, which she barely touched, and then Todd came over. I'd already told Kathy the full story, so she'd filled him in. He was so sweet, bless him. He gave Mia a big hug as soon as he saw her; even brought us a big bunch of flowers.'

'I spotted those in the lounge,' Mark replied. 'I wondered where they came from. Is Todd still here, then?'

'No, they've gone out into the city centre for a bit. Some fresh air is probably exactly what Mia needs. There was a bit of an incident earlier when she thought she'd lost her mobile.'

'Oh? What happened?'

Hannah explained how Mia had come storming out of her bedroom that morning, saying she'd looked absolutely everywhere for her phone and could not find it. 'Have you seen it?' she'd asked her aunt. 'Have you moved it some-where?'

Hannah had said not, whereupon Mia had stomped her heels and started tearing around the apartment in a frenzy, upending sofa cushions and anything else that got in her way, in a desperate attempt to find it. Initially, recognising her niece's need to give vent to her anger, frustration and grief, Hannah hadn't got involved, assuming she'd soon find her mobile and calm down. But she'd been forced to intervene after hearing Mia scream at full volume: 'Where the hell is it?'

'Okay, you need to take a deep breath and calm down now,' Hannah had said firmly. 'Panicking won't help you find it. Think when you last used it. It can't have gone far.'

Mia had burst into tears at this point and collapsed in a heap on the lounge floor in despair.

'Come on, love,' Hannah had told her, gently placing a hand on her shoulder. 'I'll help you. We'll find it together.'

Mark grimaced at his wife's recounting of the story. 'That sounds tricky. I guess you found her phone eventually, right?'

'Yes, thank goodness. It was on the shelf in the bathroom. I don't know how she'd missed it. She said she'd looked there. Clearly her head's all over the place. She apologised for getting worked up anyway, and then we tidied up the mess she'd made.'

'Sounds to me like you handled the situation just right,' Mark said as he took his jacket off and hung it over the back of one of the kitchen chairs. 'What about Sally? Did you get to see her okay today?'

Hannah nodded. 'Yes. I was a bit worried about leaving Mia, but she said she'd be fine with Todd.'

'Did your session help?'

'As much as anything can in the circumstances. It was good to talk things through.'

Mark stood behind Hannah and placed his hands around her waist. 'Good.'

Hannah guessed what her husband was thinking. He was no doubt worried about history repeating itself; her withdrawing and becoming a recluse again. It made sense for him to think that, seeing as it was her mum's death and the subsequent falling-out with her sister that had sparked it.

But she was much stronger than that now. Her recent sessions with Sally had helped her appreciate this fact. Plus she had Mia to take care of; her niece needed her to hold things together. There was also the fact that Hannah was used to life without Diane. She'd had years to adapt. For this reason part of her felt like she had no right to mourn her sister. It wasn't like they'd had any kind of genuine relationship at the time of her death, was it? She particularly felt like this around Mia, who of course had an absolute right to grieve. Every time Hannah shed a tear, which had happened a lot today, it was almost like she was waiting for Mia to tell her she had no business doing so.

Hannah wasn't even one hundred per cent sure why she kept on crying. Was it because she regretted the way she'd treated Diane on her recent visit? Was it because she wished she'd used that opportunity to try to reconcile? Maybe it was more down to guilt and the awful sense that her behaviour towards Diane might have played a role in her suicide.

She knew that at least some part of the sorrow that had gripped her by the throat since yesterday was for poor Mia, whose situation was one of pure tragedy. But Hannah also missed her sister: the fearless, independent little girl she'd grown up alongside; the yin to her yang; the left to her right; the hot to her cold.

All that time they'd been apart, barely a day had gone by when Hannah hadn't thought of Diane at least once. There had always been the two of them – even when there hadn't. That was why, back in the day, the shock of suddenly being cut off from her had hit Hannah so hard.

Having a sister like Diane wasn't something you could just shake off. Especially not when she'd been there, at your side, before you were even born. When her features were identical to your own to the extent that, as children, even your parents struggled to know who was who.

Hannah hadn't thought of Diane in that way for a long time now. She'd closed herself off to it as a way to survive without her; to be an individual. But facts were facts and, as much as she'd tried to bury the real nature of their bond – to think of her as a normal sister in a bid to ease the pain of their separation – that wasn't the truth. Nothing hit this home quite as hard as the terrible finality of death.

Her twin sister was gone. She was never coming back.

CHAPTER 20

Leaving Hannah in the kitchen, Mark went through to the bedroom to change out of his work clothes and have a shower in the en-suite bathroom. Along the way, he retrieved a handful of letters Hannah had put aside for him from that morning's post.

His wife was putting on a brave face, but he feared she was struggling to cope with the news of her sister's death. She was clearly conflicted, which made sense in light of her eroded relationship with Diane. Mark had seen Hannah fall to pieces before – and the idea of that happening again terrified him, not least because of Mia. If the teenager was to stand a chance of dealing with her mum's suicide, she was going to need her aunt's strength and support every bit as much as Mark's.

He'd not seen Hannah looking so fragile in ages. Things had been going so well for her recently, particularly in terms of snagging her dream publishing deal. Mark couldn't bear the thought of all that positivity being ruined before her debut novel had even been released.

He feared that should Hannah now learn the true nature of his relationship to Mia, it could be enough to tip her over the edge.

To Mark's relief, his earlier conversation with the policeman hadn't encroached on this treacherous territory at all. The questions put to him had been general rather than probing. He'd got the sense the officer had been going through the motions, with the phone call more of a box-ticking exercise than anything else. Mark's best guess was that the poor train driver had likely provided enough eyewitness information to make it an open-and-shut case.

When he entered the shower, he turned the water nice and hot. He savoured the feeling of it beating down on to his head and shoulders, then gradually coating every inch of his skin in a blissfully warm, wet layer. The steam snaked up and around him and, briefly, he found peace as he focused on the pleasant physical sensations and muted the warring thoughts slugging it out in his mind.

He held on to this serenity as he transferred his focus to the act of drying himself, choosing what to wear and then slowly, mindfully, getting dressed in a comfy pair of linen shorts and a polo shirt. Finally, sitting on the edge of the bed, he turned his attention to the items of post he'd picked up on the way to the bedroom.

The first couple were from the bank: a credit card bill and a reminder of a bonus period coming to an end on a savings account. The third was a small padded envelope with his name and address plus the postage details printed on self-adhesive labels. It looked like it might contain something small he'd ordered off eBay, like a phone case or a new charging cable. This wasn't unusual – apart from the fact he hadn't ordered any such item recently. Had he? He racked his brains, wondering if there was something he'd forgotten about, but still nothing came to mind.

He looked on both sides of the package for any sign of where it had come from, but there was no sender's address or postmark. The postage label was no help in this regard either. It looked like the kind you could pay for online and print off using your own equipment.

A voice inside Mark's head suggested that perhaps he ought to open it if he wanted to discover its contents, and so he did.

Inside, to his bewilderment, he found a single item – a loose white USB stick – something he knew for sure he hadn't ordered. When he turned it over in his hands and saw the bright yellow sticker on the back, his heart started pounding. Written in blue biro in a tiny version of a handwriting style he recognised straight away, were four words: *Mia was conceived here.*

What the hell? That was Diane's writing – no question. He'd read her letter enough times to know this for sure. So what was he looking at? And when had she sent it: just before killing herself? Oh God. What had she done? What was on this bloody flash drive?

Afraid to find out, Mark dropped the stick back into the padded envelope and shoved it under the foot end of his side of the mattress. Dammit. This was a nightmare.

Then an even worse thought came to mind: something potentially disastrous.

Diane's letter.

Mark had stuffed it into his jacket pocket at work when Sharon had approached his desk earlier today. He'd then proceeded to forget about it, having been distracted by the police phone call.

Meaning . . . the letter was still in there.

Inside his jacket.

Which he'd left in the kitchen.

With Hannah.

Shit.

CHAPTER 21

Hannah was sitting with her head in her hands at the kitchen table, sobbing over Diane's letter to Mark. She'd found it a few minutes earlier when she'd picked his jacket off the chairback with the intention of hanging it up. Now the jacket was lying discarded on the floor next to her feet as she fought to absorb the enormity of the betrayal she'd just discovered.

Mark appeared in the doorway. 'Hannah,' he said, causing her to look up and see him through the blur of her tears. Sorrow, disbelief and hatred all fought for precedence in her befuddled mind. 'I can explain,' he said. 'It's not what—'

'How could you?' she spat. 'With *her* of all people? And to keep it from me all of these years! I thought you loved me; that you were different from all the other guys. And there you were, having an affair with my sister under my nose. What was it: some kind of gross twin fantasy you needed to fulfil? You disgust me! You even gave her a child, Mark. The very thing you always denied me. That you said you never wanted. I feel sick to my stomach.'

'Listen, Hannah. You have to—'

'I don't have to do anything you say,' she replied, shouting now, fury taking charge. 'You've betrayed me. Totally and utterly. You've been lying to me for years. How long did it go on for – and how many others have there been? Don't you dare lie to me.'

'It was j-just once,' Mark stuttered. The blood had drained from his face and there was terror in his eyes, but at that moment she felt nothing but contempt for him. 'I swear to you, Hannah. It was a terrible mistake. I—'

'How many others?'

'None. That's it, I promise you. I can tell you the details if—'

'No, shut up, Mark!' Just the thought of that made her want to gag. 'Are you sick in the head? Why on earth would I want to know any of the details?'

'Um . . . sorry.'

'Don't you dare apologise. You can stick your apologies up your arse. So when you stayed there the other night – at Diane's house – did you sleep with her again for old times' sake? Is that why she killed herself, Mark? What the hell did you do?' Hannah raised her hands over her head before slamming them back down, balled into fists, on to the tabletop. 'How is this happening to me?'

Tears started pouring down her cheeks again. As much as she wanted to, Hannah couldn't stop them. But still she blinked over and over again, determined to stay strong. She kept her gaze firmly locked on the man she'd always loved and trusted above anyone else, demanding to know why he'd betrayed her.

Meanwhile, Mark remained rooted to the spot. He looked pathetic: like a child caught stealing from his mother's purse. Hannah watched him grab the edge of the nearest work surface and squeeze it with his trembling fingers, as if clinging on for dear life. She felt zero sympathy.

'Well?' she snapped, making him jump. 'Why did she kill herself, Mark? What did you do?'

He cleared his throat before replying in a shaky voice: 'I didn't do anything to her, Hannah, I swear. And no, of course I didn't sleep with her. That only ever happened once, around fifteen years ago, and never again. It was a terrible, terrible mistake I've regretted ever since. I don't know why she killed herself. She was cagey about what was going on with her and when Mia would be able to return home. She seemed a bit on edge, sure, like she did when she turned up here. But I had no idea what she was going to do. I wouldn't have left her alone if I had.'

'Are you sure about that?' Hannah asked.

'Of course.'

Unable to look at this pathetic creature – her so-called husband – for a moment longer, Hannah took her head in her hands and started rocking backwards and forwards in her chair. Who could she turn to now for comfort and support? How could she ever trust anyone again?

Neither of them spoke another word for some time. Hannah realised her initial anger had mutated into something else – a kind of detached numbness – when she eventually asked: 'Does Mia know?'

'Um, no. I don't think so,' Mark replied. 'I certainly haven't told her and Diane said she hadn't either. To be honest, I've only got Diane's word that I am her father. I didn't believe her at first, particularly as it only happened once. I obviously wondered when she fell pregnant and then when Mia was born, but she, er . . . she always maintained someone else was responsible. Until that letter.'

'All these secrets you've been keeping from me,' Hannah said in little more than a whisper. 'For all this time. And there was foolish, stupid little me thinking we shared everything. What a mug I've been.'

Hannah watched Mark's eyes fall on his abandoned jacket, still lying where she'd dropped it on the floor. Was he berating himself for his mistake in leaving it in the kitchen, allowing her to discover the letter? The thought of that being his main concern right now sent a fresh chill through the ice already encapsulating her heart. Well, she for one was glad he'd finally tripped up. As broken and battered as she currently felt, at least she now knew the truth. Remaining in the dark would have been infinitely worse. And Mark clearly wouldn't have told her otherwise. Why would he after he'd already got away with it for so many years? In different circumstances, she may never have found out – and the thought of that made her sick to her stomach.

'You'll have to tell her,' she said in a clinical tone, staring straight ahead rather than looking at him.

'What, now? Is that the best idea in the circumstances?'

She scowled at him before looking away again. 'No,

obviously not now, but soon. It's only a matter of time until she starts asking about her father anyway.'

'Right, but what if it isn't me? Like I said, I don't—'

'Be quiet!' Hannah snapped, startling herself with the frosty bite of her voice. 'That's not my concern. Not my problem. It's your mess: you work out what to do. I need to get away from you. I can't bear to look at your lying face any more.'

With that, she slid her chair out from under the table, rose to her feet and stormed out of the kitchen, slamming Diane's letter into Mark's chest as she passed him.

CHAPTER 22

Mark was reeling, like he'd taken a punch to the jaw. He pocketed the letter and walked over to where his jacket was lying in a heap on the kitchen floor. He picked it up and smoothed it over his right arm before taking the seat Hannah had vacated. After sitting there for a long moment, staring into space, he leaned forward to rest his forehead on the cool surface of the table.

He was sorely tempted to run after Hannah and beg her forgiveness. There were things he desperately wanted to say to her to help clear things up. More than anything, he needed to explain what had actually happened on that godawful night he and Diane had spent together, which was far from clear-cut. But it was way too soon after Diane's death for that. Plus he could tell his wife was far too upset to be able to listen, never mind comprehend such matters, on top of everything else.

So, reluctantly, Mark accepted that now wasn't the time. He would have to give her space to process everything.

261

Otherwise he ran the risk of being turfed out of their home. He was surprised she hadn't already kicked him out. Maybe she still would. The night was young.

He'd lived in fear of this moment – of Hannah finding out about him and Diane – for so many years now. It was the stuff of his nightmares, literally: his apocalypse moment. And here it was, coming true after so long, thanks to something as simple as leaving a letter in a jacket pocket.

Despite all the times he'd imagined this happening, it wasn't like he'd expected. He'd pictured histrionics, long bouts of shouting and screaming and maybe even some physical violence directed towards him. He wouldn't have blamed Hannah for any of that. But after an initial wave of tears and anger, his wife had mainly adopted a manner of cold detachment, which had thrown him.

An invisible wall had slid up between them as soon as she'd read the letter. Now he didn't have a clue where Hannah's head was at, especially in terms of her emotions about Diane, which were bound to be even more conflicted now than before.

How had he let this happen? And what did it mean for his, Hannah's and Mia's futures?

Sitting there with his head on the table, dazed and confused, Mark must have nodded off. It wasn't entirely surprising, considering his lack of sleep the night before and his desire to curl up in a ball and escape reality. But he was shocked nonetheless to be woken up by Mia, who looked as confused as he felt. She was make-up free again today and it emphasised the fact that she was still so young – barely more than a child.

'What's going on?' she asked.

'Um, what?' he replied, blinking as he took a moment to get his bearings; wiping his mouth free from the drool he could feel lingering there.

'Why are you asleep on the kitchen table? And where's Hannah gone?'

'Oh, I didn't sleep well last night. I rested my eyes for a moment and must have dozed off. Hang on, what do you mean about Hannah?'

'Todd and I passed her in the lobby on our way back. She was heading out somewhere with an overnight bag. I asked where she was going, but she was in a rush. Said there was a taxi waiting. She told me you'd explain.'

'Did she? Oh, right. I, um—'

'Is she going to Bournemouth? I was thinking about it in the lift on the way up and that would make sense. But if so, why isn't she taking me with her? It's my house; my mum who's died. I ought to be going with her.'

Mark didn't know what to say. He had no idea where his wife had gone. She hadn't mentioned anything to him, but he didn't want to explain this to Mia. Could she be on her way to Bournemouth? Possibly, but he didn't think so.

Mia was standing right next to him, with arms folded across her stomach and a furrowed brow. Her wide eyes were crying out for an answer to her question.

'Listen,' he said, after weighing up the options and deciding to tell her a version of the truth rather than more lies. 'Your aunt got a bit upset earlier. We had a row. I don't want to go into the details, but I think she's gone somewhere nearby to cool off. She's most likely on her way to a friend's house or something like that. Don't worry. I'll try to call her in a bit, once she's had a chance to calm down, and find out. I'm pretty sure she's not heading to Bournemouth. Like you say, it's your house; she wouldn't go there without you.'

'Okay,' Mia replied, looking sheepish. 'Sorry. I just thought—'

'No, don't be silly. You don't have anything to be sorry about, Mia. Listen, have a seat. Are you hungry? Hannah made a big pan of soup: carrot and tomato. Can I get you a bowl? I'm sure we have some nice bread too.'

'Thanks.'

She sat down as Mark jumped to his feet. He was glad of Mia's company and of a distraction from his misery.

As he turned the hob on to reheat the soup, he asked her how she was getting on. 'How've you managed today? You've been out with Todd, right?'

He had his back to her as he asked this and when there was no reply, turned around to see why. Mia was silently sobbing her heart out.

'Oh, love,' he said, rushing back to his seat and, instinctively, taking her hand in his. He felt a huge lump in his throat, seeing her in pieces like this.

'It comes in waves,' she said, sniffing and still crying as she spoke. 'One minute I feel kind of okay, like none of it has actually happened, and then the next . . . I remember Mum's gone. Really gone. And I'll never see her again. It hurts so much.

'I was walking past a Costa with Todd earlier and it

264

reminded me how, when I was younger, Mum and I used to go to this branch near the supermarket before doing the shopping on a Saturday morning. She'd have a latte and I'd have a hot chocolate. It was kind of a ritual – her way of making the shopping trip more fun. And then, when I was older, I told her I didn't want to go with her any more. That it was boring and I'd rather stay home or meet my friends. So we stopped doing it. Now I wish more than anything that I could go there with her again one more time.'

Hearing this, squeezing Mia's cool, slender hand the whole time, Mark found himself fighting back tears. She'd never spoken in such a way to him before, so openly and honestly; that, combined with the raw intensity of her grief, was overwhelming, especially in light of what had occurred with Hannah. To his surprise, he realised he wanted to share something with her that he hadn't told anyone for a long time.

'What happened when you saw that café?' he asked. 'Todd was with you at the time, right? Did you go inside?'

Mia slowly shook her head. She slipped her hand free from his to wipe some of the tears from her cheeks. 'I got really upset and ran off. Todd didn't know what was going on and I never really explained it to him, but I think he realised it was to do with Mum. We didn't chat about her too much. I told him I didn't want to. I asked him to distract me by making me laugh and he did. It was really good to get out with him today. It definitely helped, but when we got back . . .'

Her voice trailed off like she'd thought better of what she'd been about to tell him.

'What were you going to say?' he asked. 'It's good to get these things off your chest. There's nothing to be embarrassed about.'

Mia looked away from him as she replied. 'I feel bad saying it, but when I saw Hannah leaving earlier, she had her hair tied back and sunglasses on and . . . she looked so like my mum.' There was a catch in her voice as she added: 'It was almost like seeing her alive again. They look so alike. I've struggled with it a bit ever since I've been here, to be honest, but now . . . I don't know. Maybe it would be easier if I hadn't got to know you and Hannah so recently. I guess I'd be used to it, then.'

'That's identical twins for you. You should have seen them back in the day when they both wore their hair in a similar style with their natural dark-brown colour. They were almost indistinguishable from each other.'

Mia nodded. 'Personality-wise, they're quite different, though, aren't they?'

'Oh, definitely. They've always had distinct characters, for as long as I've known them both. They did used to get on pretty well, though. In their own way. There was always rivalry, sisterly rows and so on, but they were close. Did your mum ever tell you what happened between them to drive them so far apart?'

Mia shook her head. 'Not really. She said they fell out, but that's about it.'

Mark considered telling her more but decided it was too soon. 'It was a long time ago,' he said, getting up to check on the pan. 'No need to go into all of that now.'

After serving them both a large bowl of the soup, with some crusty bread on the side, Mark had the same urge he'd felt when Mia had spoken about passing the branch of Costa. Hearing her open up like that had made him want to do the same: to share a very personal story with Mia that he thought might be of some comfort to her as she processed her grief. For he'd also lost someone close to him as a youngster and he still remembered every little detail of how awful that experience had been. It was something he rarely spoke about. Usually he didn't even like to think about it.

Mark blew on his soup before skimming his spoon across the surface and taking a small mouthful. 'Mmm, that's nice,' he said, looking at Mia, who was blowing her nose and yet to start eating. 'Be careful. It's hot.'

After they'd both finished their soup, Mark offered Mia a slice of Hannah's fridge cake, which he knew from past experience would be delicious. She declined, saying she was full.

'Okay,' he replied. 'Let's leave it for now. We can have a piece later with a brew.'

Mia had only managed about two-thirds of her soup and Mark wanted to make sure she kept eating despite what she was going through, particularly considering her young age. He remembered how Hannah had lost a lot of weight following her mum's death.

Mark placed an elbow on the table and cupped his chin in the palm of his hand. He looked at Mia, who was staring into the distance with a blank expression on her face, and took a deep breath before starting to speak. 'I want to tell you something, Mia, which I think might be . . . useful, for want of a better word.'

Mia threw him a puzzled look.

'Don't worry,' he said. 'It's nothing that . . . well, I'll go ahead and say it, shall I? This isn't something I share with many people, but when I was a bit younger than you are now – about eleven-and-a-half – I, um, lost my younger brother. Pete was only six when he died. Have you heard of meningitis?'

'Yes, I think so,' Mia replied.

'Well, it's a very serious illness. There are vaccinations against the most common forms of it these days, but he got a particularly nasty version that poisoned his blood. It all happened so quickly. Pete was rushed to hospital, but the doctors weren't able to save him and suddenly he was gone. Like that, I didn't have a brother any more.

'Anyway, what I'm trying to say is that although I can't imagine exactly what you're going through at the moment, I do . . . have some idea. When you described your experience outside the coffee shop, I knew exactly what you meant. I remember feeling a really similar thing soon after Pete died.

'I was quite a lot older than Pete, you see; much as I loved him, I didn't always show it. In fact the day before he fell ill, he'd begged me to go to the park near where we lived in Stockport to play football with him, and I'd said no. But it was worse than that. I'd recently started at secondary school and made a load of new friends I was keen to impress. One of them had been round at the time, hanging out in my bedroom. Pete had come in with his football and I'd shouted at him to leave us alone and find some friends of his own to play with, calling him a "saddo no-mates". Little did I know he'd be dead a couple of days later.'

Mark stopped talking for a moment, feeling his eyes start to well up; he was touched when Mia placed a hand on his shoulder and whispered: 'It's okay.'

He wanted to fight the emotion, but it was no use, so he let the tears fall as he continued to speak, keeping his voice as steady as he could.

'I hadn't really meant it. It was bravado. Showing off. But the wounded look on Pete's face haunted me for years. I missed him so much after he was gone. I still do. I often wonder how different my life would be now if he was still in it. But he isn't, so there it is. Anyway, like you said about Costa, I had a similar thing with the park where Pete had wanted to play football. I refused to go in there for a very long time afterwards. I even avoided walking past if I could, because thinking about that place made me think of Pete: both the good times we had there together and that last time when I didn't go and was so mean.

'I knew if I went there, it would hurt so much and I'd cry in front of everyone. Like I am now. Sorry, Mia. I didn't mean to—'

'It's fine,' she whispered. 'Would you like a hug? I know I would.'

'Definitely.'

Next thing, Mia was crying into his shirt as he carefully

wrapped his arms around her and tried to hold himself together in the process. Why was he getting so emotional about something that had happened so long ago? His tears certainly weren't for Diane, although seeing Mia this fragile and distressed was tough to witness. And then there was everything that had just happened with Hannah, of course. Was it really a surprise he felt wretched?

As they embraced, neither speaking, Mark wondered if this was what it felt like to be a father. His feelings for Mia at that moment were certainly different to anything he'd experienced previously. Holding her like this, although it was something they'd never done before, felt right. It probably ought to have been uncomfortable, awkward. But it wasn't. The closest comparison he could make to it were the hugs he used to have with his mum when he was a boy: the ones that somehow made him feel like everything would be all right. But now he was on the other side. And more than anything, he wanted Mia to believe that everything would be all right. He desperately wished he could protect her from all the pain she felt and would continue to feel at the loss of her mother, even though he knew that wasn't possible. But he could at least help, right? He could try to ease that pain even if he couldn't get rid of it.

'Shall I put the kettle on?' Mark asked eventually, once both of them seemed to have reached a calmer place in their minds.

'That sounds nice.'

As he did so, he had an idea he immediately put to Mia. 'Why don't we watch a film to take our minds off everything? What do you think? Maybe we could find a Marvel one we both fancy.'

'Sure. What about Hannah, though? Don't you think you ought to call her to check she's okay? Where's she likely to have gone? She will be all right, won't she?'

'Don't you worry about any of that, Mia. I'll try to get hold of her very soon, I promise. But before I do, I'm not sure I made it clear what I was trying to say when I told you about Pete. Firstly, I wanted to let you know that I'm here any time you want to talk about how you're feeling. I thought that might be easier if you knew I'd experienced a loss of my own when I was a boy. It's okay to feel like you did when you walked past Costa. It's a natural part of the grieving process. But if you can, I'd recommend you go in there rather than trying to avoid it. I did that for a long time with the park where Pete had wanted to play football. It was only years later that I went in there, at the suggestion of Hannah.

'She encouraged me to face my fears and so eventually I did; she even came with me. It was emotional. I cried a lot. But it also helped me to get past that guilt I'd always felt. It was something I should have done a lot sooner. Now, when I go there, I can focus on the happy times Pete and I had. I've accepted I was just a kid when I said those nasty things to him; beating myself up about it won't make a jot of difference. It'll only make me miserable.'

After pausing to pour the hot water from the kettle into the waiting mugs, Mark asked a silent Mia: 'Does that make sense?'

She nodded.

271

'I'm not saying to do it straight away, but when you're ready, you definitely should go there. Order a hot chocolate, like you used to. You could even get a latte for your mum, if you liked. And you wouldn't have to do it alone. I'd be happy to come with you, and I know Hannah would too. We're both here for you, whatever you need.'

'Thank you,' she replied in a tiny voice.

They tidied up the kitchen together. Then Mark told Mia to amuse herself for a few minutes while he tried to contact her aunt. 'We'll find a good movie after that, okay? But if you want to start looking and come up with a few suggestions, be my guest.'

CHAPTER 23

Mark walked through to the bedroom, a sinking feeling in his stomach at the prospect of what Hannah might have to say to him. And that was assuming she answered his call in the first place.

He'd been considering where she might have gone ever since Mia had told him about her leaving – and the most likely place he could think of, assuming it was local and not a hotel, was Laura and Ralph's house in Prestwich. It was a decent-sized four-bedroom semi they'd moved to with a view to filling it with a family: something that had never happened, thanks to their fertility issues and various failed IVF attempts. There was plenty of room to accommodate a guest anyway, and although it was about four miles north of the city centre, it was easily and quickly reachable by tram. Plus, unlike a hotel, it came with a friend ready to listen to her problems. At least if Hannah was there he didn't have to worry about her safety.

He pulled his mobile out of the pocket of his shorts

and stared at it before switching the screen on. No messages or missed calls. Damn. He'd deliberately not checked it while in the kitchen with Mia, knowing it was on silent. As each minute had passed, he'd hoped against hope that the chances of Hannah contacting him might have increased. But of course she hadn't done so. Why would she? If his wife had wanted him to know where she was and what she was doing, she'd have told him before leaving.

He called her number and held the phone up to his ear as a wave of anxiety set his stomach churning. It rang several times before going to voicemail.

'Hi, Hannah,' he said into his phone. 'It's Mark. Mia tells me she saw you heading out and, well, I totally get that you need some space. You must be going through hell at the moment; I wish more than anything that I wasn't in any way responsible. It might not seem like it right now, but I love you so much. What happened with Diane all those years ago . . . it isn't as straightforward as you might think. There are things I'd like to try to explain to you, if you'll let me; whenever you're ready. For now, though, please could you at least let me know you're okay and somewhere safe?'

Mark ended the call. He had considered mentioning that Mia was concerned about her, but thought better of it. This was between him and Hannah.

Would her discovery affect how she felt about Mia? It was bound to change the way she looked at her to some degree, but Mark felt certain his wife wouldn't let it harm her newly rekindled relationship with her niece. Hannah's love, affection and sympathy for Mia would prevail, he was sure.

Unfortunately, he was far less confident about the direction their marriage would take from here. Hannah walking out on him was totally justified in the circumstances – and yet he hadn't predicted it. He'd expected her to kick him out instead. Now he desperately wanted to explain to Hannah what had really happened between him and Diane that night. This was crucial. Their whole future depended on it.

Meanwhile, ironically, Mark felt like he and Mia had grown closer tonight. He was glad he'd told her about Pete's death. The hug afterwards had been a lovely surprise. Considering how little they actually knew each other, he wouldn't have dared to instigate it himself, for fear of being inappropriate. But coming from her, it had been so sweet; for the first time he'd genuinely felt that maybe they could make the father/daughter thing work somehow. He'd have to tell her the truth first, however, and there was a good chance this revelation would in fact have the opposite effect and drive her away.

What he hadn't explained to Mia about Pete's death was the profound, long-term impact it had had on his family and his whole outlook on life. This, as he'd confirmed to Hannah a long time ago, was a key reason he'd decided he'd never wanted children.

He'd instigated the chat on a freezing winter's night in Didsbury, where they'd lived at the time, both still in their twenties. It was a conversation designed as a precursor to popping the question; a way to ensure they were on the same page in terms of their future together. Having considered the matter at length, he'd finally plucked up the courage to actually say the words after a boozy meal out together.

'I don't really get children and I don't want to be responsible for bringing another life into this world.' That was how he'd phrased it to her, emphasising that this was not going to change. Then he'd risked everything by giving her the chance to walk away if she absolutely couldn't live without having a family.

They'd discussed the subject before, but never head-on like this. Mark had always got the impression that Hannah felt, wrongly, she would be able to change his mind when the time was right. So although giving her an ultimatum – choose me or kids – might have seemed cruel on the surface, to him it had felt like the most decent, honest course of action he could take.

'Is it because of what happened to your brother, Pete?' she'd gone on to ask him.

'That's not the only reason,' he'd replied, 'but yes. I think his death and what it did to the rest of us is definitely a huge part of it.'

Hannah had nodded pensively before adding: 'Sometimes horrendous things happen. That's the reality of life. But don't you think maybe the best response is to carry on regardless; to live our lives as fully as we can rather than in fear?'

Mark had understood her argument, but his mind had been made up on this matter long ago and there was zero chance of him being swayed.

'I'm not living my life in fear,' he'd replied. 'I'm being selective and choosing my own path, based on my experiences and beliefs. Lots of people want children and that's fine. I don't. I know that's not the most common way of thinking, but that doesn't make it wrong. It's right for me. Whether it's also right for you, Hannah, is your choice, and I'll respect that absolutely. Sometimes the best way to show you love someone is to let them go rather than hold them back.'

'Isn't love also about compromise, though: give and take?'

'Yes, but I can't compromise on this. I'm sorry. It's a decision I made a long time ago and I won't change my mind.'

If Mark had to pinpoint the exact moment he'd reached this conclusion, it would be the day his dad, Patrick Cook, had left. That had been a year or so after Pete's death, which had devastated them all, but his father in particular. A self-employed electrician by trade, he'd stopped working in the aftermath of the tragedy and had fallen into a severe depression. From then on he'd spent his days staring blankly at the TV and drinking endless pints of homebrew, the creation of which was about the only thing that got him out of his armchair other than using the toilet and going to bed.

Meanwhile, Alma Cook, Mark's mum, had had to hold things together by working all hours as a cleaner: houses by day and offices by night. They'd both been dealing with their grief in different ways, with Mark stuck in the middle and left largely to his own devices. Then, one day, when he'd got into trouble at school for skipping classes with some other lads, despite usually being a model student, Alma had exploded. She'd held Mark's dad responsible, telling him enough was enough and it was time to pull himself together for the sake of his family. When Mark had got home the next day, the house had been empty. Patrick had gone, never to return or show any further interest in his remaining son.

He'd only seen him a handful of times since, usually pissed out of his head, drinking in the street or coming out of some dive bar or another. Last Mark had heard, he was living in a council flat somewhere in Reddish. He didn't have the address. What use would he have for it? As far as he was concerned, he didn't have a father any more.

Patrick had been a normal dad before Pete had been killed: out at work every day and around at home more often than not at night and on the weekends. Not the best father in the world, perhaps, in that he was very much a hands-off parent, but not the worst either. He'd never got physical with either of his sons or his wife, which was more than could be said for the dads of some of Mark's school friends. Thankfully, that hadn't changed after Pete's death, but he'd certainly become a lot more bad-tempered, snapping at him and his mum over the slightest thing and showing little interest in anything other than drinking his beer and watching his programmes on the box.

Parents weren't supposed to show favouritism towards one child over another, were they? Well, Mark had suspected from a young age that his brother was his dad's favourite. Patrick had always seemed to side with Pete when the two of them had argued about anything. He'd generally had more time for him too. Mark had tried to convince himself it was because Pete was so much younger; deep down, however, he'd sensed it was more than that, which Patrick's reaction to his death had more or less confirmed. Who knew why? Mark had long since given up caring.

But it was the fact that Patrick had abandoned him and his mother, without warning or explanation, that would forever define Mark's view of his dad. What kind of father did that? All three of them had lost Pete; Patrick's selfish response to an awful situation had only made it worse. Hence it had sealed the deal in terms of Mark's decision not to have children. Not only had he seen first-hand what losing a child could do to a parent; he also feared the possibility of becoming a bad one, like his father.

The irony was that he had become a version of his father, regardless. It may not have been deliberate on his part, but Mia had grown up without him so far. So now, one way or another, it was his responsibility to change that. At least he'd had one good role model to help him do so in the shape of his mother.

Alma had never been anything short of a fantastic parent, working her heart out to make up for Patrick's absence and pushing Mark in the right direction through school and university to play to his academic strengths. Unlike Patrick, she'd never shown any favouritism while Pete was around either.

Mark was very aware of the key role Alma had played

in shaping his life. Without her guiding and inspiring him as a youngster, he'd never have found himself in such a fortunate financial position today. He enjoyed spoiling her in return whenever he got the chance. He'd encouraged her to retire at the earliest possible opportunity, which she now had. He'd even offered to help her move to a nice little apartment somewhere nearby in the city centre, but she'd preferred to stay in the terraced house where he'd grown up in Stockport.

'This is my home and it has been for years,' she'd explained. 'My life's here. All my friends and so on. Why would I want to move?'

'Okay, Mum,' he'd replied. 'I understand. Wherever you're most happy. But if there are any improvements you'd like – a new bathroom perhaps, or whatever you fancy – I'd love to make that happen.'

Not that she'd taken him up on this offer so far. She was a woman of simple tastes, bless her. But he had at least managed to treat her to a couple of coach trips abroad. And thanks to him, she had arguably the best set of bowls out of anyone in the club where she'd started playing.

His mum had always respected his decision not to have children, while still making it clear she would have liked him to, nonetheless. He recalled what she'd told him five years earlier, having taken him aside for a private word on his fortieth birthday.

'I understand your reluctance,' she'd said, 'but you are not your father and you shouldn't be led by his failures. Having children is an amazing gift. Losing our little Pete was horrendous. I still miss him every single day; I always will. But not for an instant have I ever wished he wasn't born at all. He brought so much joy into the world in his short time here. And I'll always have those memories to counter the bad ones. It's your right not to have children, Mark. For the record, though, I think you and Hannah would make damn fine parents.'

Her message had been clear: there was time to change their minds, but it was last-chance saloon. Hannah had been thirty-seven at that point: still of child-bearing age, but not for too much longer.

'Sorry, Mum,' Mark had said, shrugging before pulling her into a hug. 'I love you to bits, but it's not going to happen.'

Looking on the bright side of recent events, maybe he would, after all, be able to give Alma the grandchild she longed for, even if Mia wasn't quite the tiny bundle of joy she might have pictured.

What if his mum had been right all along about him and Hannah raising a child together? Would they ever get the chance to find out now that he'd blown things so spectacularly with her, the woman he adored? She was his wife, his best friend, the love of his life. The idea of being without her terrified him. So could he somehow manage to do the impossible and fix their marriage?

One way or another, Mark knew he had to do the right thing by Mia, like Alma had by him after Pete's death and Patrick's desertion. But how much better would life be for Mia – for both of them – if he could do so together with her aunt? Hannah wasn't Mia's mother and never would be. But how could anyone be a better fit to raise her in Diane's place?

Glancing over at his phone, still on silent, he noticed a text had arrived from Hannah, which he opened up.

I'm okay and somewhere safe.

That was it. That was the entire message. She'd taken his voicemail request literally. Better than nothing, though. He slipped the phone back into his pocket and exited the bedroom.

'Coming, ready or not, Mia,' he said in a feeble attempt to inject some levity into the situation. 'Have you found something good for us to watch?'

CLIENT SESSION TRANSCRIPT:
HCOOK090819

H: I'm sorry to start off crying . . . I told myself I wasn't going to do this . . . If you could please give me a moment?

S: Of course. Take your time, Hannah.

H: Thanks. Let me grab a tissue or two.

S: Help yourself. Can I get you a glass of water?

H: No, I'm fine, thank you. I had a couple in the waiting room. Right. Okay, I think I'm ready to carry on now. I've had some devastating news, on top of Diane's death. After I saw you yesterday, I found a letter my sister had written to Mark. In it she revealed that . . . I'm sorry, this is hard to say . . . Diane revealed that he, um, is Mia's dad.

S: Your Mark? He's the mysterious father your sister never revealed? My God! You poor thing. Have you confronted him about it? Has he admitted it's true?

H: Yes, we had a short conversation. He swore to me they'd only ever slept together once, all those years ago; that it was a huge mistake he's regretted ever since. It also seems he knew nothing about being Mia's father until the letter, which Diane wrote in our apartment during her recent visit. But none of that helps. Obviously I'm in bits, as you can see. I walked out. I'm staying with friends. Mark's been the one constant in my life for so long. I trusted him completely – and now I learn he's betrayed me in the worst imaginable way. He also gave her the one thing he's always kept me from having: a child. You wouldn't believe how much that part in particular hurts, even though it doesn't appear to have been deliberate. I feel like my whole world has collapsed. Where on earth do I go from here, Sally?

S: Well, I think going to stay with your friends for a while was a sensible move. Clearly this is a complicated situation and you need time away from it to allow yourself to think. My advice would be to avoid making any hasty decisions while everything is so raw and emotional. And although I understand you might not want to see him at all right now, I think you do need to talk it over in more detail with Mark, to find out exactly what happened and why.

H: I guess so. Just thinking about him sleeping with my sister makes me feel physically sick at the moment, though. And it's hard to comprehend all the lies they must have told between them. I feel angry rather than surprised at Diane. But Mark? I can't express how distressing his betrayal feels, how agonising. It's like I don't know my own husband at all. I didn't think he was capable of this. I thought he loved me. Honestly, Sally, I don't think I've ever felt so conflicted before in my life. My emotions are all over the place, particularly in relation to Diane. I hate her for doing this to me. And yet she's gone forever – my flesh and blood. I still wish she wasn't, even though that's partly because I want to shout and scream at her; to slap her around the face. What an absolute nightmare!

S: How are you feeling in yourself? You seem to be holding up pretty well, considering.

H: I feel too angry to let this break me. I might not be able to stop the tears falling, but I'm not going to allow myself to go to pieces over this. Strong, successful, confident: I have those words playing on repeat in my head. I'm using them to try to drown out all the negative stuff.

S: Excellent. That's very good to hear. What about Mia? Does she know what you've learned?

H: No, not to my knowledge. Goodness knows how she'll react when she does find out.

S: Do you think this will affect your relationship with her?

H: I hope not. It wouldn't be fair on her, particularly so soon after losing her mum. And do you know what? I think it could be me and Mark who Diane named as Mia's guardians in her will. We agreed to it years ago, before she and I fell out, and I have a feeling she won't have changed it. I think that might even be why she left Mia with us in the first place, knowing she intended to kill herself. And so things get messier still.

S: Do you think you could make that work?

H: I don't even know if Mark and I have a future as a married couple right now, so—

S: What about without this latest revelation? In a world where Mark hadn't cheated on you with Diane and Mia wasn't his daughter, would you be able to picture the three of you making a go of it?

H: Um, yes. I mean, I already gave that a little thought before finding Diane's letter to Mark. My view then was that we could try to make it work. I know Mark and I are used to a certain child-free way of life, with the luxury holidays and impromptu city breaks; the regular nights out to dinner followed by a concert or the theatre. But how much does any of that really matter? I've not missed it while she's been staying with us. And it's not like you can't do any of those things when you're a parent anyway. There's just a bit more organising involved. Plus I always wanted to have a family, as we discussed before. Mark didn't, but he was there when we agreed to be Mia's guardians should anything happen to Diane. And surely she's the person who should be considered above anyone else in this matter. She's lost her mother. She's family. The only other realistic option, as far as I can see, would be for her to go and live with my father and his wife, Joan. But he's already sixty-seven and Joan is, well, not the easiest or most flexible woman to get along with, to put it kindly.

S: So what about in the real world, where Mark is Mia's father?

H: I honestly don't know. If Mark and I were to split up, who would she be best living with out of the two of us? Me, her mum's sister, or Mark, the father she thinks is her uncle? Dad would usually trump aunt in such a situation, but what if we decide now's not the right time to tell her the truth about her parentage, in light of everything else she's been through? Then I'd be the blood relative, as far as she was concerned, not Mark.

S: You've clearly given this some thought already.

H: It's all I can think about. Laura and Ralph, the couple I'm staying with, tried and failed to have kids via IVF. It sounds awful, but I remember a tiny part of me secretly feeling glad when she didn't get pregnant, because I knew I'd be envious of her if she did. I've never told anyone that before. I was feeling guilty about it as I lay in their spare bed last night after they'd both been so kind and welcoming to me. It made me realise how much I have always wanted children, even though I tried my utmost to bury that desire for the sake of my marriage. How ironic is that, considering what we now know about my husband? Honestly, what I really need at the moment is for someone to tell me what to do next to find my way out of this appalling situation. But you're not going to do that, are you?

S: It's not my place to tell you what to do, Hannah. But hopefully talking it through here with me will help guide you towards your own solution.

H: Mark wants to talk, in person preferably. I can't face that today, but maybe tomorrow. Any advice you can offer about that?

S: It sounds like a good idea, but I'd suggest doing it somewhere neutral and public rather than at home. These kinds of discussions often work best that way. It helps both parties to stay calm when otherwise they might get overly emotional.

H: Okay. The thought of seeing him terrifies and repulses me at this moment, but there's too much at stake not to do it. He claims what happened isn't as straight-forward as it might appear, but that's what cheats always say, right?

S: Meet him. Tell him honestly how you feel. Hear him out, if you can. You never know.

H: I'll try. Thank you, Sally. This does feel like it's helped.

S: That's good to hear. I wish you all the very best with it. Hopefully things can only get better from here.

CHAPTER 24

Hannah looked out of the rain-flecked window of the tram as it darted through some of Manchester's more gritty northern suburbs on its way back to the affluent city centre.

Laura and Ralph's home in Prestwich was lovely, located a stone's throw away from the sprawling green of Heaton Park; the same couldn't be said for some of the rundown, litter-strewn spots currently jarring her vision. So Hannah closed her eyes and thought back to the time she'd spent walking and thinking in the park after returning from her session with Sally yesterday, before her temporary hosts had got back from work. She'd cut a solitary figure among the many local families making the most of the warm weather and school holidays, playing and relaxing in the pleasant, leafy surroundings.

Today, in sharp contrast, it felt like autumn: a grey nothingness up above, spitting out constant drizzle. This remained true when Hannah exited the tram at Piccadilly

Gardens a short while later, but it didn't seem to matter so much, thanks to the improved backdrop of busy shops, bars and restaurants that felt like home.

She'd phoned Laura's mobile after leaving the apartment building on Thursday evening and, thank goodness, her old friend had answered straight away.

'Are you home?' she'd blurted out. 'I'm in a bit of a mess and, I hate to ask, but is there any chance I could come to stay tonight?'

Laura had agreed instantly, which was amazing of her considering how little they'd seen each other of late, and one night had turned into two. 'Stay as long as you need to,' Laura had told her that first night after they'd had a weepy heart-to-heart over the kitchen table, Ralph having made himself scarce. 'We've plenty of room. It's absolutely fine, honestly.'

Unsurprisingly, Laura had been shocked to hear everything that had happened; particularly the bits about Diane's apparent suicide and Mark being the father of Hannah's teenage niece.

'Oh my God, Han,' she'd said, her jaw on the floor. 'You poor thing. No wonder you needed some space. I can hardly believe it all. I mean, I never knew your sister, but . . . Mark . . . I'm dumbstruck. I'd never have guessed he could do something like this to you. I didn't have him pegged as that kind of person. Not for a moment. Ralph and I have always thought of you two as such a strong, well-matched couple. I'm . . . well, I don't know what to say. Did you ever have any clue or—'

'No. I didn't think he was that kind of man either. I've

never worried about Mark cheating, especially not with my twin sister. To be honest, I always thought they didn't like each other. More fool me.'

Laura had squeezed her friend's hand. 'Has Mark given you, um, any kind of explanation? I mean, I'm not saying it might be justifiable in any way, but it seems so out of character. Do you think it was a full-blown affair or a one-night thing? And how long has he known about Mia being his daughter?'

Hannah had shaken her head and sighed. She'd felt utterly drained. Beyond tears. 'He claims it only happened once and never with anyone else. He left me a voicemail saying something about it not being straightforward and wanting to explain. But how can I believe a word he tells me ever again? As for Mia, I don't think he knew about being her father until very recently. Diane's letter, which she wrote in our apartment before heading back to Bournemouth, seemed to be telling him about it for the first time. And yet there was a reference to him suspecting it in the past, at which point she'd denied it.'

'Right. And do you think her coming clean to him was linked to why she killed herself?'

'I guess it must be, Laura. That and leaving Mia with us like she did. There was definitely something going on with her. But do you know what? I'm not sure I even want to know the details. My relationship with Diane was damaged enough before this latest revelation. Now I'm struggling to feel anything but anger and hatred when I think of her.'

Soon after that Hannah had gone to bed in Laura and

Ralph's comfortable, well-appointed spare room. But neither the nice surroundings nor her tiredness had aided her sleep, which had been as fitful that night as the next, filled with nightmares of failure and frustration. Most had since slipped away from her memory, as dreams are wont to do, but the crux of one still remained. It had been about the release of her novel, which had been such a huge flop that a truck filled with thousands of unsold copies had arrived outside her apartment, with the driver insisting she took delivery of the lot.

She still vividly remembered the climax of the dream, when she'd screamed: 'What the hell am I supposed to do with them? I can't possibly store all of these books.'

'You should have thought of that before you wrote something so terrible,' the driver had snarled in reply, slapping his clipboard and pen into her hands for a signature.

Strangely, neither Mark nor Diane had featured at all, despite the two of them being at the forefront of her conscious thoughts.

After waking from this particular nightmare, Hannah had been unable to sleep for a long stretch. During this time – probably because she was at Laura's house – her mind had skipped back to that car-crash moment at her old work, when she'd made such an idiot of herself in public.

She and Laura had both been in an important meeting with several other colleagues, including two senior managers, plus a set of key clients. One of these clients, a particularly demanding type, had criticised some copy she'd worked hard on, grinning as he did so, seemingly jeering at her. Without warning, a fury had erupted from deep within. She'd jumped to her feet in the boardroom, hurled her notes and pen against the window and called him a 'self-righteous prick' who should try writing the bloody thing himself next time. As if that wasn't bad enough, before storming out of there, she'd told everyone in the room, all gaping at her in disbelief, that they were 'phonies spouting bullshit' and the whole advertising industry was 'a bloody con, a meaningless waste of time'.

They'd have definitely fired her if it hadn't been for lovely Laura speaking up on her behalf, explaining about the stress she'd been going through as a result of her mother's death and then her falling-out with Diane. Instead Hannah had been advised to see a doctor, who'd signed her off work on stress and referred her for counselling. A couple of months later, having reached the conclusion that she never wanted to return there, she'd offered her resignation and they'd accepted. Remembering the incident still made Hannah shudder to this day. It also reminded her of how low she'd felt afterwards, before the writing had given her a new purpose, to the extent that she'd even had the odd suicidal thought. Were she and Diane so different after all?

Hannah had spoken to her dad several times while in Prestwich, but she hadn't let on that she wasn't at home. She couldn't bring herself to tell him. He had enough to deal with at her sister's house in Bournemouth, where he and Joan were busy trying to piece together what had happened to lead Diane to kill herself in such a drastic and brutal manner. Her sister had disliked their stepmother even more than Hannah did; a small part of her saw the black humour in the idea of Diane shaking her fists from beyond the grave as Joan rooted through her knicker drawer and other personal items.

One significant find so far had been a series of hospital letters tucked under her mattress. Joan had found these, according to Frank, which hadn't surprised Hannah in the slightest. If ever there was someone likely to root out a good hiding spot, it was her devious stepmum. Anyway, they seemed to point to her having some kind of cancer, which was a shock to all of them.

'She never said anything to you, Dad?' Hannah had asked. 'Nothing to suggest she was unwell?'

'No, definitely not. How did she look when she came up to Manchester?'

'Well, older than I remember, but that's hardly a surprise after so long. Thinner than she used to be; a bit frazzled. She was worked up about something. She mentioned being in a big mess, which was why she wanted to leave Mia with us. But she never let on what was wrong. My first guess was money trouble, but now I think about it she could have been ill.'

'What about Mia?' Frank had asked next. 'She must have known if her mum had cancer.'

'I doubt it. I'm sure she'd have said something if so.'

'Is she there? Can you ask her?'

'Um, no. She's popped out. I'll mention it later on, though.'

Frank had sounded surprisingly together, compared to

the awful state he'd been in after Hannah's mum had died. He was most likely operating on autopilot; keeping busy rather than allowing his mind to dwell on the brutal reality of his daughter's death. The last thing he'd said to her on the phone was that he would pass the letters on to the police and the coroner in the hope they might be useful in terms of reaching a verdict at the eventual inquest.

Meanwhile, Hannah hadn't spoken to her husband once since walking out on him. He'd phoned her plenty of times, but she'd been ignoring all of his calls. He'd eventually managed to work out where she'd gone, apparently contacting Ralph directly for confirmation.

'I hope you don't mind that I told him,' Ralph had said to her afterwards. 'His call took me by surprise and, well, he sounded really worried. I did advise him not to come here, though; to give you some space.'

She'd told Mark the same by text message. He'd agreed not to come to Prestwich, but in return he'd asked her to meet him in a neutral place today so they could talk. That was where she was heading now, this busy Saturday morning, to a café they'd been to together a couple of times previously on the edge of the Northern Quarter. It was one of those places frequented during the week by trendy young folk with fat headphones and skinny laptops. She'd even tried writing in there a couple of times when she'd felt a bit cabin-feverish in the apartment. But weekends drew in a more chatty, social bunch – young lovebirds and the like – the thought of which made Hannah feel sick as she walked the last few yards as slowly as she could, dreading seeing Mark.

Why had she agreed to meet him? Mia, an innocent party in the whole mess, was the main reason. Despite everything, she was still her niece and she'd just lost her mother. Hannah wasn't about to abandon her – not for more than a couple of days anyway – and so that needed discussing, even though she'd rather not see her husband yet or hear whatever excuses he had to offer. She wondered how Mark had managed juggling work and Mia yesterday. Surely he hadn't gone in as usual and left her alone for the whole day at a time when she was so vulnerable.

Would she be returning home after this meeting or not? She could do with popping in to get some fresh clothes at least, but she couldn't see further than that right now. Maybe she ought to have kicked Mark out and been the one to stay. That was still a possibility. But if he was Mia's father, she should be with him, right? Plus Hannah had felt stifled at home, where she spent most of her time anyway.

She'd needed to get away to find some breathing space, which Laura and Ralph had been good enough to provide. It was the first time she'd seen Ralph in ages, as the last few occasions she'd met up with Laura – also fairly infrequently – it had been the two of them over a coffee in town.

So why was it Laura she'd turned to at her time of need, despite not being as close to her now as previously? In truth, other than Kathy who lived too nearby, there wasn't really anyone else. In between jacking in her job, overcoming her breakdown and carving out a new career for herself, she hadn't had much time for friends, old or new. Her life these days revolved around Mark – her supposed rock, lover and best friend – plus the fictional characters she created in her books. Or should she say book? It wasn't like she'd made any meaningful progress on her second novel in recent days. Her mind was far too preoccupied with the real-life drama erupting all around her.

Anyway, the last thing Laura had said to her, having walked her to the tram stop this morning, was that she was welcome to return and stay for longer. 'If you want to come back; if it doesn't feel right, just do it. It's no problem at all, seriously.'

Walking through the rain, her mind awash with all these thoughts and recent memories, Hannah almost stepped out in front of a black cab while trying to cross one of the city centre's busy roads.

The sound of its horn blaring jolted her back into the moment. She saw the driver shaking his fist and mouthing something unpleasant at her through the windscreen as time froze for an instant. And then he was gone. Hannah was jostled back on her way by a musty-smelling mass of damp pedestrians even more eager than usual to get where they were going to escape the wet.

Soon she was outside the café and peering through the glass door at the bustling sales counter, awash with cellophane-wrapped snacks under the shadow of steaming, gleaming coffee machines. She took a deep breath. Thought about turning on her heel and walking away. She could use this opportunity to whip into the apartment while Mark was out and grab some more stuff, couldn't she? It was sorely tempting, but no: she had to do this.

Before she had a chance to change her mind, she bit down on her bottom lip and strode through the door. She scanned the large, high-ceilinged room with its exposed brickwork and wooden floors. And then, in among the chattering clientele, she saw him stand up and wave to her from a far corner. Neither of them smiled as she walked over to the brown leather booth he'd selected and sat down opposite him with a curt, 'Hello'.

He sat down too. 'Hi, Hannah. Thanks so much for coming. I, er, wasn't sure you would. How've you been?'

She resisted the temptation to confirm that she nearly hadn't come. 'How do you think I've been?'

'Right. Yeah, sorry. Stupid question. Can I get you a drink or anything else?'

'In a minute. What about Mia? Where is she at the moment? How's she coping?'

'She's round at Kathy's with, um, whatsisname.'

'Todd?'

'Exactly. She's okay. Pretty quiet. Not really talking too much about anything. I've made sure she's not been on her own, other than in her bedroom and stuff. I haven't told her anything yet about, um, you know what. I said we'd had a row but didn't elaborate. I know you want me to tell her soon, but it would be too much for her at the moment. I'm certain of that.'

'Right.'

He hesitated before going on: 'I did tell her about Pete. I, er, thought it might be of some use to her to know I'd been through a loss too when I was a child. It seemed to help.'

Hannah nodded in silence. This actually sounded like

298

quite a good idea, but she wasn't about to congratulate him for it.

'How are things going down in Bournemouth?' he asked. 'Any talk yet of when the funeral might be?' Mark's hands were intertwined in front of him, like he was trying to keep them from fidgeting; his elbows were resting on the edge of the table.

'No, not as far as I've heard. Dad and Joan are busy trying to work out what happened. I don't think they've even met with a funeral director yet.'

'Okay, sure. It's just that Mia's been asking. Understandably, she wants to be involved.' He sighed before adding: 'I know this must be difficult to discuss with me in light of, er—'

'What?' Hannah replied in a deliberately loud voice. 'The fact you slept with my sister?'

Mark's cheeks flushed; he looked sheepishly down at the table. 'The thing is, I think she ought to be down there with them.'

'Right. Are you volunteering to take her, then? She's your daughter.'

'I can do, if that's what you want,' he replied, to Hannah's surprise. 'They know what's going on at work and they've been very understanding. I was able to take yesterday off and, well—'

'They know what's going on, do they? Everything?'

Mark pulled his hands apart and dragged them across his face and hair, giving himself a momentary facelift. 'No, obviously not everything. Just about Diane's death and Mia staying with us.'

'I see.'

At that moment a young member of staff with spiky red hair appeared at the table with a coffee for Mark. 'Here you are, sir: your flat white,' he said. 'Sorry about the wait. We've fixed the issue with the machine now.'

'Could I have a cup of tea, please?' Hannah asked.

The lad wrinkled his nose. 'Sorry, it's not table service. I—'

'It's okay,' Mark said, standing up. 'I'll go and get that for you.'

She was about to tell him not to bother, feeling annoyed, but he was already on his way.

Maybe she ought to be the one to head to Bournemouth with Mia, Hannah thought while alone in the booth. Not for her sister or Mark, but for her niece and her dad. Both of them deserved her support. They were bound to be hurting terribly over the loss of Diane.

'Here you go,' Mark said. He slid a hot white teapot in front of her followed by a cup and saucer with a paper-wrapped English breakfast teabag on the side plus a small jug of milk. 'Sorry, I forgot to ask if you'd like anything to eat. I can go back if you—'

'Could you please sit down now, Mark?' She let out a long sigh.

'Of course,' he replied, doing as she asked.

'So what is it you wanted to talk to me about?' Hannah said without looking at him, busying herself by opening the teabag and preparing her drink.

He nodded purposefully, more times than seemed necessary. 'Sure, okay. I, um, well, obviously I feel awful. I can't imagine what it must have been like for you, finding out . . . *that* . . . in the way you did, especially so soon after hearing about Diane's death. I'm so unbelievably—'

'Don't you dare say sorry to me now or I'll throw this tea all over you. You can stick your apology. If you really did regret it, you'd have come clean years ago. The only thing you're sorry about is that you got found out.'

'That's not true, Hannah. I've never regretted anything more in my life. I might not have told you about it. I hold my hands up to that. But I've spent every day since trying to make it up to you. I'm nothing without you, Hannah. I'd do anything if you could—'

'Stop!' Hannah could feel herself welling up, which made her angry, as she'd been determined not to cry in front of Mark today. She wanted to look strong, like she could manage without him in a heartbeat.

'I'm sorry, I—'

'I asked you to stop talking. Seriously. I really don't want to hear it. If that's all you have to say, then we might as well end this conversation now. Could you be quiet for a bit and drink your coffee? I can't think with you badgering me.'

Returning to Laura's house felt all but inevitable now, at least for a few more nights. Looking her lying, cheating husband in the face was too much. She couldn't get the image out of her head of him and her sister writhing around naked, laughing at her expense. And Diane: that scheming bitch was worse than him. She'd even had the bare-faced cheek to ask Hannah to be with her in the birthing room when Mia was born, knowing full well her baby was the product of her illicit union with Mark. And to think part of her had felt bad all these years about the two of them falling out: like it was somehow her fault more than Diane's; like she maybe ought to have been more understanding of her sister's situation as a single parent.

A silence had fallen over the table following the last words Hannah had spat at Mark, to which he clearly didn't know how best to respond. Having looked away from him across the café while she pondered the situation, Hannah now turned back and watched him, sipping his coffee and examining his hands as if they might hold the secret to fixing things. He looked cowed and pathetic. Despite herself, Hannah felt a little sorry for him. Not that she had any intention of letting him know.

She considered saying something to break the deadlock she'd created, but instead let him stew.

Her mind was busy now anyway. It was on a course of its own, hurtling through the years; returning to that specific time when everything had changed irrevocably for her, Diane and the rest of the family. It was travelling back to the moment, soon after their mother's death, when the two of them had had that awful row: the one that had effectively ended their relationship as twin sisters once and for all.

CHAPTER 25

October 2008

'Where's Dad going with Mia?' Hannah asked her sister after spotting their father heading out through the front door with his granddaughter in tow, both wrapped up warm.

'He's taking her out for a walk along the beach,' Diane replied. 'It was my suggestion. He clearly didn't want to be around for this and Mia was getting bored, so it seemed like the ideal solution.'

'He really doesn't want to be involved?' Hannah asked. They were about to go through Mum's stuff for the first time since her death. She'd expected Frank to be an active part of the process, but apparently Diane knew otherwise.

'No, he thinks it'll be too traumatic.'

'Since when?'

'Since he told me so earlier.'

'What if we get rid of things he wants to keep?' Hannah asked her sister.

'He says it's up to us. Besides, he won't be gone that

long. Anything we're not sure about, we can put to one side and ask him when he gets back.'

Hannah sat down on the bed. 'Do you think it's too soon, Di?' Their mum had passed away at the end of March and it was now early October: a chilly but bright and crisp day. The sunlight streaming through the large window of their parents' bedroom – now just her father's – at least helped brighten the mood a little.

'No, it was Dad's idea, remember?' Diane sat down next to her, placing a hand on her knee and giving it a reassuring squeeze. 'He might not like the nitty-gritty of actually doing it, but he knows it needs to be done. What's the point in him keeping these cupboards and drawers full of Mum's things? It's not like he's ever going to use any of them, is it? He won't be able to move on otherwise.'

'I don't know,' Hannah replied. 'He seems to be doing all right. That neighbour of his, Joan, is certainly around here a lot. He mentions her all the time.'

Diane nodded. 'Oh, you've noticed that too. I really don't like her. Dad talks about her like she's a really caring, kind person, but she's clearly trying to get her claws into him. It's one of the reasons I think we need to do this now, to make sure she doesn't try to get her grubby mitts on any of Mum's lovely jewellery. I'm sure she's a bloody gold-digger.'

Ah, the jewellery. Hannah had wondered how long it would take for that to come up. The two of them hadn't properly discussed this yet, but in her mind that was always going to be the most contentious part of this exercise.

Neither of them was likely to be too bothered about

having any of their mum's clothes. She was of another era, at the end of the day, and a different size to them. But her jewellery, of which there was a fair bit, mainly accumulated as gifts from Frank over the years, was a different matter. Some of it was probably worth quite a bit, although for Hannah it was about the sentimental value. Maggie's wishes had been that it should be split between the twins, with them deciding how between themselves. So far they'd skirted the issue: in Hannah's case, because she feared it would prove contentious and she hadn't wanted to rush to take anything away before her dad was ready. Now, however, there was no more avoiding it.

There were her mum's wedding and engagement rings, for one thing, plus a vintage engagement ring that had belonged to their grandmother. None of these items were first and foremost in Hannah's mind, though. There was one piece in particular she really wanted above everything else: a pearl-and-gold bracelet that had a wonderful story behind its creation.

The bracelet was modelled on a piece of costume jewellery Maggie had loved and regularly worn, but which had broken as she was about to head out one evening, spilling all over the bedroom floor and making her cry. Frank had picked up the pieces and, unbeknown to his wife, taken them to a jeweller together with a photo he'd found of her wearing the original bracelet. He'd secretly had a new version made with real pearls and gold, which he'd presented to her as a gift on their next wedding anniversary. Maggie had treasured it ever since and Hannah could still picture her proudly telling the story to anyone who happened to compliment her on the bracelet. Her father hadn't been known for his romantic gestures, which made this particular one really stand out, and was testament to his devotion to her mother.

Diane suggested they start the clear-out by going through the clothes. As expected, this didn't prove too difficult. Neither of them wanted much, other than the odd scarf or shawl, so there were no rows and most of it went into bags destined for charity shops. That wasn't to say the process wasn't emotionally draining. Hannah found that certain outfits reminded her of her mum in particular situations, from tending to the borders of her garden on a kneeler dressed in cords and a T-shirt, to attending a function in one of her many glamorous dresses.

'Oh my God! She wore this to my wedding,' Hannah said about one particular sky-blue frock, promptly bursting into tears. And Diane had a similar reaction when they came across the floral skirt and top she'd worn to Mia's christening.

As for Maggie's shoes, there were some lovely designer pairs. But since they weren't the right size for the twins, and neither had the heart to try to sell them, these were also earmarked to go to charity shops.

Eventually, they were done. The only things remaining were Maggie's wedding dress, which had previously been cleaned and boxed up, plus a few random bits and bobs Diane thought might be perfect for Mia's dressing-up basket.

'The cupboard looks so empty,' Diane said. 'We'll have

to take Dad out shopping for some new clothes of his own now before Joan gets any ideas about moving her stuff in.'

'Don't even joke about that, Di. A lot of widowers do find a new partner pretty quickly, you know. They don't seem to be able to manage as well on their own as widows do – particularly the ones of Dad's age with little experience of cooking and cleaning for themselves.'

'Oh, come on, Han. Dad's not bad at all that. He's been managing for a while now – ever since Mum got sick.'

Hannah flopped down on to an armchair at the foot of the bed and let out a tired sigh. 'Maybe, but he's not exactly Rick Stein. And I think we both know he'd rather be waited on than do everything himself. Do you think he'll stay here in Southport, actually, or that he might return to Manchester? He could always move in with you and Mia; kill two birds with one stone.'

Hannah had meant this to be funny, but it was clear from the furious look on her sister's face that she'd taken it a whole different way.

'What the hell's that supposed to mean?' Diane snapped.

'It was a joke, that's all.'

'No, I don't accept that, Hannah. You must have meant something by the whole "kill two birds with one stone" thing. What were you suggesting: that I can't manage by myself? Just because I don't have two salaries coming in, like you and Mark, doesn't mean Mia and I are on the breadline.'

Hannah wished she'd kept her mouth shut. 'I never said that you were, Diane.' She couldn't stop herself from adding: 'But the way you're reacting, I'm starting to wonder. It sounds like I hit a raw nerve.'

As Hannah remained seated, Diane stood in front of her, gesticulating wildly. 'What the hell do you know about it? Life's different when you have a child to consider, Hannah. It's not all about fancy holidays and swanky meals out.'

This comment made Hannah see red. 'What drivel are you spouting? If you don't have enough money, maybe you should try sticking a job out long enough to actually get a permanent contract, rather than going from one temp gig to the next. Where is it you even work at the moment? I've lost track. The reason I mentioned Dad moving in with you is because he's probably paying most of your bills already. How long is it that he's been helping you out now? Ever since you've had Mia, or even before she was born? Surely it would make more sense to get money from Mia's father, whoever he is, rather than pretending he doesn't exist. Call yourself a mother! You're nothing but a big child dressed in a parent's clothes.'

Diane's jaw hit the bedroom carpet. 'What? How dare you! And how do you even know about the money? Who told you? Was it Dad?'

'What the hell does that matter, Diane? Don't you think you ought to be standing on your own two feet by now, rather than relying on handouts?'

Diane snarled at her sister, lunging towards her like she was about to start a fistfight. 'You've always thought you're better than me. It makes me sick. You think your little life is so perfect, so much better than mine; that you know so much. Well, you don't know anything – especially not about having children. It's as well your precious Mark has never given you any kids, because you'd be a bloody awful mum.'

'How dare you!' Hannah shouted, jumping to her feet and standing toe to toe with Diane, so their noses were almost touching. She was itching to slap her or grab her by the hair, but somehow she managed to hold herself back, even as her sister's face broke into a spiteful, taunting grin.

'Oh, that's nothing,' Diane spat. 'I'm just getting started.'

At that moment, the front door of the bungalow opened. They both turned to look in the direction of the noise, which was swiftly followed by the sound of a child crying, overlaid by their father's voice: 'We're back! I'm afraid I've got a wounded soldier with me, though.'

Diane raced to the door to find out what was the matter with Mia. By the time Hannah had followed her into the hallway, she was already holding her daughter in her arms. Meanwhile Frank, who'd been joined somewhere along the way by Joan, was busy explaining: 'She tripped and grazed her knee. She did cry for a while at the time, but luckily Joan's house was nearby, so I took her there and she cleaned it up and popped on a plaster. Mia seemed fine after that. Then as soon as we arrived here, she got upset again.'

While Diane was busy calming Mia down, Hannah spoke for a few minutes with her dad, who clearly felt bad about the whole thing. She ignored Joan as much as possible, hoping she'd get the message and leave, although she kept chipping in to the conversation regardless. Diane insisted on removing the plaster and cleaning Mia's wound herself before applying another, much to Joan's obvious irritation, although even this didn't diminish Hannah's anger towards her sister.

Frank offered to make everyone a cup of tea, plus a juice for Mia. Thankfully Joan declined, saying she had a Pilates class to attend. As she was leaving, Hannah excused herself and headed back to the bedroom to get a private look at her mum's jewellery. She was feeling so annoyed with Diane that she was ready to lay claim to her favourite bracelet without her. The problem was that, despite rummaging through every jewellery box she could find, there was no sign of it whatsoever.

Eventually she went through to the lounge, where there was a cup of tea waiting, to ask her father. He had his feet up, reading the paper, while Diane was sitting with Mia on her knee, the pair of them staring at the TV, which was showing something loud and colourful on the CBeebies channel.

Avoiding her sister's eye, she knelt down next to Frank and spoke in a low voice. 'Dad, I was starting to look through Mum's jewellery and there's something I'm struggling to find.'

He lowered the broadsheet and peered at her over the top of his reading glasses. 'Oh? What's that then?'

'Do you remember the pearl-and-gold bracelet: the one you had made?'

'Yes, of course. Diane has it.' He looked over at his other daughter. 'That was the one you took a while ago, wasn't it? Didn't you want to wear it with some dress at a party or something? I thought you said you'd discussed it with Hannah beforehand.'

'She did not!' Hannah replied. 'When was this – and where is it now?' She turned and threw Diane an accusatory stare. 'Do you even know why that bracelet was so special? I bet you don't. You've never cared about that kind of thing.'

'Sure I do,' Diane replied. Her face twitched as she shifted awkwardly on the couch before lifting Mia off her knee and placing her next to her, so glued to the television she barely seemed to notice. 'Dad had it made for her.'

'I just said that,' Hannah snapped. 'Why did he have it made? What was the significance? Come on, spit it out.'

Diane rolled her eyes. 'You're such a goody two-shoes, aren't you? Fine, I don't know. I liked the look of it, that's all.'

Hannah stamped her feet on the lounge carpet, only managing to stop herself from shouting and swearing because of Mia's presence. 'You're unbelievable! Mum loved that bracelet precisely because of the story behind it. And she told it so often. Only someone as self-centred as you wouldn't remember it. You've always been too wrapped up in your own concerns to listen to anyone else.'

'Oh, get lost,' Diane replied. 'You self-righteous bitch.'

This stopped Hannah in her tracks, as she couldn't believe what her sister had said out loud in front of her young daughter. Clearly Frank thought the same, as a moment later he stood up and turned off the television –

despite Mia's complaints – telling her he needed her help with something. Leading her away, helped with the promise of a piece of chocolate, he scowled at the sisters before closing the lounge door and mouthed: 'Sort this out!'

Then they were alone again.

'So where is it?' Hannah demanded, still standing while Diane remained on the sofa, arms folded across her chest.

'What?'

'You know what: the bracelet, of course.'

'Um, it's at home somewhere, I guess.'

Hannah knew her sister well enough to be able to recognise she wasn't telling the truth. Her body language was way more defensive than it ought to have been.

'Where is it?' she demanded again. 'It means so much to me. That bracelet is the one item of Mum's jewellery I really had my heart set on.'

'You never mentioned it to me before.'

'No, because I know what you're like, Diane; if I'd told you I wanted it, you'd have wanted it too. Where is it?'

Diane kneaded her hands into the fabric of the sofa on either side of her legs, refusing to meet Hannah's eye, even though she was now standing right in front of her. It was a weird physical reversal of how their last confrontation in the bedroom had begun.

'What have you done?' Hannah asked. 'Look at me and tell me. And while you're at it, you said you were just getting started when we were arguing earlier. You know, before we got interrupted and after your bitchy comment about me not having children, which is ironic considering you've asked me to look after your daughter if anything happens to you. So please, do carry on. I'd love to hear what you really think.'

'Oh, here we go again,' Diane said, standing up. 'You love to paint me as the villain, don't you? As I recall, you were giving as good as you got, accusing me of stealing all Dad's money and being a crap mum.'

Things carried on like this for a while, the insults and language getting progressively worse and the volume creeping louder and louder. Years of unresolved, bottled-up conflict spilled over as the pair faced off against each other – toe to toe and nose to nose, insults and accusations flying fast in both directions – the row teetering once again on the brink of a punch-up.

'I'm going to ask you one more time: where the hell is Mum's bracelet?' Hannah bawled.

'I don't know, okay? I lost it.'

'You what?'

In a suddenly quiet voice, Diane explained: 'I wore it on a rare night out. It was that summer ball I told you about at the Midland Hotel. The bracelet must have slipped off at some point. I didn't realise until the next day.'

'Bloody hell, Diane! Did you even bother to try to find it?'

'Of course. I phoned them a couple of times, but no one had handed anything in like that.'

'You phoned them? You didn't even bother to go back?'

'What difference would that have made?'

'And you never thought to mention to Dad, or to me, that you'd lost it?'

313

Diane shrugged. 'I didn't know what to say.'

'Oh, that's all right, then. I guess you hoped no one would notice, didn't you? You stupid, careless cow! You don't have a clue what that meant to Mum, Dad and me.' Feeling herself start to cry, Hannah fought off the tears by channelling her emotion into more angry words. 'You really don't give a toss about anyone or anything apart from yourself, do you? I pity Mia growing up with you as her mother. I really do.'

'Screw you, Hannah! God, I hate you.' As Diane said this, her hand swept up and slapped her sister hard on her left cheek. It caught Hannah unawares, stunning her and causing her to step backwards, stumbling on a discarded doll belonging to Mia and landing on her bum. 'You're going to regret that,' she growled, still catching her breath on the floor. 'And trust me, I hate you more. I wish it was you that had died, instead of Mum. The world would be a better place without you.'

She was about to get back up and throw herself full force at Diane when the door swung open and Frank bellowed: 'What in God's name is going on here?'

'I'm leaving, that's what,' Hannah replied, jumping to her feet and bustling past her father into the hallway. 'I can't spend another minute here with her. Ask her what happened to Mum's bracelet, Dad. Ask her.'

And with that she stormed out of the house. Her whole body was buzzing with adrenaline as she slammed the front door behind her. And then, through the glass panel next to the door, she glimpsed Mia's scared eyes, wide like CDs, silently watching her from further down the hall.

And she felt awful for her. But still she left, not realising she wouldn't see those eyes again in person – the beautiful light-green eyes of her beloved niece – for more than a decade.

CHAPTER 26

Now

Neither of them had said a word for nearly fifteen minutes, Hannah noted, looking at the clock on the wall above the serving counter at the café. Mark's eyes had landed on her occasionally as he patiently did as she'd asked and stayed silent, offering no more unwanted apologies or appeals for her to give him another chance.

They'd both finished their drinks and, since neither of them had resorted to looking at their smartphones to keep occupied, they were now literally twiddling their thumbs. Hannah had read the menu from top to bottom at least ten times, in between eavesdropping on nearby conversations, none of which had proved very interesting. The young couple in the booth behind them were looking through wallpaper samples, trying to make the right choice for the lounge in their new flat; to their right were three female friends catching up on each other's latest news, from one of their cats being run over by a bus to another's racy dating experiences.

Hannah was actually impressed that Mark had done as she'd requested and stopped talking for so long, not that she had any intention of telling him. But it made her decide to give him another chance to say his piece.

'Right,' she said with a sigh. 'Let's try this again without the bullshit. What do you want to talk to me about?'

Mark nodded slowly. 'Thank you. I'll cut to the chase. I received something in the post from Diane. She must have sent it just before she—'

'What the hell? When was this? What is it?' Hannah suddenly felt out of breath; her heart was hammering in her chest. There was no way she could have seen this coming.

'Do you remember that small padded envelope that arrived for me on Thursday?' Mark asked.

'Yes, vaguely.'

'That was it. There was a USB stick inside containing two short video messages – one for you and one for Mia. There was also a text file containing a short message for me. Diane had written that it was my choice whether to show the videos to you both or not, and that these were the only copies. I think she must have recorded the videos that night I stayed down in Bournemouth – after I'd gone to bed. She was wearing the same clothes anyway.'

'And you only told me this now?' Hannah said, for want of anything better springing to mind. She still couldn't believe what she was hearing and it was like her mind had split into two camps: one part that had no interest in learning what that husband-stealing bitch had to say; another part desperate to understand why her sister had killed herself after leaving Mia in her and Mark's care.

Again she thought back to that awful row they'd had in 2008 in Southport, surprised Diane hadn't let it slip then about her and Mark. She'd been over every nasty little thing they'd said to each other that day countless times in her head, particularly in the immediate aftermath of the fight, when she still had no idea how long a feud it was going to spark between them.

Diane's words about Mark not giving her any children were even crueller in light of what Hannah now knew. And when Diane had told her that was 'nothing' and that she was just getting started, she must have been considering telling Hannah the terrible truth about what she'd done with her husband and the child he'd given her. Goodness only knew what had held her back from doing so. It must have been more about protecting Mark and Mia than her, whom she clearly hadn't cared about in the slightest. Or perhaps it had been about hiding the truth from their father for fear of him cutting her off financially as a result.

Anyway, days of not speaking to each other had quickly turned into weeks, months and then years. Frank had tried at first to mediate between them, even splitting Maggie's jewellery in half and distributing it between them himself. But neither twin had been open to any kind of meet-up or conversation to try to resolve matters. Following previous fallings-out, which had admittedly been far less severe, Hannah had usually been the one to offer an olive branch, knowing how stubborn Diane could be. But this time, still grief-stricken following her mum's death, she'd stuck to her guns. Then she'd had her meltdown at work and slipped into a vast depression, which had incapacitated her until she'd sought help through counselling. When Diane and Mia had made their surprise move down south, this had more or less sealed the sisters' fate.

Back in the present, Mark hesitated before replying to Hannah's comment about him not mentioning the USB stick previously. She could tell he was treading carefully. 'I'm sorry, but this is the first chance I've had to speak to you. Mentioning it by text hardly seemed appropriate.'

He had a point. 'So what do they say?' Hannah asked 'Have you already shown Mia the one Diane made for her?'

'No, not yet. I wanted to talk to you first. I wanted to let you see both videos for yourself.' Mark reached under the table, pulled out his tan leather briefcase, opened it and removed Hannah's laptop followed by a white flash drive and a pair of headphones.

'You want me to watch the videos here? Now?'

Mark held up his palms. 'Not if you don't want to. You can watch them wherever you like. They're only short – it won't take long. Come back to the apartment, by all means, or watch them somewhere else. It's totally up to you. I didn't want to make any assumptions. I've, er, made a backup copy of the files, which I've left at home, but that's the original. That's the USB stick she sent me. The password to access it is, um, "Lowry".'

Hannah didn't reply for some time. She was weighing up her options. Should she go back to the flat or to Laura's house, or should she watch the videos here in this public place? Eventually, curiosity got the better of her and she made a decision. 'Fine. I'll watch them here, but first I want you to order me another drink, so no one bothers me, and then leave me alone here to do it. I don't want you staring at me the whole time.'

'Okay,' Mark said. 'Can I speak to you afterwards, though?'

'Yes. I'll call your phone when I'm done; then you can come back.'

He slipped off to order her another tea, brought it over and, leaving his briefcase with her, said: 'Goodbye. I won't go far.'

She watched him leave the café. Pulse racing and shaky of hand, she gingerly opened up the laptop and slid the stick into the right slot. She typed in the password 'Lowry', and first selected the text file Mark had mentioned. It was just two sentences, stating what he'd already told her: that it was his decision whether or not to show the videos to them and that there were no other copies. Well, that last part was no longer true, since Mark had now backed the files up. But at least it meant there was no chance of her dad or nosy Joan coming across the messages while rooting around Diane's house.

Next Hannah clicked on the video file with her name and, a moment later, her dead sister appeared, staring right at her out of the screen.

She was in a bedroom – presumably her own in Bournemouth – and judging by the closed curtains and artificial light it was night-time. Diane, wearing an olive tank top and no make-up, had dark bags under her eyes;

her short, bottle-red hair only served to emphasise how pale and drawn she looked. She appeared to be lying propped up with a couple of pillows on her bed, recording herself from the webcam of a laptop or similar device. So only her upper half was visible, including her bare arms, which were painfully thin.

'Hello, Hannah,' she said into the camera with a tired smile. 'If you're watching this, I'm most likely not around any more and, well, you've probably received this from Mark. I wanted to give him the choice of whether to show it to you or not. That's the very least I owe him, considering everything I've done. Whatever you know so far, it's probably not the whole truth. But that's what I want to give you now. You've little reason to believe anything that comes out of my mouth. I know that. But I swear from the bottom of my heart, based on all the good times we shared before things turned sour – one twin to another – that everything I'm about to say is absolutely true. Consider this my last promise to you.'

Hannah reached forward and stopped the video. She felt like she could hardly breathe. It was too much, considering everything she'd already discovered and knowing what Diane had done after recording this; knowing she was gone forever. Seeing her late sister brought back to life on the computer screen was like looking at another version of herself: a desperate, more broken version. And how come, despite everything, she felt something more than hate for Diane? There was still love there too; sorrow over her death; emptiness, knowing that she would only ever be one now, when she used to be one of two. Had a part of her died with her twin? It felt that way.

Conscious of the tears welling up in her eyes and the overwhelming strength of her emotions, Hannah looked around the café, fearful that everyone might be watching her. But it was pure paranoia. No one was even looking her way. They were all too wrapped up in their own issues. Even the customers sitting alone were more likely to be checking the weather or playing some mind-numbing game on their phones than watching her.

Still, she didn't feel ready yet to watch the rest of the video, so instead she opened the one created for Mia.

The scene was identical. Diane must have recorded it immediately before or after the other video. However, as soon as Hannah saw her twin's misty-eyed gaze into the camera, heard her hesitant, wavering first words, she knew the tone was going to be very different. This was a mother saying goodbye to her daughter. It felt wrong for her to even be watching it, but she couldn't stop herself.

'Mia, my darling girl, I'm so sorry I've left you. I can't expect you to understand why, but please know it's not because I don't love you. I love you more than anyone else in the world and, although I'm sure it doesn't feel like that right now, my intention is to spare you pain; to leave you in the best possible place, which I firmly believe is with Hannah and Mark.

'The fact is I'm dying. I have pancreatic cancer. I've only known for a short time, but it was already incurable when I got the diagnosis. I'm sorry I didn't tell you, but I wanted to spare you the pain. I know it must seem like I've caused you more of that now, but having watched my own mother die a slow and painful death from cancer, I didn't want you to have to go through the same thing, Mia.

'I did hope to end things in a more, um, civilised manner. My plan was to go abroad, to a place where they'd let me die on my own terms with dignity, but as it turned out, there was too much red tape involved. It would have been impossible to make it happen in the timeframe I needed and without informing you and other family members first, which I never wanted to do.

'Gosh, that must sound terribly cruel, my love. I meant it to be the very opposite. I wanted to spare you all of that. I know we lost our chance for a proper goodbye this way, but sometimes as a parent you have to make difficult decisions you feel are best for your child. That's why I left you with Hannah and Mark, so you'd have a chance to get to know them beforehand. I want them to be your guardians – something I asked of them a long time ago when things were very different between us, but which I hope they'll honour. I can't think of anyone better to bring you up in my absence; I know they'll do an amazing job of it. The truth is that they're both far better people than I am, which leads me on to something rather difficult I need to tell you . . .'

Hannah paused the video, taking a moment to absorb everything she'd just heard and to compose herself. She took a big swig from the cooling tea in front of her on the café table, followed by several deep breaths. Then she pressed play again.

'I've never really told you anything about your father.

I encouraged you not to ask about him and, on the few occasions you did, I always painted him in a bad light, as someone not interested in being a parent, so not worth bothering about. I thought I could be enough for you, but obviously that's no longer the case.

'Anyway, the truth is . . . well, let's say it was unfair of me to present him in that way. He's a good person and the reason he hasn't been in your life is purely down to me. He didn't even know he was your father until very recently. I hid it from him until I found out I was dying. Now he does know, it's clearly a big shock. I wish I could tell you who he is, but things between us are, um, complicated, and I'm the one to blame for that. I've left the ball in his court. It's the only fair thing to do in light of the way I've treated him. He and I are the only ones who know, so there's no point in asking anyone else. But I'm confident he will come forward when the time is right. And in the meantime, you have your aunt and uncle, who I'm sure you've already discovered are wonderful people, plus of course your grandad, who loves you dearly and will always be there to look out for your best interests.

'You're probably wondering about why Hannah and I kept apart from each other for all those years. Trust me when I say I wronged her infinitely more than she ever did me; I treated her terribly. I won't go into details. The past is the past. But I'll let you into a secret: I always thought of Hannah as the good twin and me the bad one. Ever since we were children. She has a heart of gold; I don't. I always envied her that – wished I could be more like her – but jealousy made me worse rather than better.

Anyway, what I'm saying is please don't let our falling-out colour your view of Hannah or Mark. Leaving you with them and sparing you the pain of watching me die is meant as my final gift to you, Mia, and to them. Somehow, you're the one thing I got right in this life and I hope you'll understand my actions one day, even if you don't now.'

Diane's face crumpled and tears began to flow. She struggled to speak for several moments and then finally concluded: 'I miss you so much already, Mia. I hope more than anything that you live a long and happy life without me; that one day you meet someone special and have a family of your own. Know that I would never have left you if there was any way to beat my fate, and please try to understand that my only intention in speeding things along is to spare you pain rather than cause it.

'I wrestled with my conscience doing things this way. Keeping the truth from you like I have has been so hard. It still weighs heavy on me now. But honestly, if I had told you about my cancer and my intention to go before getting really sick, I know you'd have tried to change my mind. And how could I have said no to you?

'I have to go now, my daughter, my love, my everything. All I leave behind is yours. In time, I hope you'll forgive me. Goodbye.'

Tenderly, she kissed her hand, touched the camera lens with it and then the video ended. Hannah removed the headphones, turned off the screen of the laptop and saw her stunned reflection staring at her from the black background, like a ghostly echo of her twin. She rubbed her hands across her cold, wet cheeks and slowly exhaled. Gosh, that had been tough to watch. Throughout, part of her had felt awful seeing it before Mia, although Mark must also have watched it. Surely it was only right that her niece got to see this as soon as possible, but what an incredibly tough watch it would be for her. How could a child be expected to comprehend any explanation her mum might offer for stepping out in front of a speeding train? Hannah couldn't understand it herself, having also lived through the slow, painful death of their own mother. Sure, it was awful, seeing her fade away like she had, gradually succumbing to her fate; losing herself to pain, weakness and powerful drugs that befuddled her mind. But was this drastic, brutal way out that Diane had chosen really so much better?

And yet Hannah didn't doubt that Diane's intentions, however warped, had been good. As strange as it sounded, her sister had genuinely seemed to believe she was acting in her daughter's best interests. And her words to Mia about Hannah and Mark had shown a maturity – a recognition of her own wrongdoing – unlike anything Hannah had witnessed from her previously. This made her feelings towards her late twin even more conflicted than they had been before. Then there was the fact that she'd held back from naming Mark as Mia's father. Was this in recognition of the fact that it would be hard for the teenager to absorb right now, on top of everything else, potentially impacting the way she viewed her new guardians? Or maybe leaving Mark in control of this matter was intended as a way to increase the likelihood of him actually showing Mia the video.

Who could say for sure what had been going through Diane's mind when she'd recorded it? The fact that she'd killed herself hours later wasn't exactly a ringing endorsement of her sanity. And yet her wording had been carefully considered, particularly in the way it freed Mark and herself from potential questions about Mia's father's identity, by suggesting they had no clue. She was also very clear about wanting them to be Mia's guardians.

So what had she recorded in the other video message? Had she come clean about her sordid fling with Mark? Hannah finished her tea. She wondered where Mark had taken himself off to and what he was thinking and doing at that moment. And then, unable to resist any longer, desperate to learn whatever else Diane had recorded, she turned the laptop screen back on and restarted the video meant for her.

CHAPTER 27

Hannah rewound Diane's video by a few seconds. '. . . everything I'm about to say is absolutely true. Consider this my last promise to you.'

She gritted her teeth and sucked in cool air as the video continued past where she'd watched up to previously and she braced herself for whatever was to come.

'So around about fifteen years ago I did a terrible thing,' Diane said on screen. 'But before I go into that, let me first say how much I've missed you since we fell out, and how often you've been on my mind. I thought about contacting you on countless occasions prior to this summer, Han, but . . . something always stopped me. The more time that passed, the harder it became. I wonder if it was the same for you, or were you glad to be rid of me? I wouldn't blame you, if so, particularly knowing what I'm about to tell you.'

Diane took a deep breath before continuing. 'So back to this terrible thing. It's arguably the worst, most calculated and deceitful act of my life. And I'm afraid it involves you and Mark. I've always been jealous of you, Hannah. Did you know that? As a child I felt that Mum and Dad thought of you as the bright, sensible, capable one. And it was the same at school. Our teachers always compared us to each other. Of course they did. That's what people do with identical twins. The problem for me was that I always came up short. I was the stupid one – the black sheep – and that feeling of inadequacy stayed with me into adulthood. There you were with your great career, your loving husband and your amazing life, while I could never find a good job or a boyfriend who made me happy. I scraped by in your shadow: a constant disappointment to myself and everyone around me.

'Do you remember that time at primary school when I convinced you to swap places for the day; to pretend to be each other and see if we could get away with it? We did it, didn't we? And not one person guessed. I loved that. It felt amazing to be the good twin for one day. I wanted to do it again, if you recall, but you never would. You said it was wrong to trick people. That moral compass of yours was installed at an early age, wasn't it?

'Anyway, about fifteen years ago, I did it again as an adult. Without your knowledge this time. And it worked just as well as it did that first time. All I had to do was wear a dress I'd borrowed from you, style my hair like yours and be careful what I said and how I said it. It was an Oscar-worthy performance. So much so that I convinced your husband. I felt what it was like to be truly loved by a good man for one night, because he thought I was you, and I got greedy. I took things much further than I'd ever intended.'

Hannah's jaw was on the table by this stage. She was shocked, revulsed and yet transfixed by what she was hearing from Diane's lips. And as much as she wanted to shout and scream – to hurl the laptop off the table in disgust – she couldn't stop watching. She had to find out more.

'I'm getting ahead of myself,' Diane added, taking a big gulp of air and turning away from the camera for a few seconds before she continued. 'I'm not proud of this, Hannah, especially from my current viewpoint, with death breathing down my neck. However, I need to confess. Mark had a big work do at the Lowry Hotel. You were invited too, but you weren't well that morning – you had a stomach bug or something. So you told him to go without you; to keep the room at the hotel he'd booked for you both and make the most of the night regardless. You told me about it on the phone that day and then I remembered the lovely emerald cocktail dress you'd lent me for another function a few weeks earlier. I still had it. I saw an opportunity – and I pounced.

'Mark was shocked to see me, of course, when I turned up unannounced at the hotel. But wearing your dress, presenting myself like you in every way I could think of, it was too easy to convince him I was you. He'd already had a few drinks by that point and I spun a yarn about feeling better and deciding to surprise him. He fell for it. He had no reason to suspect anything. He was just glad to see you – or me pretending to be you – and, as I say, things got out of hand.

330

'My original intention was to mess with him. To spend a couple of flirty hours in his company. To feel what it was like to be you again, like I did that time at primary school. And then to come clean before things got too serious. I really didn't intend to sleep with him at first, Hannah. Maybe a kiss or two, if I'm honest, to see what it was like, but no more. I figured he'd be too mortified to ever tell you – and I was right, even when things did go further. I told him the next morning, after we woke up together, and he was devastated. Hannah, you have to know that.

'Mark never showed the slightest romantic interest in me before or after that night. I know guys who cheat only too well, and he's not one of them. I'm sure a part of him wanted to confess. But he was so distraught and ashamed at not being able to tell the difference between us, even during the most intimate of moments, I don't think he knew how to tell you – not without ruining your marriage. To be fair, by the time things got out of hand, we were both very drunk. Had that not been the case, he might have suspected something.

'Anyway, I certainly didn't plan to get pregnant that night. No way, I swear. But he wasn't used to using a condom with you because, unlike me, you were on the Pill. So I risked doing it without. You know what happened next: Mia was conceived. Beforehand, I hadn't been particularly interested in having a child, but something changed when I learned I was pregnant. I found I couldn't bring myself to get an abortion. So I kept her, refusing to identify the father. When Mark inevitably got suspicious,

I fended him off with a convincing story about how she was definitely another man's child.

'The fear of him suspecting the truth as Mia got older was one of the reasons I chose to move so far away. Our falling-out, Mum's death, and Dad's new relationship with Joan all played their part too.

'So there you have it, Han. Now you know what a backstabbing bitch your twin sister really is after all these years. Worse than you ever thought, right? I did feel bad afterwards, if that helps, although at the same time I know my actions resulted in Mia being born. She's the best thing that's ever happened to me, so how can I regret that?'

Hannah stopped the video for a moment to let everything she'd heard so far sink in. It was a huge shock to learn all of this. It was particularly hard hearing the sordid details of Diane and Mark's night together. And yet, as awful as it was, the truth was actually easier to bear than some of the scenarios that had been running through her mind ever since she'd found Diane's letter to Mark the other day. If Diane's story was indeed the truth, and she got the impression it was, then it shone a whole different light on Mark and his involvement in this one-night stand.

If he'd been tricked into sleeping with Diane, thinking she was his wife, that was a whole different ballgame. That was not the same as consciously cheating on her. It was a silver lining – a glimmer of hope for their future together – although it didn't excuse the fact that he hadn't told her, or the numerous lies he must have fed her over the years as a result, not least in recent days.

However, Hannah could sort of comprehend why Mark hadn't come clean. It must have been a horrendous discovery to make. And she could well imagine how hard it would be for him to accept he hadn't been able to tell one twin from another, even in bed. The fact that he could have been tricked in this way was less of a surprise to Hannah than it would have been to him. She understood how easily it could be done, particularly with alcohol involved, and considering what a skilled manipulator her sister could be. There were times as children when even the twins' parents hadn't been able to tell them apart, for goodness' sake.

Lies aside, Mark was a victim – even more than she was really. The only truly guilty party here was Diane, whose actions were despicable and unforgiveable. But she was dead and gone now, so hating her was pointless. Plus it had all happened so long ago, and Mark had been such a good husband to Hannah in the time since then. How would she have ever recovered from her breakdown without his unwavering support?

Strangely, considering everything Hannah had just heard, she saw her reflection in the dark laptop screen and realised there was a faint smile on her face. Learning what she had about Mark the other day had been horrendous. It had felt like being torn away from her life raft during a ferocious sea storm and left to drown. Everything had looked so bleak. Try as she might, because love wasn't a tap you could simply turn off, she hadn't been able to see any way forward for them as a couple. Her life as she knew it had appeared all but over. Now there was hope.

It wouldn't be easy, but suddenly, unexpectedly, she could at least picture a future for them again: one where they eventually got past this.

She continued watching Diane's video message from where she'd stopped it.

'I don't expect you to ever forgive me for what I've done to you and Mark,' her sister said, still sitting propped up on her bed, looking straight into the camera. 'But for what it's worth, I'm truly sorry. Knowing you don't have long to live really focuses your mind. I'm sorry about losing Mum's bracelet too – the one that was special to you and which sparked the big argument we never found our way back from. I did feel awful about it at the time, even if I didn't appreciate its true meaning. That was probably why I was so prickly with you. We were both still grieving, weren't we? Losing Mum was so hard.

'I, um, have to ask you something now – even though I have no right to do so, and you surely hate me more than ever. It's not for me. It's for Mia, who I need to ensure is well looked after in my absence.

'Do you remember that time we were walking in the park soon after Mia's birth and I asked if you and Mark would be her guardians in case anything happened to me? Some guy had just been staring at us because of the twin thing; I'd given him a mouthful and you'd told me off for being aggressive. Anyhow, I asked you and, soon after-wards, having spoken to Mark, you agreed. So I wrote it into my will.

'You might be surprised to hear I've never changed my mind. I still believe there's no one better to bring up Mia.

It's not only because Mark's her father either. I'd totally understand if you didn't want to tell her that for the time being. It's not exactly going to be easy for her to digest. But no, it's because of you too, Hannah. I think you'd make a wonderful parent. I know that's not what I said when we had our big fight in Southport, but it's the truth. In fact you'll probably be better than me at it, because you've always been a better person overall.

'Part of you always wanted to be a mum, isn't that right? I'm sure this was something you gave up for Mark. You never said so, but I still remember you talking about having kids before you met him. Is it too much for me to suggest that this is your chance? Okay, it's a weird starting point for a family, and yet I think the three of you could make it work.'

As Diane repeated some of the things Hannah had already seen in the video to Mia, such as her cancer diagnosis and her desire for her daughter to avoid watching her die a slow and painful death, like their mother, Hannah found her mind wandering. She was imagining how a world in which she, Mark and Mia lived together might look – and, surprisingly, it felt like a genuine possibility. It wouldn't be easy, particularly at first. She'd need plenty of time to heal from the wounds inflicted on her marriage, while Mia would be struggling with her grief for a long period to come. It didn't feel impossible, though, and Mia deserved that shot, even if her mum didn't.

Hannah thought back to Mia's terrified eyes as a young child, silently watching her storm out of Frank's old house following that blazing row with Diane. She never wanted to upset her niece or let her down like that again; she intended to do her utmost to protect her. Sure, it would be messy at times, especially once the moment arrived to reveal the truth about her father. But that could wait a while in light of the current situation, assuming Mark was on the same page.

'I have to go now, sis,' Diane said as Hannah tuned back into the video still playing before her. 'It's over and out for me, but not for you. If anyone can turn this chaos I've created into something good, it's you. Mia reminds me a lot of you sometimes, particularly her love of books, her creativity and warmth of heart.

'At the start of this video I pledged to tell you the whole ugly truth, Han. I've done that. In return, would you please, please honour the promise you once made me to look after my daughter when I'm gone? You may well struggle to understand the way I've chosen to end things. It's controversial, I know, but I genuinely feel it's for the best. Losing Mum like we did was so awful. I wouldn't wish that on my worst enemy. And if my final actions turn Mia against me – make her want to forget I ever existed – then so be it. Maybe that could help bring you together as a new family unit. Goodbye, my sister, my twin. I love you. I miss you. I'm so sorry for all the pain I've caused.'

CHAPTER 28

Mark scowled at the front door of the café where he'd left Hannah with her laptop and Diane's videos. Then, with a sigh, he started to walk around the block yet another time. How long was she going to take? It already felt like forever. He knew the videos weren't that long, having already watched them, but he was well aware of the need for him to give her whatever space and time she needed.

He wondered in which order she'd chosen to view them. Had she started with the video file created for her or the one for Mia? And what the hell was she making of them both?

After Mark had received the USB Diane had posted to him, he hadn't dared open it initially, fearing what it might contain. But late on Thursday, the same day Hannah had found Diane's letter and walked out on him, he'd eventually tried to open it. Mia had gone to bed and he'd been unable to switch off his whirring brain, so he'd decided to look.

The message – *Mia was conceived here* – which he'd found attached to the USB on a bright yellow sticker, had actually made him fear the memory stick might contain a video of the night he'd spent with Diane all those years ago. He had no idea how she would have made it back then, when decent video recorders weren't on everyone's mobile phones like nowadays. But he hadn't been thinking rationally and he knew from bitter experience never to underestimate his sister-in-law and what she was capable of doing.

In the event, he'd realised the sticker merely referred to the password she'd used to protect the files, which he'd worked out after a couple of tries to be 'Lowry', after the hotel where it had happened. Where she'd tricked him into thinking she was his wife and, like a dumb idiot, he'd fallen for it hook, line and sinker. He'd never forgiven himself for that – and he'd never managed to find a way to tell Hannah either. He'd wanted to, particularly at the start when the guilt felt like a gaping wound in his chest. But he'd been so ashamed. How could he have not known the difference between the twins? What kind of husband did that make him?

It probably ought to have been the first thing he'd told Hannah when she'd finally learned the truth via Diane's letter, because it was obviously better than a deliberate act of infidelity. But having kept the truth from Hannah for so long – telling so many lies in the process – he hadn't been able to find the right words. Also, it somehow felt wrong to reveal this about Diane in light of the fact she'd killed herself.

Thankfully, she'd done it for him in the video she'd made for her sister. She'd chosen her words very carefully in the video for Mia too, leaving the choice of how and when to tell her that he was her father firmly in his own hands. Mark's current view was to show Mia the video message now – just the one meant for her, not the other – and wait to tell her any more until a calmer, more suitable time. Possibly a good way into the future. It all depended on Hannah, really, and how she reacted to these videos, because if things were over between them, then the whole thing would be up in the air. But if she was at least prepared to try to work on repairing their marriage, going to relationship counselling perhaps, whatever it took, maybe the three of them could make a go of it as a family, like Diane wanted.

Of course, not telling Mia the full truth now could eventually backfire spectacularly. But how could the poor girl be expected to process the idea of her uncle – her mum's twin sister's husband – being her father, while she was still grieving for her mother? No, as far as Mark was concerned, that and any potential DNA testing that might emerge as a result were definitely best kept for the future.

In Hannah's absence, he and Mia had continued to get closer. They'd spoken a number of times about how she was feeling, which had led to several bouts of tears; he was just pleased she felt able to open up to him. Telling her about his own experience of losing his brother, Pete, had been the right move. Not that their discussions about Mia's emotions had been particularly detailed. Most of the time it had been a case of her saying she felt sad, numb, confused or angry and him nodding in response, telling her it was normal to feel that way and good to keep talking about it. It wasn't like he was a trained therapist or anything. He was doing his best, although he knew she'd get more insight and useful advice from Hannah, who knew first-hand what it was like to lose a mother and also had the advantage of being Diane's twin sister.

Mia had asked a couple of times about how things were going with Hannah and when she would be coming home. Her unexplained absence was obviously bothering her, so he'd played the seriousness of the situation down, telling her not to worry and that things should be back to normal soon. If only he was so confident of this in reality.

The hardest conversation so far had been when Mia had queried whether Mark knew why Diane might have killed herself, based on the time he'd spent with her. Fortunately, he'd suspected she might ask this, so he'd had an answer ready-prepared. 'Goodness knows what must have been going through her mind,' he'd said. 'She seemed quite upbeat when I said goodbye to her. I'd never have guessed what she was about to do. One thing I can definitely tell you is that it had nothing to do with you. She loved you so much and she was so proud of you. That was really obvious from the chat we had. We spoke about you at length. She wanted to know everything you'd been up to in Manchester and kept saying how much she missed you.'

'If that's true, why would she do what she did?' Mia had replied with a catch in her voice. 'Why would she leave me without even saying goodbye? Do you reckon . . . maybe she was ill or something?'

'Um, what makes you say that? Did she seem ill to you? Had she been seeing a doctor or anything?'

'Not that she told me, but . . . I don't know. I guess she just didn't seem like herself recently. The more I think about it, the more I wonder if she could have been hiding something from me. She seemed to be tired a lot in the last few weeks before we came here, and she'd lost weight. There were a few times when she had a belly ache too. She told me it was because of her time of the month, but it seemed to happen more regularly than that.'

Mia had fallen quiet after saying these words, like they were eating her up inside. This had made Mark feel awful and desperate to let her see Diane's video. However, having already decided to show it to Hannah first to get her opinion, he'd forced himself to hold back.

'There's no point thinking about that stuff, love,' he'd told her instead. 'If she was ill and had wanted you to know, she'd have told you. Parents often try to protect their children from such things so they don't worry.'

'I'd rather be worried and still have a mum,' Mia had said in little more than a whisper, her words like a hammer to Mark's heart. He'd stayed silent, for what reply could he have offered her?

On a more light-hearted note, Mia had confessed something to Mark that had sounded very serious when she'd first mentioned it, but had actually amused rather than annoyed him. 'There's something I need to tell you,' she'd said as they'd sat down to eat some pasta he'd cooked for their dinner yesterday. 'You and Hannah have been so good to me and, well, I feel awful for not coming clean about this sooner.'

'That, um, sounds serious,' Mark had said, placing his fork down in his bowl and giving Mia his full attention

Her face had turned bright red. 'It is. I stole something from you.'

'Okay. What was it? Have you returned it now?'

'I would have, but I can't. It's gone. I can't buy another one myself either, but I'll definitely pay to replace it.'

'I see. So how about you tell me what it was you took?'

Mia had looked down at the table as she'd replied. 'It was a small bottle of alcohol. Kirsch, I think it was called. I found it under the sink. It was before Mum, um . . . when she was still alive and I was worried about stuff. I thought if I got a bit drunk, I might feel better. Less anxious.'

Mark had had to bite the inside of his lip to avoid smiling; to remind himself he needed to be parental rather than reminisce about similar escapades of his own as a teenager. Kirsch, though: what a choice of alcohol to swipe. They only kept it in the cupboard for the very occasional time when they had a cheese fondue. It was unlikely they'd have even missed it. Mark had never tried actually drinking kirsch, but based on the smell, it probably tasted foul, especially to a teenager unused to alcohol.

'I see,' he'd replied. 'So you drank it?'

'No, I dropped it. I didn't drink any at all.'

'Where were you at the time? Who were you with? Todd?'

She hesitated for a second before replying: 'No, I was alone. It was in town, in a back alley near the library. I'm so sorry. It'll never happen again, I promise.'

Mark had told her he was glad she'd come clean and the important thing was that no one had got hurt. But he'd added: 'Please never do anything like that again, Mia. Promise me? Alcohol is very dangerous, particularly spirits. You can die from drinking too much and, as a young, vulnerable teenage girl, you risk getting yourself taken advantage of, or worse.'

'I won't do it again, I promise.'

'Is drinking alcohol something you do when you're out with your friends at home?'

'No, honestly it isn't. I've tried it literally twice at parties, but that's it. I don't know what I was thinking. I'm so sorry.'

Mark hadn't had the heart to punish her after what she'd already been through and everything she still had to face, such as her mum's funeral and moving house. Plus she'd confessed of her own volition, which was impressive. In truth, he hadn't a clue what would be an appropriate punishment anyway, thanks to his total lack of experience as a parent. He suspected Hannah would know. She was much better than him at these kinds of things: yet another reason why he so desperately hoped they could resolve their problems.

As Mark continued walking in the present, his mind occupied by the past, his phone finally rang. It was Hannah.

'Hello?' he said, his fingers having fumbled to pull the

343

mobile out of his pocket and answer the call. 'Can I come back now?'

'No,' Hannah's voice replied.

Mark's heart sank. 'Oh, okay. What—'

'I do want to see you, but not here. I need to get outside. Find some fresh air. Where are you now? Is it still raining?'

'Um.' Mark looked up at the sky. He'd been so caught up in his thoughts and memories, he'd barely noticed the weather while he'd been pacing around. It had been raining earlier, right? Hence his damp hair and clothes. But now it was dry. He could even see a glimmer of sunshine peeking out through the clouds.

Mark looked at his wife, sitting next to him on the bench in Piccadilly Gardens. He wanted to kiss her, squeeze her tight, hold her hand. But he didn't dare push things, so he gave her the sweetest smile he could muster. 'I don't know what to say, Hannah. This is . . . you are . . . amazing. Are you sure? I really don't want to rush you. You can take all the time you need.'

'It sounds like you don't want me to come back to the apartment with you,' Hannah replied, looking more beautiful than ever to him in that moment, despite her tear-stained cheeks and bloodshot eyes.

'No, not at all. There's nothing I want more – and I know Mia will be over the moon to see you too. She's been worried.'

Hannah frowned. 'How much did you tell her?'

'Only what I had to. Nothing specific. Just that we had a row and you were upset.'

344

'Things between us aren't going to return to normal straight away. You realise that, don't you, Mark? It'll be a long time, if ever, before I feel like I can really trust you again. All those lies over so many years. You should have trusted me with the truth from the start. I need you to be one hundred per cent honest with me – no exceptions – from this point on. That's the only way we have a chance of making this work.'

'Of course. No more lies, I promise. I'm so happy you're giving us another chance. As long as it takes. Whatever you need. You're in the driving seat.'

'Good. And you're definitely okay with the idea of us taking in Mia permanently; being her guardians, like Diane wanted? What about Pete? What about never wanting to have children?'

'Things change. I've changed. She's a great kid, despite her mother, and it's absolutely the right thing to do – the only thing. I've no doubts whatsoever. I just hope Frank's happy. He's not likely to challenge it, is he, on the basis that he's had a lot more to do with Mia over the years?'

Hannah shrugged. 'I don't see why, especially if that's what it says in Diane's will and since she specifically left her with us. Dad's not getting any younger and can you really see Joan wanting to take a teenager into her oh-so-perfect house?'

'True. So we're agreed to show Mia her mum's video straight away but not to say anything about me being her father for now? That can wait until sometime in the future, when we both think it's best, right?'

Mark couldn't help but notice Hannah wince at the

mention of the paternity issue, but she replied: 'Yes, agreed.'

Would there need to be a DNA test eventually to confirm Diane had been telling the truth? Possibly. Probably. But that was a matter for another day. There were other, more pressing matters to deal with in the meantime, like trying to repair his marriage – to never let his beloved Hannah down again – and to make the best life possible for Mia. It was going to be incredibly hard for her to move past the death of her mum unscathed, but by offering her their love and support and a permanent place in their hearts and home, they could at least give her a fighting chance.

Slowly, tentatively, Mark lowered his right hand on to Hannah's left, which was resting between them on the bench. She flinched as he first made contact, causing him to jerk it back up. But then he looked into his wife's eyes and, despite the hurt still clearly visible, they told him that small step forward was all right. So he gently lowered it again and rested it on top of her hand, surprised how cold her skin felt, his fingers sliding in between the gaps of hers.

For several long minutes they remained like that, neither making a sound as life moved on around them in that busy, noisy pocket of central Manchester. Then Hannah spoke a handful of words that would have sounded innocuous to a passer-by but meant so very much to Mark. They made his heart skip with hope.

'Okay. Let's go home, shall we?'

EPILOGUE

Several days later

Mia entered the crematorium to the sound of an organ playing something sombre. Everything was a blur. Lots of people had been gathered outside the chapel when she'd arrived, but she hadn't been able to focus on any of them. They'd all merged into one mass: a sea of glum faces and dark outfits. None of what was happening seemed real. She didn't even feel like she was actually there, in her own skin, but rather an observer watching from afar.

'Are you okay, love?' she heard her grandad's voice whisper from nearby, accompanied by a gentle touch on her arm.

She nodded in reply, even though she clearly wasn't okay. Her eyes remained trained on her black leather school shoes, which were shuffling forward on autopilot, led by her aunt and uncle. Hannah was holding her hand and Mark had his arm wrapped supportively around her lower back. They guided her to a pew at the front of the chapel. But she couldn't look at them. She couldn't look at anyone. The

347

only face she wanted to see was the one she couldn't –
and never would for real again.

As she sat down on the hard wooden bench, Mia realised that, despite everyone else present, she'd never felt
more alone in her life. She cast the briefest of glances at
the light-wood coffin a few metres in front of her and it
was like she'd been thumped in the stomach, leaving her
winded and nauseous. The idea of her mum's body, or
whatever was left of it, being in there, so close to her, was
awful. She felt an urge to run – to get as far away from
all of this as possible. And then a cool, calm hand came
to rest on her bare knee and gave it a squeeze of reassurance: Hannah.

'Don't worry,' her aunt whispered close to her ear, in
that voice so similar to her mother's. 'You can do this.
We're going to get through this together. I'm right here
next to you – and so is Mark.'

'I am,' her uncle said into her other ear. 'We've got you,
Mia. You're not alone. You'll never be alone.'

She allowed herself one look at Hannah, who looked
so like her mum today, with her hair tied up in a bun and
her kind blue eyes, that it almost felt like it was her. And
although Mia knew the painful truth only too well, she
let that slight feeling of relief wash over her for a moment.
She closed her eyes and imagined the person she missed
so much – every minute of every day – really was at her
side.

In her mind's eye she pictured the two of them walking
hand in hand along the beach on a sunny day like they
used to so often when she was younger. They were both

barefoot and on the edge of the water as the tide slowly clawed its way towards land, lapping over their toes at regular intervals. The water's cool, eager swirl soothed away the anger and confusion Mia had felt ever since learning of Diane's suicide, leaving only sorrow and love.

'I've been dreading this day, Mum,' she said. 'I don't know how to let you go. I don't want to. I can't bear the thought of you not being in my life any more. I love you so much.'

'I know, my darling. I feel the same. You're so incredibly precious to me. I'll never truly leave you. You know that, right? You grew inside me. My blood runs through your veins. I'll always be there if you look deep enough. Now go and be strong for me. You can do this.'

Mia opened her eyes as the white-haired celebrant began to speak into the microphone at the front of the chapel and the funeral service began. She did her best to listen to the warm words this kindly man said about her mother, having spoken to her family and friends. But still she felt detached from the proceedings, like she was in a dream and might wake up at any moment. She spent more of her time focusing on the photo they'd selected for the front of the order of service: a snap Mia had taken on her phone the previous summer. It showed her mum looking so happy, sipping a glass of wine on a blanket on the beach, during an impromptu picnic they'd enjoyed together one balmy evening. Little had they known what a cruel fate awaited them a stone's throw into their future.

When Mia's grandad took to the microphone to speak,

reality kicked in; the numbness that had protected her so far was stripped away as she focused on his familiar figure. He looked so frail, standing there in his black suit and tie, arms quivering as he gripped the lectern before him and spoke from the heart.

'I thought losing my first wife was hard,' he announced to the busy room with a catch in his throat. Then, after taking a slow, deep breath, he added: 'But let me tell you, nothing prepares you for the agony of losing a daughter.'

Pausing again, blinking repeatedly in a futile bid to stem his tears, he exhaled into the microphone. 'Your children never fully grow up in your heart. Part of you always thinks of them as the little ones they once were. So how can my precious girl have gone before me?'

Frank raised his trembling hands to his face, cupping the palms around either cheek and shaking his head like he refused to accept what had happened.

Hannah's hand, also shaking, gripped Mia's in response. Their eyes met for an instant, Hannah's every bit as tear-soaked as those of her niece. She and her mum may have fallen out for a long time, Mia thought, but she clearly still loved her. She'd lost her twin. If anyone could under-stand her own grief, it was Hannah. And her poor grandad too, of course, who'd lost one of his children.

'It's not natural!' Frank exclaimed, his face crumpling. 'I . . . I'm sorry. I thought I could do this, but I can't . . .'

His resolve to push on with his speech collapsed. He staggered to one side, breaking down in tears as Mark, Joan and the celebrant all raced forward at once to support and comfort him. The sight was too much for Mia. She also started sobbing uncontrollably and was barely able to register anything else that happened as the proceedings continued with some readings. Then one of her mum's favourite songs was played: Eva Cassidy's 'Over the Rainbow'. This had Mia in bits. She could picture her mum singing along while playing it in the kitchen at home. She could actually hear her voice in her head – and it was like all of her pain and sorrow came billowing out in a huge plume of emotion.

She was way too distraught to lay a wreath on the coffin, as they'd planned, lacking both the physical and mental strength to step out in front of everyone at this moment of intense personal grief.

'Don't worry,' Hannah whispered in a shaky voice, slowly moving her arm away from where she'd placed it around her. 'I'll do it.'

'No!' Mia cried, louder than she intended, reaching out to her, desperate for her aunt to remain at her side. 'Please stay here with me.'

'Of course I will,' she replied, as Mark leaned in and offered to place the floral tribute instead.

Mia felt a terrible wrench when, soon afterwards, the coffin disappeared behind the curtain to the tune of 'Lay Me Down' by Sam Smith. This was another song her mum had loved. Mia remembered her swaying along to it on one particular occasion as she'd driven them to the dentist. 'He's got such a wonderful voice,' Diane had said. 'Every single note he sings is jam-packed with emotion.' Mia hadn't replied. She'd been in a sulk about something un-important, which she now regretted. If only she'd known then how precious such moments spent together would turn out to be.

Everything felt so final, so raw, it was all Mia could do not to howl her lungs out to express how utterly devastated she felt, like her entire essence had been shattered into a million little pieces.

Later, as her uncle drove them to the reception Frank had arranged at a nearby cricket club, Mia stole a glance at Hannah, sitting next to her in the rear seat of the BMW, and then at Mark, behind the wheel. Neither was speaking at that moment. They both looked tired and anxious; lost in their thoughts, staring out of the car into the distance.

She hadn't known either of them for long at all, having no memory of the time she'd spent with them as a tot before moving down south. Only a few weeks had passed since her mum had left her with them in Manchester, but they'd already been through so much together, it felt way longer.

Hannah and Mark had both been brilliant at the funeral, watching over her like a pair of bodyguards. They'd been amazing with her generally, as she'd explained to her grandad when he'd taken her aside in her bedroom last night for a private chat.

'How do you honestly feel about going to live with your aunt and uncle in Manchester?' he'd asked, sitting next to her on the bed. 'Yes, it was your mum's wish for you, but as your grandad – someone who loves you so very much – I need to know you're definitely happy about it. Manchester is a long way from your home and I realise you're still getting to know them, so . . . does it feel right?'

'Um.' Mia hadn't been sure how to answer.

As if reading her mind, Frank had added: 'For the record, I'm not trying to get you to say you'd rather stay with me, kid. You're absolutely always welcome, but that's not what this is about. As much as I'd love to have you come and live with me and Joan, Hannah and Mark are a more sensible choice. They're much younger, for a start, and it's obvious how fond of you they are already. I think they'd do a great job of looking after you and you'd want for nothing. But I'm conscious of how fragile you are at the moment and I have to be certain you're okay with everything.' He'd leaned over and planted a kiss on her forehead. 'Does that make it easier to answer?'

'A bit,' she'd replied. 'The idea of moving – leaving my home, my friends, my school behind – is scary. But I know I can't stay here and, well, Hannah and Mark have made me feel really welcome. I'll probably never get my head around why Mum left me like she did. Why she didn't say a proper goodbye. But the one thing I do kind of understand is that she thought she was doing the best for me, right or wrong. And leaving me with them like she did . . . that's the easiest bit for me to grasp. So, yeah, I think I'd like to give it a go. But I hope you'll visit regularly.'

Frank had pulled her into a tight hug. 'You just try to keep me away.'

What Mia hadn't told him was that a part of her also hoped that by being in Manchester she might finally get to meet and, perhaps, start up some kind of relationship with her father. Her mum had always given her the impression he lived somewhere up there. Now he actually knew about her, would he try to contact her? She hoped so, even though she was partly terrified by the idea. What if he didn't like her? What if she didn't like him? Gosh, life was complicated these days.

Mia felt like she'd aged ten years since her mum's death. But as sad and broken as she was, at least she had Mark and Hannah. They were trying so hard, bless them, despite their lack of experience of raising children. And, thank goodness, things between the two of them seemed better now after that blip when Hannah had briefly stayed away. Mia knew how lucky she was to have them, today more than ever.

As the car continued towards the cricket club, Mia tried to steer her thoughts away from everything that had happened at the funeral. She needed a break from the tears and heartache. Instead she considered how similar Hannah looked and sounded to her mum. She'd found it weird when she'd first arrived in Manchester, but now it gave her comfort, like a part of her mum was still with her. As different as they were personality-wise, there were also similarities in their behaviour. Hannah's facial expressions and the way her nose wrinkled up when she laughed, for instance, were just like her mum's. They even had the same fastidious way of scrubbing, rinsing and stacking the pots and pans while doing the washing-up. Mia noticed new little things all the time.

'How are you doing, Mia?' Mark asked from the driver's seat, flashing her a reassuring look in the rear-view mirror.

'I'm okay,' she replied. 'A bit nervous about facing everyone at the reception. Do you think there will be a lot of people there?'

'Don't worry about that,' Hannah chipped in. 'You can talk to as many or as few people as you like. Everyone's on your side. There are no expectations.'

Her aunt hesitated before reaching into the seat pocket before her and pulling out a small package wrapped in brown paper, which she handed to her niece. 'I'm honestly not sure if this is the right time,' she said, 'but Mark and I thought it might put a smile on your face on a day when you need it.'

'Oh, thank you,' she replied. 'What is it?'

'You'll have to open it to find out.'

She tore the paper apart and out fell a book. But not just any book – it was her aunt's novel.

'The proof copies arrived the other day,' Hannah said. 'That one's all yours. I hope you like it.'

'Wow,' Mia said, grinning for a moment in spite of everything. 'It looks amazing. So professional. I'm going to start it tonight. It'll take my mind off things.'

Hannah smiled gently. 'No rush. Whenever you feel ready.'

'How does it feel to see your name in print?' Mia asked.

'You tell me. Look inside, on the page where I've placed a bookmark.'

Mia was confused. She'd already seen her aunt's name, Hannah Cook, on the cover. What was she talking about? She opened the book regardless, and then she saw it – the dedication. It read:

For Mia. So glad to have you back in my life.

She gulped, feeling herself start to cry again. 'What? How?'

'Do you like it?' Hannah asked.

'I don't know what to say. But yes, I love it.'

'Good. I thought you would. I barely knew you when I wrote the book, more's the pity. But now – and after everything you've been through – well, it seemed perfect. I contacted my editor and luckily I was just in time before they printed it.'

'What about Mark?' Mia asked.

'Oh, you deserve it far more than I do,' her uncle replied. 'Besides, I reckon your aunt's got dozens of other books in her. Plenty of time for me to get a dedication, if I'm lucky.'

'Thank you so much,' Mia said. 'It means a lot.'

'Good, because you mean an awful lot to us too, Mia,' a dewy-eyed Hannah said, her voice unsteady. 'Things have been really tough recently. Today especially. But we're going to get through this together: first the funeral reception and then everything else.'

'All for one and one for all, like in *The Three Musketeers*,' Mark chipped in.

Hannah gave a sarcastic shake of her head. 'Sorry about him. He tries his best.'

'What?' he shrugged, winking at Mia. 'That's a nice literary reference. I thought you'd appreciate it.'

As Mark pulled the BMW into the cricket club car park, Mia found herself short of breath at the prospect of facing everyone. She felt so anxious and fragile – but at least she

356

didn't have to do it by herself. Her aunt and uncle had her back, as did her grandad, and there was strength to be drawn from that, as well as hope for her future. Her mum was gone. She was never coming back. But at least she'd left Mia in a safe place, with people who truly cared for her and would protect her.

'Like family?' the teenager said quietly. 'We can get through this like family, right?'

Hannah nodded. 'Exactly.'

'Yep,' Mark added. 'Definitely. That's the one: like family.'

ACKNOWLEDGEMENTS

Thank you to everyone who's helped me to produce this, my fourth novel, including all my family, friends and readers. It was a tough one to write at times, but I'm delighted with the end result. My editor, Phoebe Morgan, was fantastic as always. Victoria Oundjian was also a huge help, particularly when I was first developing the idea. Hats off to you both plus Sabah, Elke and the rest of the amazing team at Avon.

Big thanks also to:

The best wife, daughter, sister and parents that anyone could ever wish for.

My brilliant literary agent, Pat Lomax, and everyone at BLM.

Jill, Matt, John and Darren, who were all kind enough to help me with various aspects of research. Much appreciated!

How do you leave the person you
love the most?

Is there ever a right time to let go?

time
to say
goodbye

S. D. ROBERTSON

A heart-rending story about a father's love
for his daughter.

Is holding on harder
than letting go?

How far
can love
carry you?

if ever
I fall

S. D. ROBERTSON

A beautiful story of love, grief and
redemption.

Best friends since the day
they met . . .

True friendship can last a lifetime . . .

'A heartbreaking tale' *Sun*

stand

by

me

S.D. Robertson

They'll always have each other,
won't they?